MISTRESS

OF THE

RUNES

A MYSTICAL ROMANCE

by

ANDREWS & AUSTIN

2007

MISTRESS OF THE RUNES

ISBN-10: 1-933110-89-9
ISBN-13: 978-1-933110-89-9

THIS TRADE PAPERBACK ORIGINAL IS PUBLISHED BY
BOLD STROKES BOOKS, INC.,
NEW YORK, USA

FIRST EDITION: SEPTEMBER 2007.

CREDITS
EDITORS: SHELLEY THRASHER AND STACIA SEAMAN
PRODUCTION DESIGN: STACIA SEAMAN
COVER DESIGN BY SHERI (GRAPHICARTIST2020@HOTMAIL.COM)

By the Authors

Richfield & Rivers Mystery Series

Combust The Sun

Stellium in Scorpio

Visit us at www.boldstrokesbooks.com

Acknowledgments

Thank you to Bold Strokes Books and its award-winning publisher and author, Radclyffe, who continues to break ground in lesbian fiction. Thank you to the witty and brilliant Jennifer Knight for her leadership, and a huge thank you to our personal and extraordinary editor Dr. Shelley Thrasher, who wrapped her arms around this book and nurtured and encouraged and improved our work over many months. Also thanks to our talented line editor Stacia Seaman and to Sheri for great cover art. Special thanks to consulting publicist Connie Ward for her dedication and friendship.

Dedication

To Ellen DeGeneres
who in 1997 told 42 million people that it's okay to be gay
Take a chance—dance

PROLOGUE

Corporate turf wars are ancient battlefields reincarnated—warfare waged on laptops, cell phones, and PDAs by warriors whose armor is Armani and who fight to the death for promises made on paper held in brokerage houses they'll never visit, backed by government gold in vaults they'll never see. Like all fighting, it's essential or senseless depending on how long one has been at war.

Born to corporate combat, and adept at outthinking the enemy, I pick my crusades carefully and, once committed, never give ground. My staff is loyal. They know with certainty I may lose a battle but I will always win the war.

"I'm not hiring her, Jack," I said. A laser beam of sunlight broke through the tall glass windows, ricocheted off the stainless steel banding of my angular glass desk, bounced off the gold entertainment trophies behind me, and pointed like a radiant celestial finger at my crystal desk clock. 11:11 a.m.

Jack fiddled with the button on his vest and slouched against one of my pale green leather chairs, looking battle weary. "She's bright, eager, talented, and a Harvard grad."

"She's sleeping with our CEO. Why don't you hire her for your sales division?"

We both knew why. CEO Anselm Radar didn't trust Jack when it came to women.

"She's summa cum laude, Brice."

"In what?"

He paused, obviously trying to spin it, and finally gave up, muttering, "Microbiology."

"Sounds perfect for network programming or talent management. In fact, she's precisely what I lie awake nights wishing I had—a microbiologist!"

Jack looked down at the rug. "Well, I'm glad, because she's right outside. Anselm told me to bring her over. She's your new vice president of strategic development."

He glanced up, perhaps to see if he was in any immediate danger of being run through with a letter opener. I glared at him in silence until he dashed out of my office and, seconds later, ushered in a tall, thin, dark-haired, young woman with alabaster skin and overly bright lips. She was wearing a tight, black V-neck shirt that hugged her body like a leotard and a matching black skirt that stopped mid-thigh to embrace her legs.

"Brice Chandler, Megan Stanford," Jack said, and bolted out of the room.

"Ms. Chandler, I'm so glad to meet you. Anselm has said nice things about you."

I sat down, crossed my legs, propped my chin up on my hand, and stared across the desk into her eyes. "How is it that a microbiologist gets a job in an entertainment conglomerate as vice president of strategic development?"

"Anselm just feels I have something to offer," she said, quite composed, turning her head away as she spoke, in the bored and idle fashion of someone who doesn't have to make an impression.

"I am an extremely frank woman, Megan. Since you have been added to my senior staff, without my permission, let me clarify how I work. You will do what is right for the company at all times. You will become a cooperative member of the senior team. You will not become Anselm's spy in my camp. And if I learn that you are violating company policy by sleeping with the CEO, as rumored, I will fire you without hesitation. Are we clear?"

She batted her fawn eyes, giving me her full attention.

"Good. Because, Ms. Stanford," I smiled coldly, "you will not be under me, if you are under him. Now, get out of my office and go find something to…strategically develop."

CHAPTER ONE

It was the fourth year—that time in my relationships when everything always exploded like fireworks at a Chinese New Year. I had lived the four years so many times I could trend them. Year One, the Year of Finding—locating the love of my life. Year Two, the Year of Fooling—pretending this was the love of my life despite obvious signs to the contrary. Year Three, the Year of Fucking—albeit diminished and periodic, banging the love of my life who I subconsciously knew was actually not. And finally, Year Four, the Year of Forgetting—obliterating from my memory everything that had taken place over the last three years so I could merrily return full circle to the Year of Finding—the love of my life. Clare and I were in the fourth year.

I knew I should leave Clare, but I couldn't handle one more breakup in which a woman screamed, cried, and carved her name in my furniture, my partners always seeming to exhibit far more emotion upon my leaving than upon my staying.

I glanced in Clare's direction as I tossed my Birkin briefcase onto the couch and headed for the bedroom to change clothes for that evening's fund-raiser. She was seated on the edge of a straight-backed wooden chair, staring intently at her sheet music propped up on the metal stand in front of her, her body bent over the beautifully polished cello, her arm sawing out melodramatic moans. I waved hello.

Clare lifted her head and smiled in my direction as if I was only a slightly annoying distraction. Her long, thin arms enveloped the body of the cello as she caressed the notes from its strings with the grace and dignity befitting a symphony performer. I paused to watch her push her body into the backside of the instrument with a rhythmic pulsing, moving with the soft melodic sounds erupting from its burnished soul, gripping the instrument with her knees, an urgency overtaking her as her strokes became more fervent, controlling the instrument's every mood and melody, and soon she was forcing it into an intense and richer longing. It dawned on me, as the music reached its climax, that the cello was the only thing Clare had tightened her thighs around since I'd known her.

❖

"Be back late," I said as I whisked across the room, this time dressed in a black Armani pantsuit and heels.

"Have a good time," she replied in our detached but friendly style of exchange.

"I can't have a good time at these events. Why don't you go, and I'll stay here and play the cello." But I knew she couldn't hear me over the instrument's renewed moans.

As I maneuvered through the maze of one-way streets to get downtown to the Montemart, one of Dallas's older hotels, I dodged cars and checked my makeup in the rearview mirror and noted that at forty-four my eyes were still bright and focused, my hair thick and, while not totally wild, at least parochially punk. Giving myself a smile in the mirror, I looked for lipstick that had gone awry while cognizant that my smile was one of my greatest assets. I used it even when I didn't feel smiley. Perhaps later in life, when all the other parts had worn out, I'd simply arrange to meet people at drive-thrus.

Minutes later, I valet-parked my car and took the elevator along with other people in ridiculous ruffles and rhinestones up to the massive ballroom on the seventeenth floor and the St. Albert Children's Medical Center Fund-raiser. I dutifully smiled at total strangers, spoke warmly to people I purportedly knew, slogged through the buffet line, and found a seat at one of the larger tables where I settled in, nodding at guests on the opposite side of the table who could not have heard me even if I'd introduced myself, thanks to an orchestra that was miked up so loudly we were in danger of otologic collapse. The roast beef shimmered under the chandelier with a greenish-purple iridescence, and I decided against eating it. I was bored, but not suicidal. I settled on a piece of chicken that looked like it had been prepared by the Smithsonian.

Surreptitiously checking my watch under the table, I didn't see a woman in her early forties join me. I glanced up as her plate slid onto the table next to mine, and I recognized her from her television show. She was wearing a tight, electric blue satin dress that enhanced her ample breasts and showed just enough cleavage to make me forget the time. Her short hair was so golden it almost looked eighteen karat, boyish in cut, but just curly enough to be feminine. She had with her a handsome, prosperous-looking man in expensive dress pants and black leather suspenders who was drunk right down to his socks.

"Enjoying the evening? I'm Liz Chase and this is Harry," she said as Harry collapsed into the chair next to me.

"I'm Brice Chandler. Hello." I nodded at Harry, who obviously had no idea where he was.

"I was just wondering if I had to eat this prehistoric fowl before leaving," I remarked as Harry let out a large, dangerous belch that turned into gagging sounds, then escalated to near vomiting. The man adjacent to him snatched him up and hoisted him from the chair, propelling him toward the men's room.

Liz watched the retreating Harry slobbering down his own suit front and pushed her plate away, rolling her eyes in humorous dismay. "I don't think I'll be eating now at all. In fact, I'd like to leave."

"Do you need a ride?" I tried not to make too big a deal out of what had happened, certain Liz Chase would be fine with Harry finding his own way home.

"That would be wonderful."

We both slid discreetly out of our chairs as if headed for the powder room, but instead we dashed through the lobby, wanting to get out before anyone noticed we were in full retreat. I glanced at Liz, assessing her frame of mind, and caught her suppressing a giggle, I assumed over the ridiculous situation she'd found herself in and the near–projectile vomiting of her date. I grinned at her, liking her ability to find humor in embarrassing situations and to roll with the punches— but then that's probably what TV people did.

At valet parking, I handed the young boy my ticket stub, and he dashed for my car. The wind caught Liz's perfume and washed it over me, making me light-headed. Women always smelled so good. It was one of their immediately irresistible qualities. That's what I told myself because my heart was racing in an uncharacteristic pattern as I tipped the sprinter and a second man, who held the car doors open for us.

The moment we settled in, Liz said, "I was watching you tonight. I've heard about you forever and never had a chance to meet you. Tonight, I…thought you looked very handsome, powerful, unlike other women."

That could have been a come-on, but since moving back to Dallas from L.A., I'd found that perfectly straight women often made astonishingly intimate remarks to other women without being at all concerned that they'd compromised their heterosexuality. I thanked her and confessed that while I'd only watched her show occasionally, due to my work schedule, I thought she was very good at what she did.

As we headed north, chatting amicably, she suggested we cut through Turtle Creek. Why we would take the scenic route when it was too dark to see any of the park's creeks and flowers was a bit mystifying, but I obliged her, thinking it a shortcut. She continued to talk nervously, telling me that the man she was with at the party worked at the television station and his wife had just left him. When I asked why, Liz replied, "Puking in public." She paused, then we both burst out laughing.

"That's not true." I continued to chuckle.

"No, I made that up," she said, getting control of herself as my heart happily skipped around in my chest. Liz Chase was, in addition to being attractive, a great deal of fun.

I turned left off the main thoroughfare, up the winding hill that in daylight was home to a myriad of flowers.

"Stop here for a minute," she requested.

I pulled off into a parking indention and looked at her, wondering if something was wrong.

"It's taken me a while to even meet you, and with our schedules, who knows if I'll see you again anytime soon." She paused and I frowned. "I'm a TV anchor, so I have a lot to lose with what I'm about to say, but I've vowed recently that I'm going to trust my instincts and take chances when the outcome matters." As she stared into my eyes, I felt my heart lurch and a tingling sensation break out somewhere in my lower abdomen.

"I'd like to see you," she said, then let her breath out in a there-it's-done kind of way.

It was as if she knew I'd never been good at nuance. So there she was, looking me directly in the eye and asking—*What, to date me? Liz Chase is gay?* That was my first thought, followed immediately by the ingrained corporate suspicion that for all I knew, maybe she wasn't! *Maybe she's setting me up. Maybe her station is doing an expose on closet execs.*

I found myself physically stiffening, becoming internally tense, my voice rising in cold alarm. "Could you be more explicit?" It was a supercilious response, but I was suddenly nervous in a city with so many closeted executives the skeletons were having to sleep double.

After a beat she answered with a wry smile. "Probably not." She slowly reached toward me, her wrist extending beyond the tight blue satin sleeve of her dress, her fingers long and beautiful stretching out across me for what seemed like eons until they caught the loop of the seat belt by the driver's side door and slowly dragged the strap across my chest, the tips of her fingers brushing my breast. I stopped breathing entirely and thought I might faint.

My reaction wasn't lost on her. She gazed up into my eyes, and I could have taken her in that instant; she was that lovely, and her look was that erotic. The metallic click of the belt into its lock snapped my heart back into my chest and punctuated all that she hadn't said.

"Better buckle up." Her smile carried a warning that went beyond this particular ride. I certainly didn't *want* her out of my car, but I *needed* to get her out of my car. I didn't want to be on the front page of the city's paper under a headline that read TWO PROMINENT WOMEN ARRESTED IN LOCAL PARK.

We drove on in silence. A few blocks later I let Liz off in front of a small but stately two-story brick home in the older part of town. Getting out of the car, she thanked me, her eyes lingering for just an instant on mine, then turned and walked up the steps to her house, and I noticed Liz Chase had a perfectly engineered derriere. Perfectly.

❖

I drove directly across town to a small but neatly kept duplex not far from SMU, my heart pumping out of my chest, my breathing short as I jumped out of the car. Taking the wooden steps two at a time and the porch in two more, I knocked on the paint-peeling white door in search of Madge Mahoney, my university drama coach and longtime confidante, the person I always turned to when I needed guidance.

Madge, approaching a rather liberated seventy, her flaming red hair in wild disarray and wearing a silk Japanese kimono flared at the bottom and belted at the waist, flung open the door. She spread her arms wide in welcome, as if taking in the entire second-floor balcony instead of just me.

"You shouldn't open your door to strangers in the middle of the night," I admonished.

"You should show up occasionally and you wouldn't be a stranger! Come! Sit! Drink! What can I get you?" She jutted her head forward like an inquisitive turtle and stared, most likely trying to decide what was going on with me at this hour. "You're too well dressed to be running away from home—"

"Fund-raiser. I left early."

"—*and* you have a certain glow about you."

"I gave Liz Chase a ride home."

"The TV anchor? They don't pay them well enough to afford a car or cab?" she said slyly, not having had a talk about my love life in quite some time and presumably relishing it since it allowed her to live vicariously—akin to experiencing childbirth without pregnancy. She drifted into the kitchen.

"I'll have coffee!" I called out.

She appeared moments later and handed me a cup of tea, fully aware I wasn't a tea drinker and not caring. If Madge drank tea, the world could drink tea. Her repertoire of guest formalities exhausted, she plopped down in her huge leather chair across from me. "So what's Ms. Chase like? She's attractive, I know that. I watch her on TV."

I took off my suit jacket, kicked off my heels, and curled up on the white couch across from the wall of R. C. Gorman prints of Native American women, which in my college days I had viewed as extremely erotic, their black, sleek locks blowing wildly in the wind. In contemplating the artwork, I had delayed too long for Madge, and she ordered me to speak up or go home. I recited the entire evening's events, and she listened without interruption until I reached the scene at Turtle Creek when Liz's hand brushed my breast.

"What kind of a woman does that? She doesn't even know you!" Madge was up on her feet pacing now as if she held the lead in *Medea*. "What if you called the station and reported her? She's a fool to take that chance."

"She admitted that, but said—"

"—that she's crazy and you should stay away from her? I'm

hoping that's what she said!" She threw her arms up to the heavens in supplication of the unseen.

"I *intend* to stay away from her."

"You have a lot to lose too, you know."

"I'm fully aware of that, Madge," I said as she suddenly collapsed into her chair and picked up her tea.

"Living with the dead makes you vulnerable," she warned in a heartless attack on Clare. "If nothing else, this Liz Chase person has revived you. The blood's all up in your head again. You're excited. You're nervous. You're aware that you're alive! What does that tell you about your life?"

"Nothing's wrong with my current relationship. You've just never thought Clare was right for me. You don't see her as sexy," I said dismissively.

"That makes two of us then, doesn't it?" She sipped her tea, eyeing me over the half lens of her glasses.

I looked past her into the dimly lit garden. There was nothing more to say.

❖

I returned that night to Clare's elegant north Dallas estate, the house I shared with her but in which I'd never felt quite at home, in a neighborhood of the near famous whose mansions had undergone as many face-lifts as their occupants. After pulling into the three-car garage, I kept my car doors locked until the electric door was down, an odd safety precaution promoted by the local police, who seemed to think that if a burglar managed to slip into the garage before the door was fully down, it would be best for me to be locked in with him.

My routine was so ingrained that my body could operate on automatic pilot while my mind did other things—enter the house, punch in the code to de-arm the alarm, toss my car keys on the counter, and wander down the long hall to the bedroom where the lights were already out—as my mind wondered what I was still doing here, in this house, in this moment, with this woman.

As I slipped out of my suit and pulled on a silk nightshirt, I glanced at Clare, who was asleep. Crawling into bed with her, I started to draw myself in close to her back and wrap around her long, angular form, but she somehow sensed my presence and moved away, as if to make room for me, but I felt she was avoiding me.

I'd been attracted to Clare's aristocratic roots, her elitist friends, and of course to her talent as a cellist in the Philadelphia Orchestra and now the Dallas Symphony. If I were honest with myself, she'd been attracted to my liberal leanings in a conservative city and to my status—a highly paid woman executive doing well in a man's world. But now here we were with no executive suite, only our bedroom suite; no orchestra, only the music the two of us could make together. And if we listened honestly, the sound was cacophonous.

I put my hand on her shoulder and asked her to talk to me. She groaned, letting me know she wasn't interested. I knew it was rude to awaken her for mere conversation, but part of me said, like Rabbi Hillel, if not now, when? Clare was either in rehearsal at the Meyerson Symphony Center, in practice in the living room, or driving between the two.

"We never really fell in love, you know. We merely got involved—ended up in bed together," I said, starting in the middle of the long conversation I had been having in my head. I wanted to add that because of that emotional accident, a hereditary heterosexual DNA-imprinting had kicked in, and without analyzing it, we took the obligatory sequential steps: calling each other lover, moving in together, sharing property—a sort of self-inflicted shotgun wedding for the terminally gay.

"Why are you waking me up?" She frowned, looking at the clock. "It's past midnight."

"The way we are isn't working," I said quietly in my direct way. "You and I aren't really connected. I feel alone. I might as well be living alone."

She studied me dispassionately. "Have you met someone?"

"No. But I do think I'm vulnerable to meeting someone because we share so little."

She rose up on one elbow and pivoted slightly, addressing me over her shoulder. "I think we make a good team, actually." She spoke in that removed way she talked about us.

"Athletes make a good team. Horses make a good team. Lovers have to make more." My tone was flat.

"It's the sex thing again, isn't it? I don't need it in my life the way you do."

"Sex is not an act. Sex is a language that communicates love for one another. That said, you and I haven't spoken in a very long time." I felt calm now. It was out.

Clare paused for several beats, then turned her back to me and went to sleep.

CHAPTER TWO

Nothing is by chance. I had forgotten that fact when I stumbled upon the yellow-bodied toy horse, with dark mane and tail, mounted on wheels like a miniature tricycle sitting on the junk-store shelf.

It was a lazy Saturday, on the heels of the fund-raiser dinner, and having deserted high-style North Park shops in favor of funkier finds near Crossroads, I was trying to corral my emotional life back into the safety zone. I wasn't sleeping well lately. Restless and irritable, I was trying to think about gardening or antiquing or anything I might do with my hands or my mind.

"Well, look at you," I said softly to the twenty-four-inch tricycle-horse as I hoisted it up into the air, allowing light from the dirty windowpanes across the store shelves to filter down on the horse and give it a surreal quality.

"Hi!" Liz Chase popped up above the store shelves like a prairie dog. "Not stalking you—we're here for a live shot," she joked. Her sudden appearance in such an unexpected place caught me completely off guard. "Looks like an Icelandic horse. Now who would think you would like a horse from a cold place," Liz said, the light dancing playfully in her eyes.

"You should get a real horse," the elderly shopkeeper interrupted us, and her ice blue eyes twinkled at me from behind the counter. *She reminds me of someone,* I thought. *She looks worldly, as if she might have been in the theater in her youth.*

"I have absolutely no experience with horses," I said, uncharacteristically shy now. "Just some vague middle-aged fantasy of riding effortlessly across rolling hills in a light wind, my hair blowing in the breeze like some Clairol girl on steroids."

The shopkeeper pulled her long silver ponytail around to the front of her shirt, stroking it and giving me a deliciously mischievous smile. "Then buy the toy horse," she urged, casting her eyes on it. "It will take you places you've only dreamed of!" And her voice was as melodic as wind chimes in a soft summer breeze.

"All right, I will." I made the decision almost as much to please this charming older woman as to please myself.

She snapped her fingers in the air, in a little burst of glee. "You've made the right decision. Your journey begins! Horses always bespeak a journey." And she took the horse, twirling away from me and swinging it through the air, the ebullient gesture breaking the rubber band on her long platinum locks that now swung freely around her head, startling me with their beauty and reminding me of the tail of a magnificent horse. I blinked, somewhat disoriented, then silently laughed at myself. *I can't tell the difference between a woman's hair and a horse's ass... could be definitive of my relationship issues.*

"Its hair's falling out," Liz observed as the shopkeeper set it on the counter.

"Tail," I corrected.

"Hair, tail, whatever." Liz rolled her sky blue eyes skyward and picked a few loose strands of horse tail off the floor, then held them to the light. "I think it's got mange, Brice." And I detected a smile in her voice. "We may have to call the antique vet." She lowered her voice conspiratorially. "Shopkeeper's pretty happy. Must have been trying to unload this for quite a while. For the record, this purchase falls into my old-ladies-collecting-crap category." Her voice had a little too much edge for my taste.

"For the record, it's not crap you'll ever see." I cut my eyes at her and gave her a smile designed to let her know she was out of line. *How dare she put me in the old-lady category, even in jest.*

"Ouch!" she grimaced.

Liz's cameraman shouted for her to hurry up, they were going live in two minutes.

"Gotta go be a talking head," she said.

I left the shop thinking that Liz Chase was a dangerous woman: too familiar too fast. Madge was right—steer clear of her.

❖

Clare backed up as I lugged the antique horse through the laundry room from the garage.

I placed it atop a tall handy-kitchen that my grandmother had given me. It had held potatoes and pies and memories long before the signers of the Declaration of Independence had held a quill. The toy horse looked ominously unsteady on its weathered surface, so I carefully lifted it back down and set it on the floor, where it seemed to disappear into the highly polished terrazzo. As I sighed and hoisted it up again, Clare followed me, always at the ready to protect pristine areas of the house from clutter. I finally set the horse down on a long, low parson's table under a picture of two women in faux kabuki garb.

"There!" I said triumphantly as I slipped out of my shoes and loosened my belt after a tiring weekend of errands. "It looks like a very expensive antique. Really."

"Lysol," Clare said, and smiled. We were on friendly terms again, my recent late-night confession buried. Like cats in a litter box throwing sand on their own feces, Clare and I kept the shit out of our lives by covering it with civility.

Moments later, Clare called to me from the garage, reminding me that I needed to unload the car: groceries, dry cleaning, hardware, plants, and various miscellany.

"I want servants," I said, struggling to yank the one-by-two-inch wooden slats I'd purchased for the small rose trellis out of the back seat of the Jag.

"Servants are not in vogue."

"I'm not talking about slaves," I said, assuring her of my political correctness. "They could be eunuchs, or cowboys, or really big dykes—anyone to lug this stuff other than me." Clare plopped the bookstore sack on top of the lumber I was balancing and patted my behind, urging me forward as one would a mule.

The car unpacked and groceries put away, I headed out to the terrace with my new book. It was spring, that fleeting but glorious time in Texas when azaleas and wisteria overpower patios, brick walls, and the sides of buildings, turning every living space into a breathtaking vista of hope and promise.

My goal for the weekend had been to lie on the patio, feel the wind blow softly on my body, listen to the distant church bells, and read. I was obsessed with books: the feel, the smell, the design. I thought about Liz Chase and imagined she would hate books, preferring the speed of the Internet—with its hip, hot, happening ether-info. *Typical talent—all air and hair,* I thought, happy to find a reason to chase the thought of her from my mind.

I made myself focus on Clare. She had been very attentive today, insisting on rendezvousing with me at the bookstore, to make sure, amidst all my errands, that I did something nice for myself. We were a good match, really. *Everyone fights occasionally. Everyone feels unloved on this day or that. I need to unwind and not blame her for my own internal turmoil.*

Part of my discontent centered around my obsession with corporate life despite the fact that I knew it to be dysfunctional on the whole and not worthy of such fixation. During the handful of years I'd been division president of A-Media Entertainment, we had already experienced two corporate takeovers: one in which we were the eaters, followed quickly by one in which we were the eaten.

Our leadership consisted of a disparate group of board members, none of whom wanted to share a planet, much less a company. And then there was Anselm, the crusty, conniving CEO who lay awake nights like a lizard on a hot rock with one eye open waiting for opportunity to present itself. Boards of directors are accustomed to sharks, and snakes, but lizards with fast, clever tongues that can snatch lesser life forms out of the air and eat them—boards are wary of such creatures. It would be fair to say that the new board, created in the most recent merger, was wary of Anselm.

I'd gotten a look at the new org chart, and it had more dotted lines than a subway map. I would have a dual reporting structure: continuing to report to Anselm, but also reporting to the new CEO, Walter Puckett. I fretted over this news—two CEOs and six directors all trying to steer the same ship. I was reminded of legendary ad mogul David Ogilvy's comment, "In all the parks, in all the cities, there are no statues to committees."

Perhaps the board viewed dual CEOs as one would redundancy in an aircraft: if one system failed they had a backup. However, rumor had it that we had two CEOs solely because an egregious snafu in legal had snarled up Walter Puckett's employment contract and basically given him Anselm's job title. Anselm threatened to sue. The board gods were angry and someone would have to be sacrificed.

Other office tales reported that Walter Puckett drank and ran around on his wife, but the only rumor that troubled me said he knew nothing about the entertainment business. I couldn't bear the learning curve with another corporate CEO. Of course, I could always quit, but corporate dysfunctionality had its trade-offs—financial gain, and its own peculiar and addictive adrenaline rush not unlike war.

And that's why I'd taken Clare's advice and met her at the bookstore today—to think about something else. There I'd chosen a glossy hardback book about horses, and Clare had given me a quizzical look that clearly asked what I was up to.

Frankly, I didn't know. Why am I interested in reading a book on horse breeds, as if I were ten years old?

A light breeze rippled the book's pages, as I lay on the white slats of the Adirondack chair reading the short paragraphs that accompanied the large color photos stating the horse's origin, use, gaits, and temperament. Midway through the book, I came upon a photo of a small, muscular horse with Tina Turner hair and chunky legs. The caption read *Icelandic Horse—Famous for its tolt, a four-beat lateral gait so smooth a man can drink a stein of beer while riding and never spill a drop. Horse size 12.5-13.5 hands.* I tried to concentrate on the book again but felt my eyes grow heavier and heavier until I could not stay awake. The combination of the soft church bells in the distance and the even softer spring breeze rendered me happily unconscious.

In the depths of my sleep, a vivid scene projected on the screen of my subconscious.

A man with soft but thick pale red hair and a golden-red beard that fits neatly against his face and eases its way across his upper lip. His eyes are green and weary; he is young—yet old for his occupation.

The man is well proportioned, with muscular legs and massive arms. His shoulders are cupped in intricate chain mail, held to him by thick leather thongs that cross his bare chest, light red chest hair visible through the strappings. His circular shield bears the symbol of war, a stylized arrow pointing toward the heavens; his skirt, blades of leather, fans out around his thighs that clench the body of his muscular horse—small but thick-coated, its mane and tail massive and silver in color. Its ready stance and fearless eye communicate the horse knows it is about the business of war. The man is dressed as a Viking warrior. He is among the better men, one whose name men fear and on whose strength they rely.

His band of men tears across the landscape, moving with speed and surprise; they kill villagers and burn their homes, showing not the slightest empathy for the afflicted as they flee screaming and burning. A horn sounds in the distance, signaling riders approaching from the south...

I awoke to the low notes of the cello and Clare rehearsing her symphonic solo and opened my eyes, startled by the realism of the dream. Through the porch screen I could see Clare, so furrowed and focused and fierce, her tall, supple frame almost graceful when wrapped around and stabilized by the heavy instrument she played, her hair streaks of dark and light gray pulled back and secured at the nape of her neck. She was older than I but wore no makeup, having the good bone structure of a New England matron, which in fact she was, her family having traced its lineage to the Founding Fathers.

"I had the strangest dream—a battle scene and people being burned—must be because I watched part of that old Charlton Heston movie," I called out to her.

For a long, unanswered moment I thought she hadn't heard me, but finally her voice came from far away. "Sounds like office stress." Another long pause and then a detached follow-up. "You haven't mentioned Anselm lately, or his girlfriend." She stopped playing, perhaps more to rest her arms than to give me her full attention.

"She's probably giving him a blow job right now and telling him what an impossible bitch I am," I said, and she grimaced. I started to elaborate on the office politics, but Clare was leaning into the sheet music again, studying the notes as if they were rubbings from a cave wall. She was all-consumed, and any conversation would be an irritant.

❖

I hadn't been in my office for more than an hour when Walter made the obligatory CEO-to-president phone call to assure me he liked what I was doing and we would be a great team. CEO Walter Puckett was testament to the disconnect between the board, its deal makers, and its pledge to operate the company effectively for shareholders. But in a world where deals were slam dunks, executives were benched, and everyone strove for a win/win, tall, graying former basketball star Walter Puckett was a male fantasy incarnate—a leader who could jump four feet flat-footed and who took the corporate slang right out of full-court press.

"I had an amazing weekend," he said, making small talk. "I was in Yankee Stadium and there were thousands of cheerleaders, I mean *thousands*. They had come from all over the country to audition. It was mind-blowing. They were jumping and dancing. I never saw so many huge tits! And I said, we have to do this—create an event to honor young women. They typify All-American athleticism—they're healthy, robust, and full of life like our corporation. We'll have a corporate tent stocked with great food and booze." Walter waxed on, blending inflammatory phrases like "great ass" with more palatable ones like "scholarships for women."

Jack walked into my office at the tail end of my Walter Puckett call, looking a lot like Jack Lemmon; in fact, I was convinced that was why he had no difficulty getting sales appointments or jobs, for that matter. People like look-alikes—genetic shorthand.

"Hey," Jack said, as I hung up the phone. "Sorry about the other day, but I had no choice. How's she doin'?" he asked, referring to Megan Stanford.

"Does it really matter how she's doin' since we hired her for *who* she's doin'?"

"Let up, will ya, Brice? She's scared of you."

"Smart girl."

"Hell, *I'm* scared of you. You're like having my mother around—if she had a sexy smile and great tits." Jack got a smile out of me. "You talked to Walter Puckett since he came on board?"

"Just did. You'll love him. He's only interested in getting laid." I smirked.

"I know! I had to pull teeth to get him an invite to the Lakers party to bed this redheaded groupie." Jack gave me another Cheshire-cat grin.

"Glad you two have bonded," I said, irritated over how quickly men could find common ground in sports, sex, and war.

"I'm head of sales. That's what sales guys do. We find out what rings your bell and give you the ringer—ding-a-ding! Advice, Brice?"

He didn't pause to get my permission. "Cut him some slack. You don't need Walter thinking you're, you know—"

I knew exactly. "A bitch, a dyke, a middle-aged bat spoiling his fun with young girls?" Jack grimaced, not unlike Clare. "My goal is to make him look good by dropping lots of cash to the bottom line, despite the fact that Walter believes the bottom line is the point at which a girl's panties stop."

"You make it worth comin' to work," Jack snorted. "Ya wanna go see the Lakers next time you're in L.A.? I can get ya tickets," he offered, knowing I wouldn't take him up on it.

What am I doing here? I caught myself wondering as I stared at the back of Jack's worn pinstripe suit and sloping shoulders as he retreated from my office. *Peggy Lee was right to ask "Is that all there is?"* I turned back to my computer thinking I needed to win the lotto. I thought of a recent news report of a man in California who won the lotto and said he'd continue to work in the city's sanitation department as a trash hauler because he loved his job. *Crazy bastard,* I thought. *Lotto recipients should have to prove their worthiness by running from their offices shouting, "Fuck you, I'm free!"*

An e-mail pinged onto my desktop. It was from Liz Chase. My heart leapt into my throat and my stomach sank, two critical organs seeking solace in opposite directions, though I had no explanation for my immediate nervous attack. Her note contained a succinct apology for her behavior and an invitation to attend a video shoot at an Icelandic horse farm in Washington state in a few weeks. She had attached a map with directions to the farm.

I paused, then e-mailed her back, thanking her for the note but saying it was doubtful I would be on the West Coast at that time. Then I printed out the map and put it in my briefcase, telling myself I might want to visit a horse farm on my own someday and I should keep the driving directions.

CHAPTER THREE

Ensconced in one of the larger Hollywood executive offices, I waited for Elgin Aria to arrive and contemplated the irony that a man named Elgin could not tell time. Meetings with Elgin were legend; he had turned tardiness into an art form. I was there to sell him a television series showcasing A-Media's Stinett Stone—an Olympic diver who performed like a dolphin in the water but floundered on dry land—and if I allowed myself a moment of truth, I was there for what might happen after the meeting—a plane ride north to Yakima and the Icelandic horse farm and, not coincidentally, Liz Chase.

Why do I want to see a woman who's insulted me and whom I've insulted in return? Because I find her interesting and clever and she's not afraid of me. In fact, she's shown no deference at all, which I'm sure I'll find only briefly charming. So I'll see horses and be briefly charmed.

Half an hour after I'd been seated in Elgin's office growing moss, I heard him breeze past his assistant heading my way. Elgin was a diminutive, charismatic man whose wild, curly mop of hair looked like forest creatures could live there and go unfound for weeks. He entered talking, waggling his index finger at me.

"Who cares about another Jacques Cousteau if he's unbearably uh-gah-lee—your client is sooo ugly he makes the show bo-ring! And don't tell me he's in a diver's mask because that's the best he ever looks! Let's deal with prit-teee people, shall we? Submerge the entire Bolshoi Ballet in a sunken ship! Sort of what-happens-to-this-dance-troupe-in-the-last-few-minutes-before-they-die kind of thing. Of course no one dies, so the Standards and Practices goons don't get all worked up. It will be great, greeeeaaaat!" He dashed out of the room and his very thin, very gay assistant poked his head in to say Elgin would be back in an "eentzy teenzy," a phrase that made me want to behead him.

"I can't do a damned show about submerging the Bolshoi Ballet! What the hell does that mean, anyway?" I moaned.

"It means you could have a series," he said.

"Ballerinas swimming for their lives—is that a series?"

"If Elgin wants it to be." The assistant gave me a princely smile, letting me know who was king in this realm, and once again I was face-to-face with the insanity of my profession.

❖

I booked a late-afternoon flight to Yakima, still muttering under my breath over my Elgin Aria meeting and wondering how I was going to get him off the Bolshoi Ballet idea. I made it to LAX on time, but my flight was delayed on the runway due to mechanical difficulties, and the hour grew later and later, jeopardizing my arrival at the shoot and my chances of seeing Liz Chase.

When we finally touched down, I was so irritable and antsy that I literally ejected myself out of first class, jogged to the car-rental counter, and took whatever they had available that was fast and ready to go. I threw my luggage into the backseat, grabbed the directions, programmed the nav system, and drove off at high speed.

Ninety minutes later, I wheeled the rental car through the elegant front gates of the B Famous Ranch, proceeding cautiously along the short and narrow gravel drive to Tina Bogart's home. Mountain wildflowers hung from pots and peered out of trellises, but I saw no sign of human life. I relaxed when I spotted a production van—the crew and Liz were still here.

Suddenly the front door of an arty ranch-style bungalow swung open, revealing a warm and welcoming blonde about my age, with ample thighs. I admit I wondered how my own thighs might look pressed flat, in mammogram fashion, against the sides of a horse. It's not that I have the bulging thighs of an Olympic speed skater; it's more that I don't have the thighs of every woman ever pictured in an ad involving riding apparel. Over the years, advertisers had programmed my brain, encoding an image of the perfect female rider: thirtysomething, just under six feet tall, long, natural blond hair, and Rockette legs.

Being five foot eight, with light auburn hair, sturdy thighs, and having thirtysomething in my rearview mirror, I felt *Town & Country* was definitely warning me off horses. But now here was Tina Bogart, who happily did not bear the traditional stork legs. There might be hope for me. I introduced myself as Liz Chase's guest.

"You missed the big filming. Everyone's packed up and left except those two boys," she said, pointing to the grips by the remote truck loading up equipment. My heart flopped leadlike and I was irretrievably disconsolate. *Liz is gone. Why didn't she wait for me? Maybe because you told her you most likely weren't coming, idiot!*

"I can still show you the horses under the arena lights," Tina said, stepping out of the house and steering me around to the side of it and down a lane toward the barn. There, in small corrals, several Icelandic horses stood solemnly. I don't know what I'd expected—perhaps that she'd fling open the back door, and, just as it happened in the Irish Spring commercial, I would be transported to a land of green, grassy tundras lashed by cold winds that whipped the manes and tails of the most glorious creatures on earth. Instead, I was looking at some rather chunky, pony-sized animals, each having its own issue with life in America. A freshly scrubbed young girl with an Icelandic accent, looking tall and Spartan without makeup and wearing a riding helmet, walked past me leading a beautiful bay horse who seemed healthy but hot.

Tina said her horses weren't used to the heat but that they'd have to *get* used to it because when a horse or its tack left Iceland, it was never allowed to return, thus protecting the small country from imported disease. Even horses that left the country to attend horse shows had to be sold afterward because they couldn't return home, a fact that could make me teary if I dwelled on it; but then in middle age, I could no longer differentiate between a sad story and a sudden lack of estrogen.

Tina said the Icelandic horses' intelligence and temperament were extraordinary, as the Icelanders were known to slaughter and eat the willful ones, a practice I found abhorrent.

"They go from being one with the horses, to eating one of the horses?"

Tina shrugged. "It's a rough life."

A young grip came running up to me and interrupted to ask if I was Brice Chandler. When I replied that I was, he handed me a note bearing the name and address of a restaurant, driving directions, and Liz

Chase's cell-phone number, asking me to call to confirm I could meet her there. My heart fired up like a generator and I thanked Tina, said a quick good-bye, got into my car, and turned left out of the ranch gates in the direction the hand-drawn map indicated. Only then did I dial Liz's cell phone, taking a deep breath. Liz answered almost immediately, the sound of her voice relaxed and intimate.

"We missed you." She seemed to know somehow that I would show up.

"My plane was delayed," I responded, trying to regulate my breathing.

"Can you meet me for dinner?"

"I don't know how long it will take me from here."

"Twenty-two minutes. Not that I clocked it for you or anything."

"Well then, I'm nineteen and a half minutes away," I replied and hung up, realizing, somewhere in the depths of my subconscious, I was headed for trouble and anxious to get there.

CHAPTER FOUR

The restaurant was an old mill, circa 1800, right on the Yakima River, and when I opened the car door, the cool river breeze sent a chill across my chest. I was nervous about how I looked, which was uncharacteristic of me and due perhaps to my awareness that Liz Chase was a TV personality and they were always obsessed with how they look. *This is completely ridiculous,* I chastised myself. *Go in, say hello, and eat, for God's sake! This isn't a date. But it feels like a date. Madge is right. I've got to get my personal life straightened out.*

Liz waved to me from the old front porch. She was wearing khaki pants with loose net pockets, a white linen shirt with the sleeves rolled up to her elbows, sandals, and a smile. I thought she looked even better than she did on TV or at dinner the night I'd first met her. On those occasions she had looked completely female, and now with the sun angling off her tall frame, her khakis slung loose on her slender hips, and no real jewelry, she looked rakish, almost a tomboy. I liked that. The short, loose curls were in strange contrast to the strong, angular jawline, high cheekbones, and sculpted good looks. The combination was stunning. When she hugged me, I noticed that she was about two inches shorter than I.

"You smell good!" she said in a tone that assured we were merely two good friends exchanging compliments. She asked immediately if Tina had shown me the horses.

"They didn't look as proud and dramatic as I expected," I ventured as we entered the restaurant.

"I guess not—ripped from the tundra, corralled for weeks or months waiting for enough horses to make a planeload, shipped in crates by air to New York, quarantined, waiting for three days for the blood work to get back that determines on the spot whether they get to live or die."

"Please, I'm going to cry!" I said.

"Can you tell I don't like the whole process? Get one that's here already!"

She led the way into the decaying old building and down jagged stone steps to a sitting area overlooking the river. A young woman was waiting for her with rapt attention; I assumed Liz had her cued up to make sure our every need was met, TV people being quite anal about time. She dismissed the woman with a slight gesture and a smile, saying we'd like to talk for a while and we'd let her know when we were ready for our waiter. Liz reached for my wineglass, and I held up my hand.

"You don't drink?" she inquired.

"I do but—"

"You're afraid some insane woman will get you drunk and demand to see more of you?" Her eyes danced. "Look, let me get this out of the way so we can relax. My comment when you gave me a lift home was a one-time-never-going-to-happen-again inappropriate proposal. You were just really smashing and I was…smashed! What can I say?" She poured me a glass of wine, ignoring the fact that I'd refused it.

"Thank you. It's fine, really." I felt embarrassed by the apology—actually that I should be the one apologizing. Liz had merely expressed an honest emotion, and I had acted like a 1950s nun in a brothel. I started to say something about my behavior, then feared that might take us back in the wrong direction. Liz saved me by abruptly changing the subject.

"So you saw Tina's ranch? Did you see the black-and-white photo of Tina in competition on her Icelandic stallion doing the flying pace?"

When I told her I hadn't, she said, "The horse's right front and right rear legs, and left front and left rear legs, stay in sync, like a cross-country skier."

"I missed that. I was fixated on her TRUST IN JESUS sign on the corral gate." I rolled my eyes and Liz laughed. "Those who hang signs for strangers to observe, observe strangers for signs they should hang!"

She stared at me transfixed.

"What? Is my shirt unbuttoned?" I laughed, but thought I saw in that look an appreciation for the way I could express the very emotions she was feeling, and from that slender thread of knowing the evening unfolded.

She had graduated from Chapel Hill and worked at CNN Atlanta, ending up back in Dallas years later when she started dating a Texas boy—which I found off-putting, to say the least. She'd become a producer at KBUU and two months later was plucked from her behind-the-scenes duties to temporarily replace a woman on pregnancy leave, and never gave up the chair again. Now her life was an endless sea of groundbreakings, storm chasings, and all the gang-banger crime stories a girl could ask for.

"And everybody knows your name, as they say in the *Cheers* bar." I toasted her with my wineglass. "Do you like your job?"

She began a rehearsed response, touting all the celebrity and excitement, then broke off midsentence as if suddenly injected with truth serum and simply said, "No."

I arched my eyebrow in a playful question mark.

She locked eyes with me, her voice lowering in pitch, and said, "For the same reason you don't like being division president of a big corporation—we're enacting men's fantasies, pursuing men's goals, and making men rich while wasting our potential and our lives."

I sipped my wine, unable to stop gazing at her, taking the measure of this outspoken woman and how far this shared moment would go. *Is it our work experience, our femaleness, or our very souls that have connected?* On that last thought, I sat up straighter in my chair, changing the energy, and Liz clearly felt it.

"Let's find you an Icelandic horse to ride, since you managed to miss the shoot. You wouldn't buy a car unless you at least test-drove it," she said, doing a one-eighty from the intimate moment before.

As she quickly shifted psychological gears, I was caught off balance. "I'm not *buying* a horse," I finally managed to say. "I have no place to put one."

"Well, not tonight." She laughed as the waiter came to our table offering bread.

"I shouldn't eat any. I'll never lose weight." I sighed, trying to distract myself from thoughts of Liz.

"You look fabulous," she said, and I felt heat rise from my collarbone to my ears.

"Are you sisters?" the waiter asked.

"No," I said kindly.

"You sure do look like sisters," the waiter continued, his expression puzzled.

"Actually, we're closer than sisters." Liz jumped into the conversation. "We share the same likes and dislikes, and, by being together this evening, we have saved two other people from the certain misery of our opinionated, high-energy, New-Age-meets-middle-age lifestyle."

"I'll give you some time," he said and left.

"Too much sharing," Liz critiqued herself. "I'm sorry. Did that make you uncomfortable? But 'are you two sisters?' Really! I hope he never takes a job in California's Russian River. He'll have 'sisters' coming out his ass. This is such a great evening and it feels so...familiar. Do you ever have those moments of déjà vu?"

"I had a really bizarre dream. Does that count?" I smiled, wondering again why I was here—on this planet, in this state, at this table, with this woman.

"Tell me."

She must ask herself that question all the time. She's doing the news. Is that what she came into this world to do—report traffic conditions? She knows that's not it.

"I don't know..." I hesitated, not wanting to make a fool of myself. "My dreams seem to center around why we're all here. I mean, what difference does any of it make? You, me, any of us? I can't seem to get philosophical clarity on what we're all doing...besides getting drunk." I took another sip.

She leaned in, propping her elbows on the table and cupping her wineglass in both hands, and stared over the top of it at me as if I were the most profound human being she'd ever met. I wondered if she practiced that kind of visual intensity merely to get good interviews, but her stare captivated me nonetheless.

"Are we here to make the earth a better place for the next generation? Because that makes about as much sense as a beauty contestant saying her mission is world peace. Are we supposed to ignore any human return on investment in this lifetime and hold out for celestial ROI? Because frankly, I just don't know if I can hold out," I said, and finished off the wine.

"You're very passionate..."

My chest tightened. Now the heat around my collar was sweeping up my throat and flushing my face.

"…about life and about horses." Liz finished the sentence. "I have a feeling you're about to own a horse."

"'Fraid not," I protested.

"Now if I follow your philosophy, you should stop holding out. You should give in—let go," she said, her voice sensual. "If you wait until life is perfect before you act, then you never take action or your actions are too late. Do what feels right, then life falls into place. At the end of the day, when you're lying on your deathbed, do you say I'm so happy I never took that risk on the horses, or do you say I'm so glad I did that?"

I laughed at her commentary and she gave me that penetrating look again—the one that was just this side of sexual. "How about taking a trip, just you and me, to a few Icelandic horse farms?" Her eyes glistened. "Let's take a long weekend and drive around."

My mouth went dry and my mind, repository of standard thought, seriously considered her offer while my intellect, seeker of higher standards, gave me a sound puritanical slap.

"Clare wouldn't really appreciate that," I stammered, inserting my lover between us like body armor.

"Probably not," she finally said.

Those were the very words she used that night in the park. Why am I intentionally creating distance between us again? I'm supposed to create distance—I live with someone. I'm not out to pick her up!

After an awkward moment Liz took a deep breath as if she'd been underwater for a long time and had nearly died. When she said she needed to get back to her hotel and get some sleep, her tone changed. She explained she was subbing for someone on air tomorrow night and had to catch an early flight so I signaled the waiter for the check, but she had already taken care of it, having given him her credit card before I arrived. She was definitely a woman who planned and who took charge. I appreciated the forethought that took.

"Drink this entire cup of coffee before you leave, promise me?" she said, touching my arm, and I nodded in acquiescence, wondering just how drunk I appeared to her. "Thank you for coming to dinner…it was great fun," she said as she stood up.

"It was," I echoed. She extended her hand in the formal way businesswomen say good night, and despite the brevity, I felt her tenderness and strength. She didn't linger in touching me but pulled away and grabbed her bag, slinging it over her shoulder.

"Well, take care. And have a safe trip back," she said in that tone that sounded very much like this was a wrap—whatever might have been between us, now not possible. I nodded and wished her the same. Liz walked briskly out the door, and I noticed once again that her derriere was perfectly engineered. Perfectly. *God, my head is stuck on that!* I thought, irritated with myself.

I was suddenly too warm and too agitated to stay inside. Taking my coffee with me, I wandered down the narrow lamplit path just outside the restaurant to the river where large flat rocks had undoubtedly provided resting places for countless diners over the decades. Across the river in a large pasture, black-and-white cows, visible in the moonlight, were chewing placidly and sauntering through the high grass—the embodiment of nowhere to go and all night to get there.

After slipping off my socks, I plunged my feet into the icy stream, which immediately numbed any sensation all the way up to my knees. Relaxed, I let out a great sigh, my feet feeling no pain for the first time in weeks. I stretched my arms out behind me, placing my palms on the warm rock surface, and leaned back, gazing up at the stars. How was it possible to feel restless and calm all at the same time? *This feels so good; I could stay here for the rest of my life. I wish Liz had stayed and she was sitting here with her feet in the water beside me, continuing our conversation.*

It had been a long time since I'd had an interesting conversation with Clare, one in which we focused intently on one another and not the stove as we cooked, or the sheet music as she played, or my computer as I worked. *Perhaps only strangers focus on one another intensely.* I felt loneliness, or guilt, or something nameless stir in me, and I speed-dialed Clare. It took five rings for her to answer, and she sounded groggy. I told her I was sitting on the banks of the Yakima River and knew how much she loved the out-of-doors and just wanted to say she would enjoy it here and maybe we should take some time to be together. She hesitated, which I took as silent inquiry as to the timing of my call.

"Did I awaken you?" I asked.

"It's okay. I just have an early morning."

I apologized and hung up, wondering if one should have to apologize to one's lover for calling her on a starlit night while away from home to say she was missed and to share vicarious moonlight. A light breeze picked up, moving the leaves so the moonlight flickered overhead. It was sheer heaven, and I decided not to let anyone take this moment away from me.

I was surprised to see a man and woman standing on the embankment just to my left; I hadn't heard them approach.

"Wonderful, isn't it?" The woman smiled at me.

She looked like she was forty-three. Maybe. She was wearing khaki pants and a white shirt, dressed much as Liz had been, a loose jacket thrown over her shoulders, not the look of a tourist wanting to put her feet in the water.

"I'm very familiar with this stream. My family lived on that farm across the river for centuries. In fact, the town of Samuelsville was named after my great-great-grandfather. So you're just passing through, is that it?"

"Leaving in the morning. I just stopped to have dinner with a friend and to put my feet in the river. It looked so cold and beautiful. In fact"—removing my feet from the water, I sighed and pulled on my socks—"I have to get going."

"Why do you have to go?" She seemed genuinely sorrowful about my leaving.

"A business meeting tomorrow, back home."

She frowned slightly. "Why would you let a business meeting take you away from all this?"

"That's the question, isn't it?" I smiled wistfully.

"Well, now that you're finally here—a remembrance of your trip to these healing waters." She bent over slightly and handed me a postcard, and the tiny lights lining the pathway reflected off her beautiful blue eyes, as if drawn to their particular brilliance. I imagined her eyes were the color of this very stream in the daytime. I glanced down at the postcard in my hand: it showed the Yakima River photographed at just about the point where we were standing. The caption at the bottom read, *Home of Edward Samuels until 1892, when he moved to San Francisco to start a ferryboat operation.*

"Well, thank you," I said, looking up from the card, but she and the man had disappeared. *That was odd. The way they seemed to just fade into the bucolic scenery. Almost ghostly!* A shiver danced across my shoulders, and I jumped up from the rock, slapping at the seat of my pants in a parentally engrained Pavlovian response to perceived dust and dirt.

Now I was even more restless than before I'd sat down by the river. Something had happened to me. What, I wasn't sure. But I knew I needed to cancel my hotel reservation. I had suddenly decided to take the red-eye home that night. *Why unpack, toss and turn, repack, and take a plane home at dawn? I'll sleep on the plane, then sleep in until noon and go into the office late.*

For the first time in years I felt completely confused and restless. Always, I'd known where I was headed, what I wanted to accomplish, conquer, own—and now I was adrift. Nothing had the same significance for me. I didn't want anything I had, and I wanted things I didn't have. *I have a great job and good health and a wonderful life!* I told myself brightly. *I need to pull myself together. What I really need to do is talk to Clare. We're not in sync, that's the problem. We're just not in sync. We don't share enough experiences together. We've got to fix that.*

❖

It took me two and a half hours to drive to SeaTac, the Seattle/ Tacoma airport, and I caught late flight 111 outbound. The weather was perfect; it was dark outside and the cabin was quiet, people either sleeping, reading, or drinking. I didn't awaken until the seat-belt sign dinged and we were told to put our tray tables in the upright position and prepare for landing. When the wheels touched down, I was congratulating myself on this smart move. Feeling rested and alert and having saved myself half a day, I had many things I could get done before dark.

The sun was up when I pulled my car out of the airport parking garage. I'd asked Jane, my assistant, to cancel the limo service for this trip because the drivers could never refrain from quizzing me: Where was I headed? Was I from here? What kind of work did I do? Jane had spoken to the owner of the limo service who said he'd have a talk with the drivers, but somehow they couldn't stop themselves. Jane said it was my kind face; I thought it was their poor training. A limo service should have drivers, a call center should have talkers. Although driving my own car meant I had to fight traffic, I could do it in silence.

After paying the gate attendant I merged onto the freeway toward my house, Clare's house, actually, but after four years and some minor redecorating I had come to think of it as my house as well. Ten minutes later, turning down the oak-lined street of two-story colonial homes, I pulled into the driveway, dodging a red convertible someone had left jutting out in the street two feet too far.

I put my key in the lock, punched the entry code into the keypad, and headed for our bedroom. My heart hammered my chest as I spotted a woman, naked to the waist and wearing flannel jockey shorts with a black-and-white cow pattern on them, charging toward me in the hallway. I stood stock-still.

"Who the hell are you? Clare!" I shouted, wondering if she was all right.

"Shit!" the woman said, and ducked back into the bedroom.

Moments later Clare appeared in the hallway clutching her robe, trying to wrap it around her half-naked body. My mind locked up. I couldn't think. It made no sense. Clare was the one who didn't want to discuss a breakup. *Now she's screwing around?*

The chest-of-drawers-shaped woman bolted out of the bedroom again, this time wadding her clothes up in a ball and tucking them under her arm like a running back. She mumbled something over her shoulder to Clare.

How long has this been going on? Have Clare and this woman exposed me to some STD? Those thoughts fueled my actions and I flung myself into her path, infuriated and unwilling to let her off that easy.

"Look, you two don't have anything going, so don't blame me!" the woman huffed in my face. I could hear Clare screaming my name over and over, as if to reason with me or distract me or stop me from what I was about to do.

"Don't blame you for fucking my lover while I'm away? Don't blame you for exposing me to some sexually transmitted Mad Cow Disease? Or don't blame you for running naked down my hallway begging me not to shoot you?" And with that I reached into my briefcase for a gun—well, she thought it was a gun. It was actually my car keys.

"Brice, please don't!" Clare screamed.

The woman flung herself back against the wall, gasped, gathered energy, and charged me, apparently thinking she was about to be killed.

"I'm out of here!" she yelled and dashed past me, but not before I swung my briefcase like a bowling ball into her kneecap. She drew up short, howling, Clare alongside her now bawling, the two of them in harmony like coyotes on a moonlit night.

"You stay, I'm going," I said flatly. "It will save me having to burn the sheets."

I could hear Clare whimpering my name and pattering after me on the wood floors as I left the house, slammed the door behind me, and backed the car out of the driveway and, in demolition-derby fashion, smacked it into the cherry red convertible whose owner I now knew. I was happy about the crunching metal and the hours cowgirl would spend in the body shop with a mechanic whose biggest smile would most likely emerge from the back of his pants.

CHAPTER FIVE

Madge opened her door after my loud and urgent knocking and stood there in her long silk pj's staring at me with a twisted smile.

"I just got in on the red-eye and caught Clare with another woman."

"How great is that!" Madge said, rubbing her hands together with more-than-obvious glee. "You're free and it happened surgically. Cut, amputate, done!"

"Why didn't I know this was going on?" I asked as she held the door for me, signaled me to take a seat on the couch, then went to the kitchen to pour me tea.

"Because you're not in tune. You're a smart, talented executive, but when it comes to women, you're thick, Brice," she stated as merely fact.

"Well, when I'm done, I'm done. And nothing gets me done faster than being somebody's seconds! Maybe Clare's fucking the entire ladies' basketball squad, for God's sake! I should go get checked." I was pacing and snorting and stomping around like a horse in a stall. "She said she didn't need sex in her life the way I do. Here I thought she was freaking asexual, and she was only freaking asexual for me!

"It all brings back terrible memories of my blue-fronted Amazon parrot who bit through my finger to the bone on the first day I had him. If I answered the phone, or spoke to someone, he screamed, shook his mammoth cage condo off the table, and shredded all the newspaper flooring in a rage. I was convinced he was insane, and I knew I had to keep him to save him from being killed by someone less tolerant. Then one day, my nerves could no longer take the screaming—not being able to speak above his shriek—so I gave him to a medical doctor who called that night to say my bird bathed with him in the shower and sang 'Yankee Doodle Dandy.' My parrot who had dive-bombed me and shredded my scalp until it bled sat happily on the naked doctor while he showered, and serenaded him with 'Yankee Doodle Dandy.' Here I was trying to save the bird, and it was trying to tell me that it hated me and wanted to move on. Jesus, Clare is my parrot!"

A long pause. "If that works for you, good," Madge said, tilting her head to one side and peering at me not unlike a large bird. "You need some help getting your stuff out of there?"

"No, it'll be fine. Clare is nothing if not civil," I said, thinking of how many boring, civil evenings I'd had with Clare.

❖

I ducked as my peau de soie dress shoes came flying across the room at my head and Clare shrieked at me like a blue-fronted Amazon. "You don't want to talk it over, great! You just want to walk out, great! Get the fuck out of my house!"

She had been crying for two hours and looked absolutely horrific. It flashed through my mind that I had never seen Clare do anything but mist up, and here she was wailing. It was shocking to hear her utter the word "fuck" because, in addition to never doing it, she never said it.

"Frankly, I don't give a shit how upset you are, darling," I said archly, moving at a slow and deliberate pace. "You, and not I, were found fucking some cunt in the bed in which I sleep!" I whirled and put my face within an inch of hers, wondering if I would actually strike her and deciding I should leave rather than develop a bad habit like battery. "You who never looks *up* from her sheet music apparently found time to go *down* on a cow! The bovine jockey shorts were the piece de resistance—they make her ass look like a Gateway Computer box."

"You're never here and we don't talk! Brice, I love you."

"And you demonstrate that by butt-fucking some bovine in boxers?" It was a crude remark but I was mortified, embarrassed, and not myself.

I picked up my dress shoes, stuffed them into the last bag, and said the movers would arrive in an hour to collect the boxes and my furniture. My computer was already safely in my car, and with that, I left Clare squawking in the foyer.

❖

Exhausted, disgusted, and angry, I drove in deeply ponderous silence to the Chinese drive-thru and grabbed dinner for Madge and me. She'd offered to put me up until I'd found a place to stay. Having already called one of the townhouse communities that had rentals, I knew I'd be in within a day or two. *That's one thing money can do for me—make the tactical aspects of crises more easily manageable.*

The kid at the drive-thru took my order, then eyed the backseat of my car jammed with clothes and high-tech gear, books, and a tricycle horse.

"You move?" he asked.

"No, just taking my stuff for a ride," I said sourly, thinking of Jeff Foxworthy.

I phoned my office, lying to Jane about not feeling well and blaming the plane's air-vent system. The only remaining issue was telling Jane I had a new address. I hated telling her anything. I had hired her upon learning that her boss had been fired and she was about to be summarily dismissed because of her age, although the age issue was not overtly discussed. Jane had been with me for only a few weeks when I discovered that she was a professional busybody, and her hair, which seemed to have been given electric-shock treatment, might well have received it from her own central nervous system, which seemed to have shorted out, making her supremely sensitive and causing her to spend a good deal of her day inordinately addled. My hiring her simply proved Clare Boothe Luce's point that no good deed goes unpunished.

I drove to Madge's house late in the day and used the key she'd left under the mat for me, saying she'd be at the store when I arrived. After tossing the Chinese food on the kitchen counter, I undressed and fell into bed, planning only to nap, but ending up sleeping for hours. When I did awaken, I was staring at a strangely different ceiling—lower and spackled like old, dirty popcorn.

Disoriented, I began thinking it might be morning, but I wasn't certain. *Where is the clock?* 1:11a.m. It was always 1:11. In fact, for several years I'd noticed how ones were everywhere. But at the moment, I had bigger problems to contemplate than my predilection toward only checking the clock at 1:11.

Where am I? I thought, catching sight of the Shaker rocker in the corner. I sat straight up in bed, feeling as if I'd just been captured by aliens. *Madge's spare bedroom.* My mind made sense of the surroundings. Madge's tiny house where everything smelled different and looked different and the bed was lumpy. I rolled over and covered my head with a pillow and wished I had a sleeping pill.

Four hours later I awoke again, this time depressed, and crawled around trying to locate my clothes and makeup. I was in a daze and came out of the bedroom forty minutes after the alarm went off, feeling only somewhat disheveled.

"I've never lived with anyone, so how does it go...Hi, honey, sleep well? Can I get you some coffee?" Madge handed me a cup of thickly brewed caffeine.

"Omigod, real coffee, thank you!"

"Yes, well, you're pathetic so I went out and bought some," Madge said gruffly.

"Not a bad morning greeting. You might also try, 'you look smashing in that suit.'"

"Don't press your luck, the sun's not even up," Madge growled.

❖

I pulled my Jaguar into the parking lot and sat for just a moment, practicing breathing.

Do not share your breakup with anyone, that's a sign of weakness. Yeah, well, weakness is having a goddamned breakup in the first place! I chastised myself before gripping my briefcase, slinging open the car door, and picking up my step. Pace was everything for an executive. Pick up the pace and own the place.

Papers were piled high, phone messages were in neat stacks, and my phone was ringing. Jane was on lines one and two, so I picked up line three.

"So how have you been?" Michael Kaloff boomed. Michael was a dark, dapper, self-absorbed man in his mid-fifties—a board member rich enough not to have to care how things turn out in the end.

"Great, just great," I lied.

"Good!" Pleasantries over, he lowered his voice as if people were lurking just outside his office door desperately wanting to overhear this information. "I'm an advocate of Anselm's, I think you know that. He's not the easiest person to be around, but he drives the business. I'm less than happy right now with this two-headed monster we've created," he said, referencing Anselm and Puckett's power wars. "As things begin to shift, just hang on to the rails and don't bail."

"What's shifting?"

"Let me put it this way. It's time to surgically separate the conjoined twins, and I don't think they'll both survive. Keep this to yourself. Got another call, talk to you later." He hung up.

"Line two," Jane said over the intercom, "Jonathon King." I picked up the phone to speak to Kaloff's nemesis on the board.

"How are you doing?" he boomed. Jonathon King was a diminutive, middle-aged, brown-suited guy with sandy blond hair and a Midwestern attitude. He wasn't as rich as Michael Kaloff, nor was he as clever.

"Great, just great," I lied again.

"Good!" he said, not meaning it. "Listen, we've got a few board members, I don't want to name names, who are stirring the pot. They're not giving the new structure the support it needs to work. For the record, Walter Puckett is a hard driver who is fired up and will turn this place around, given the chance!"

I thought about Walter's tits-and-ass comments and wanted to ask how Jonathon King defined "fired up," but I bit my tongue.

"I'm aware you've known Anselm longer, but I don't want you to take a bullet for him. Just lay low, keep your skirts clean. We've got a lot to do this year!" King chortled over nothing, to let me know he was a warm, friendly guy, and hung up.

Jane stuck her head through the doorway, saying Anselm had summoned me. I walked over to his office and coded myself in through the two sets of double doors that separated him from the rest of the working world.

"You're back," he stated, not wanting a reply and not pretending to care whether I'd had a good time. I had to give him points for being direct. "Gotten calls from anyone on the board?" Anselm never looked up from his scribbling, but I could tell from his tone that he knew I had.

"Kaloff and King."

"Stay out of it." Anselm disliked the fact that I had a passing acquaintance with several of the board members and that they phoned me from time to time. "Let me know what you hear?" He never looked up, to underscore that what I might hear was of little consequence.

On the way back to my office, I mused that other entertainment companies were breathing up our collective shorts while our leadership was busy trying to kill each other off, as if we were suffering from corporate autoimmune disease.

I had plopped into my chair and was staring out the window when the pinging sound associated with arriving e-mail broke the silence. Expecting it to be from Anselm, I glanced at my computer. It read lchase@kbuu. I stared at it breathlessly for a moment before clicking it open and reading *So you'll know what you missed.*

It took me a minute to realize she was referring to the photos attached. I clicked them open and saw pictures taken during the photo shoot at Tina's ranch. The horses frozen midchew on my screen looked darling in the confines of my air-conditioned office separated from the heat and the flies. The third photo showed Liz standing next to a horse, her arm around it, looking directly into the camera with those piercing blue eyes. She looked spectacular: her hair blowing in the wind; her beautiful, strong, slightly androgynous face aglow in the superb light; her eyes softened by the presence of the gentle animal resting against her. I had to remember to breathe. As I was forwarding that single picture to my PDA, I thought, *I want to see her again.*

I replied to her e-mail: *Beautiful pics, thanks. Would next weekend work for our horse adventure?* When my finger hit Send, my heart zoomed up into my throat and a voice in my head said, *What in the hell are you setting in motion?* Too late.

The instant reply: Yes. I'll set it up. Meet me Friday morning, my house at 7 a.m.

She has audacity, presuming to set the time. I wrote back that I was working Friday.

Her e-mail reply was: You're the boss; give yourself a day off. See you at 7 a.m.

I smiled in spite of myself.

❖

It was as if everyone on the planet had been assigned the job of subverting my trip with Liz. By Thursday evening my office looked like a deli, the line stretching back six people deep, each trying to get one last approval or decision or opinion. Talent acquisition, networks, and research stood in a clump waiting for Jane to quit reciting the phone messages that needed an immediate return.

"I assume you haven't formed a singing group but are gathered here for some business reason," I said to the trio of humanity looming nearby.

Maxine, head of research, smiled, apparently enjoying my particular brand of humor, and spoke up on behalf of saving the networks' ratings. "Jack is demanding we sign a guy whose entertainment representation to date, not to mention talent, is marginal at best—starred in infomercials about depilatory remedies, penile dysfunction, and right-wing religious groups."

"Does he have a following?" I kept from grinning.

"Not unless you count the very hairy, impotent guy seeking salvation," Maxine said dryly as I dialed Jack.

He answered immediately, saying he thought I was out of town, then addressed me as his own personal goddess of talent, a sure sign that he was up to something.

"Why are we signing a piece of talent who's starring in a penile dysfunction commercial?" I asked.

"Because his brother lives with the network exec who is three layers above Elgin Aria and can get your poor-man's Jacques Cousteau series green-lighted at a time when programming slots are scarcer than virgins at a rock concert."

"That kind of crap erodes our credibility. Not doing it," I said flatly.

"Okay, look, no one's supposed to know this, but…are you alone?" he asked, and I glanced up at Maxine and her entourage and politely waved them off.

"Go ahead," I said into the phone.

"Puckett traded out a penile implant for our handling this kid's career for a year." Jack spoke as if he were residing inside his own desk drawer.

"Jeezus," I snorted. "I hope the talent isn't the one who did the surgery."

"The talent's brother, who's a doctor, did Puckett's surgery. So you get the kid's career up, Puckett gets his gear up, and I get to cheer up…because the sonofabitch will be off my ass." Jack snickered at his own joke.

"We're turning into whores," I moaned, syncing my PalmPilot with my computer.

"That would be a step up. They get paid every time they get screwed," he said and hung up.

I threw my computer into my briefcase, gathered up the phone messages to be returned while I drove, waved good-bye to Jane, and dialed Madge as I exited the office. When she answered, I told her I would be out of town for a few days because I was going on a horse-sightseeing trip with Liz Chase.

"I thought you were going to leave that alone."

"I am. It's about horses."

"It's about sex. Otherwise you'd be inviting *me* to go look at horses," Madge said dryly.

"Point taken. But I can assure you I'm not going to have sex with her. I'm not going to share a place, space, or my life with her. Can I just go spend a weekend in the country and admire her nice ass?"

"You're on the rebound, so just be careful. And don't mount anything you can't ride." Madge hung up.

CHAPTER SIX

On business trips I always traveled with too many pieces of matching luggage bearing suits and shoes of every description, so it was freeing to throw a duffel bag loaded with nothing but riding gear and an extra pair of jeans into the back of the car and head off on our three-day horse adventure.

I picked up the phone to dial Clare and tell her I was leaving… then I stopped. There was no Clare. It was a bit like a death. I was off balance, almost out of my body, my life upside down again and no one to discuss it with. It didn't matter that Clare was the wrong person for me; it mattered that she was there—the person who kept the house from being empty, the person who allowed me to say I lived with someone, the person whose name I wrote on the line that said whom to contact in case of emergency. *Clare could have been almost anyone,* and this disconcerting thought made me uneasy—the idea that I missed Clare only because I didn't want to be alone.

I chose to pack that thought away and live a life free of self-analysis for three days. It would all be there waiting for me when I returned—the fact that I was now alone again.

Focus on Liz's derriere, I told my sad self, and immediately I could feel tingling throughout my body, and that instant physical response made me smile. It proved I wasn't emotionally dead and that as a general category, hormones were better than drugs.

I was as excited as a teenager as I pulled into Liz Chase's driveway and nearly danced up the walkway to her house. She greeted me with a hug and I felt exhilarated. I sucked in air as if breathing in the countryside before we'd even gotten there.

"Don't you own a pair of jeans?" I held her at arm's length to check her out.

"There's nowhere I can wear them. The station doesn't like its talent to be seen on the street looking any less attractive than we are on TV."

"Well, you've certainly accomplished that. But we're leaving town, so maybe you want to grab a pair that you can change into once I have you safely over the state line."

She grinned and dashed back upstairs, giving me a few minutes to look at the foyer and into the twenty-by-twenty-foot living room. The colors were off-white, the textures were linen, the leather butterscotch tan, and the fabric pale green accents, all put together with casual elegance. *Now I know what her taste is.* My mind contemplated that phrase in a way it never had. *I would like to know what her taste is.* I almost laughed at myself. *Too many years in the company of men,* I thought, excusing myself.

Liz reappeared with a pair of folded blue jeans and reached down to lug several bags out of the foyer. I took the heaviest one from her and carried it out to the Jag, wondering why I was suddenly turning into a butch.

"Let's stop at Starbucks. I hear you're a bear without it," she said and I drew back, surprised. "Always befriend the secretaries. Part of my line of work."

❖

We drove north on I-30 and then took I-40 through Arkansas, picking up I-55 to Missouri, then all the way up to Illinois: miles and miles of tiny towns, fields of nondescript crops, and fresh air. I loved car trips. They put me in touch with weather and people and roadside greasy spoons and my own thoughts.

"Watch where you're driving! Are you okay?" Liz warned as I swerved across the center line, mesmerized by a clothing billboard for men.

"Did you see that sign? Work clothes, size 20X! If you're 20X, you define chapped thighs!"

Off to our right, over the top of a crew-cut-crested field of corn, we saw the largest man to ever sit astride a John Deere tractor, riding right at us in a pair of overalls that flopped over the sides and back of the tractor seat like three denim inner tubes jostling for the same resting place.

"That could be 30X," I said in awe as the radio blared "John Deere greeeeen"—the color Billy Bob painted the water tower proclaiming his love for Charlene. I looked over at Liz, then away when she looked back. That glance elevated my nervous system a few frequencies above just getting away from the city and taking a vacation. The two of us together in one small space, strangers really, but sharing the same sense of humor felt so good it was electric.

Liz had made all the arrangements, surfing the 'net until she'd found Willow Bend Farm and its owners, the Coltons—a friendly couple willing to entertain gawkers. As we neared the farm, a huge storm was gathering, so Liz turned up the car radio to hear an announcer interrupt programming to warn that a tornado was headed our way. From the looks of the wall cloud just to our west, all hell was imminent! Liz went into meteorologist mode, shushing me every few minutes so she could hear the dire predictions, possible evacuations, and historical comparisons of other such storms. I refused to acknowledge even a dark cloud in the sky.

"It's going to miss us," I said in a Pollyanna tone. The possibility of seeing more than a dozen Icelandic horses and being close to Liz Chase gave me a bigger rush than any drug.

The grass-rich pastures of Willow Bend appeared around the next curve, and a big barn stood just a few dozen yards in front of our car. I jumped out and walked over to shake hands with Ann Colton. It was dark as she waved us to the corral, the wind was picking up, and lightning was barely visible on the western horizon.

I can't describe Ann because the time I spent looking at her was infinitesimal in comparison to my staring at her horses. I was like an archaeologist who'd come upon a rare find and could not take my eyes off it. The newest Icelandic horse was a mottled black and well proportioned, but not as massive and muscular as I'd envisioned one should be.

A clap of thunder and bolt of lightning came out of nowhere, and a young Icelandic girl spoke in her native tongue to the little horse as she took him back to the barn. I was mystified how every Icelandic horse farm in the U.S. seemed to have acquired a young Icelandic girl. Tina Bogart had one, now Ann had one. Apparently, if one ordered several Icelandic horses, the Icelanders threw in a teenager for free.

Ann led us into the barn where she had several other horses, and every one of them quickly turned its butt to us and unceremoniously ignored our presence, the human equivalent of giving us the finger. Ann led one of the horses out of its stall for us to admire, but by now, the wind was howling like a she-cat. While the horses were unconcerned, Liz was almost apoplectic.

Even I was forced to admit the weather had turned inclement, to say the least. Ann insisted we take shelter in her home, but I assured her that we were just a few miles from our hotel. I wasn't going to risk being trapped with strangers—I'd take my chances in the car with Liz. The fact that I would brave the elements to be alone with Liz registered briefly on my subconscious. We said quick good-byes, and Liz and I dashed to the car just as all hell broke loose.

Liz flipped on the radio only to be assured that indeed tornadic storms encircled us. The tornado alerts had progressed to the take-cover stage, and rain we couldn't see through was slashing against the car windows.

"Good grief, where did this storm come from?" I leaned into the window as if putting my eyeballs closer to the rain would let me see through it.

"I've been trying to tell you! This is the same storm that's been tracking us for two hours. I just find it really odd that it's tracked us right to this barn. It's not a good sign."

"What do you mean it's not a good sign?" I maneuvered off the country road and merged onto the interstate.

"I just don't feel good about it."

"About what—the barn, the horses, the town?"

"All of it," she muttered in an all-encompassing way.

"Well, that makes me feel better. We need to just go with the flow. I've never *seen* so much flow."

Cars pulled off the highway, their lights unable to penetrate the dark rain. Roadways were suddenly eight inches deep in water. Semis flew by, throwing veritable rivers of water up into our faces, blinding us for what seemed like treacherous minutes. Exit signs were completely unreadable in the downpour.

Liz dialed the hotel number on her cell phone, trying to get directions, but it didn't matter what the desk clerk shouted above the water pounding on our roof; we couldn't hear him. We couldn't see road signs, or intersections, or anything but buckets of water and howling, wind-driven rain.

"I'm going to need a freaking chiropractor by the time we get there," I said, clutching the steering wheel as if it might suddenly leap off its column and fly out into the windy night.

"Just keep your eye on the road," Liz directed me.

"I can't see anything."

"Do you want me to drive?"

"Now how would that work?" Pressure always made me sarcastic. "We're in a tornado! Do I pull over in the middle of the highway and let you out to walk around and drive?"

"You're not exactly grace under pressure," Liz said, eyeing me.

"Omigod!" I shouted as I dodged a truck that was hydroplaning into our lane.

"We've got to get off this road. There's your exit! Turn, turn, tuuuuurn!"

"I'm not *deaf*. I just have to find the road!"

"There it is." She pointed to the hotel.

We whipped into the driveway at the last possible second, coming perilously near a drainage ditch. After I put the car in park, we stared at one another, not believing what we'd gone through and not believing we'd made it safely.

The hotel had no overhang, no way to keep me dry between our car and the front door of the lobby. I waited a moment, thinking a young bellman or valet parker or anybody under forty with an umbrella would jump out and save us, but no.

"Stay!" I mimicked a dog trainer.

Throwing open the car door, I dashed for the hotel entrance, arriving in the lobby seconds later, totally soaked. I stood dripping on the carpet requesting the appropriate form that would put me in a warm, dry place.

"Is the tornado near here?" I asked as I scribbled my name.

"Seems like it," the young man said.

"Do you have an umbrella?"

He shook his head. Chivalry was indeed dead. I made another dash out the front door and back to the car, squished into the driver's seat, and looked at Liz. "I cannot remember the last time I stayed in a hotel without...an awning," I said through clenched teeth. Catching a glimpse of myself in the rearview mirror, I realized for the first time that I resembled a mad, wet cockatoo. Liz started giggling, which made me laugh.

"I am a fucking sponge."

"Your hair's a mess," Liz said, and she made an effort to gently wipe away the water streaming down my face. For a split second I felt a claiming, as if I belonged to this woman, as if I'd always belonged to this woman. I sat perfectly still.

"You'll have to dry your hair before we go to dinner," Liz whispered, caught in that same feeling, I was almost certain.

Her touch rippled all the way down to a spot somewhere between my legs, and that heat surge made me tense up. "That's been my concern for the past half hour, being sure I look good for dinner," I said, trying to muster sarcasm to short-circuit the electric ties that were forming.

I put the car in gear, then pulled around to the back of the building to our designated entrance nearest the second-floor elevators. Again no overhang.

"You make a break for it and stand inside," I ordered. "I'll make a couple of runs and hand the bags to you. Can we just take one of the bags in?" I refrained from saying that she was traveling as if CNN might suddenly want to do a quick live shot of her.

"No, I have clothes in one bag, makeup in another, and hair stuff in the third."

"Organizing your luggage requires the skill of a field general."

"Stop giving orders, and I don't want you running in the rain. You'll catch pneumonia," she warned.

"I'm already soaked. The faster we do it, the sooner I can change clothes. Go!"

Liz bolted out of the car and arrived inside the hotel's side entrance, only partially soaked. I made three runs, summoning every expletive I'd ever learned and linking them together in creative configurations. After my final run, I stood in the hotel hallway, dripping on the hideously ornate red carpet, and tried to catch my breath.

"We can always go home," Liz said.

"And miss this experience?"

"That would be the idea!" Liz grinned. "You're a piece of work to travel with."

I snorted, turning over custody of her third piece of luggage. "For the record, this falls under my old-lady-lugging-her-crap category."

"Touché!" She wrinkled her nose. "It appears that we're both type A—and we never forget a slight. So for the record, I wasn't making fun of you that day in the antique store. You made me nervous, and I was just trying to be funny and make you like me, and then you snapped at me like tyrannosaurus rex."

I stopped walking. "For the record, I do fine with you, up until the time that you label me: old lady collecting crap, tyrannosaurus rex, type A."

"Oh, please! If that's the worst thing you've ever been called, count yourself lucky." She blew me off. "You are such a pampered executive."

"I just carried your luggage in for you through a thunderstorm to keep your air-hair from getting wet."

"Air-hair? Like I'm a television airhead, which by the way is terminology that trips *my* hot button. And furthermore, no one asked you to carry my luggage. I have carried my luggage through many a third-world country without any executive assistance."

"This is helpful," I said and continued walking. It usually takes me living with someone to find out they annoy the hell out of me. Just saved myself at least two years! Liz Chase and I are friends and nothing more. And even friends will be a bit hard if she keeps this up.

"Helpful how?" she asked, sounding equally piqued.

"Creates perspective, that's all."

"No, say what you mean. You mean, 'Thank God I didn't have a relationship with this woman because we would have killed each other.' Well, what would have happened is I wouldn't have let you talk down to me, or walk over me, or be in charge all the time, which would probably have rendered you catatonic, so yes, it *is* a good thing." And Liz Chase walked on ahead.

She has a cute walk, I thought, smiling to myself. It's the mouth that would drive me to drink.

Chapter Seven

An hour later, having changed our clothes and blown our hair dry, we were on friendlier terms as we got ready to go to dinner. I'd mentally written off our confrontation to fatigue, mostly because it was just too damned difficult to be in close proximity to someone as sexy as Liz Chase and remain angry. Nonetheless, I was seeing a side of Liz I never suspected existed beneath those curls. *She is an absolutely maddening woman,* I thought. *Way too strong! Would have to constantly argue with me over who's in charge. But at least after a blowup, she gets over it right away...like changing channels.*

I sat on the edge of my bed, and from that angle I could see Liz applying her makeup in the bathroom mirror—leaning into the glass like a theatrical performer, searching for any little imperfection, meticulously blending every line, assessing every shadow. It was a slow, sensual transformation to perfection, from boyish road companion to elegant dinner companion, that was erotic to observe.

Pretending to be reading, I watched her as she drew back from the glass and saw her entire demeanor change. She moved catlike and seemed to be more aware of her body as she stepped out into the bedroom, her head held high, struck a pose, and asked, "How do I look?" I smiled over the fact that she would unabashedly seek a compliment; however, perhaps in her world it was a question asked a dozen times a day.

"You look breathtaking." I said it lightheartedly, but I meant it.

"Oh, that's a nice word. Thank you. Let's go."

My eyes panned down to her cleavage, which was exposed to a greater degree than I would ever attempt, and I wondered if it was for my benefit or if she buttoned all her shirts that low. I also wondered what it would feel like to rest my lips between those soft pillows of perfection. *Purely a hormonal reaction and a natural one,* I psychoanalyzed myself. *I can be attracted to how someone looks without being attracted to who they are.*

"What are you thinking?" she asked when I looked up.

"I'm starving, that's all!" I sprang from the bed and led the way to the restaurant.

❖

To avoid having to step outside in the deluge we walked through a rat maze of buildings, connected to one another by strange corridors, until we finally found the musty restaurant. By now the winds were howling so horribly they sounded like a train outside the building. A powerful breeze swayed the treetops in front of the twenty-foot-high restaurant windows, lightning crashed, and the windows went electric-white for a nanosecond, then diabolical shadows flashed on the wall beside us. The old English pub took on a centuries-old dankness.

"Kind of a spooky place," I said.

A young waitress with her hair in a ponytail took our order and returned with it five minutes later, as if we'd phoned it in ahead of time. Liz frowned, and I surmised that she was thinking someone else had sent it back.

"A lot of people must order roast beef," I said in a roundabout attempt to find the answer. The waitress didn't respond but instead pulled up a chair and joined us, staring directly into my eyes with her piercing blue ones.

"So why are you two in town: business or pleasure?"

Although put off by a waitress joining my table, I was grateful to be safe and dry, so I was tolerant, thinking she would leave soon before our dinner got cold.

"We're looking at horses."

"I love animals. You know what I've always wanted?" she asked as I paused in cutting my beef.

Since we'd met only seconds before, I found that an odd question. I had no idea who she was or why she'd felt compelled to join us, much less what she'd always wanted. She continued, "I've always wanted a Viking hound, actually a Norwegian elkhound. They're my favorite dogs."

"I've had two elkhounds."

"I'd get a male, the biggest male Norwegian elkhound I could find," she added, as if I hadn't spoken.

"It's strange that you'd say that"—I was slightly more interested now—"because my male elkhound was one of the largest elkhounds on record."

"I bet he's wonderful," the waitress said. "I'd name mine Odin, if I ever got one."

"That was my dog's name—Odin." I put my fork down uneasily.

She never acknowledged me. "Odin is so great. Odin, the giant male elkhound."

"My dog died."

"Oh. But then really, when you think about it, dying only occurs when we believe in the past and the future, right? Like forward and backward? You know, knights in armor are in the past and aliens are in the future. Of course, no one we know has personally seen real live knights or aliens. We go by pictures, right? Pictures other people have painted for us. But we could raise a child and teach it that spaceships were here long ago and that one day in the distant future, we will be so strong that we can march around wearing heavy armor and be able to kill with our bare hands. Now what is backward and what is forward?" she asked sweetly.

"But we know there is a past—" Liz began.

"I don't personally know that." The waitress shrugged Valley-girl style. "I mean, suppose we could take the beginning and connect it with the end, in a circle. The circle of life." She grinned mischievously. "Elton John sang that. At any rate, we wouldn't be saying why am I back. We'd be saying see you around." And she giggled endearingly, rising to her feet. "Leaving is so subjective." She brought her hand down suddenly and covered her entire body, head to toe, in a thin white tablecloth—like a curtain separating us. "Have I left?" She laughed, her voice echoing in the cold, barren room.

"Well, no," I said, thinking her quite adept at magic as she deftly rolled the cloth back up and tucked it under her arm.

"But I've got to leave now, for real. Enjoy your dinner."

"What are the odds of that?" I asked Liz as the waitress left.

"God, the hair on my arms is standing straight up. I'm freaked!"

"Think of it, out here in the middle of nowhere, elkhound. I mean that's not a common breed—"

"Then he's this gigantic one—"

"And his name is Odin," we said in unison, then both sat perfectly still, trying to comprehend what had just happened.

"And how did she do that with the tablecloth? That was some parlor trick. Maybe they do magic acts here," I offered. "And what was all the forward, backward, around thing?"

"It's a sign," Liz whispered. "I'm telling you." Her voice rose in pitch. "I just feel like this place is in some sort of strange energy vortex."

I summoned a waiter and asked if he could send our waitress back. He said he didn't know who we were referring to, but that he would be happy to handle our check for us.

Suddenly neither of us was hungry. We agreed it was fatigue and walked back to our room chatting about our weird restaurant experience.

Liz turned most of the lights out and undressed for bed as we talked. She unbuttoned her shirt and shrugged it off her shoulders, then unzipped her slacks and stepped out of them. The dim glow from the bedside light outlined her body, making it hard for me to maintain visual contact, my eyes begging to drift southward to warmer climes. She unhooked her bra, then turned away from me at the last moment to slip it off and slide on the nightshirt that had been lying on the bed. I suppressed a sigh.

Even her back was beautiful and I wondered if she'd ever modeled. She had what I considered the perfect body: long legs that rose to narrow hips, her waist only slightly smaller than her hips, saving the big curves for her somewhat oversized breasts. Her silhouette in the dim light captivated me. She removed her underwear under the cover of her nightshirt and threw it across the room onto an armchair with her other clothes.

When her lace-topped panties set sail, I left port as well, grabbing my nightshirt and dashing into the bathroom. I needed to rest my hot forehead on the cool sink tiles, to practice breathing, and to make the ache between my legs stop. I accomplished that by focusing on brushing my teeth, then scrubbing my face so hard with a washcloth that I nearly dermabraded it.

All the lights were out, the room was silent when I came out of the bathroom, and I was aware of Liz lying in the dark.

"Aren't you going to call Clare?" she asked softly.

"She's out," I said, only partially lying since "out" might qualify as a metaphor. I crawled into bed under the cool sheets with no intention of telling Liz Chase that I no longer lived with Clare. I wasn't going to leave myself open to another relationship of convenience brought about by being away from home, lonely and in the same hotel room as an attractive woman. No sleeping around. I had my word on that.

"Is she in rehearsal?"

"I don't know." *Also the truth,* I thought. *Oh hell, am I really lying to Liz Chase in order to keep myself under control? Maybe I just don't want her to think I've been dumped. Well, I have been dumped!*

"Actually, we aren't living together anymore," I blurted out. I could hear Liz breathing. "We'd planned to split. We just never got around to it. It was a rather unemotional breakup. No kids, no pets—"

"So why now?"

I paused before admitting the truth. "I came home and found her in bed with another woman."

Liz began a slow, low laugh. "That wouldn't have been unemotional for *me.*"

"We were actually very mature about it: I smashed her lover's convertible with my car, then later she screamed and threw things at me," I said and laughed along with her. "Now that I think about it, it's ironic that she was hurling things at *me,* when I should have been chucking her cello at her!"

"How long were you together?" Liz asked gently.

"Four years. That's my limit. I've done four years four times—a total of sixteen years. I'm forty-four—I had my first live-in relationship when I was twenty-eight. Four partners, four years each. In the end, I always walk away from everything we owned jointly—which is usually everything but my underwear—and I start over financially. Personal penance, I guess, for walking out on them or perhaps for having started the relationship in the first place."

"You give them all your money?"

"Easier to make more than fight over the spoils." I wondered why I was sharing my financial status with her. *Do I think she's interested in me only because of my money, or am I interested in her and don't want her to think I have more than I do?*

"Wow," she said quietly, then, maybe sensing my self-consciousness, changed the subject. "You waited until you were twenty-eight to live with someone?"

"I suppose you were eight when you had your first relationship with the girl next door?"

"Eighteen." Liz smirked at my sarcasm. "Toni Davis, my college roomie and star of the basketball team."

"Now that's butch." I smiled.

"I guess not. She got married to a weird guy and had four kids."

"Ever hear from her?"

"Sometimes, but not about that. She's into her kids and her life. So back to you," she said as if the interview had gotten off track. "What happens in the fourth year of these relationships you have?"

"I think it starts happening right away and just crescendos in the fourth year. Speaking of which, are you shaking my bed?"

"How could I be shaking your bed from over here?"

"Do you see it shaking?"

"Maybe we're over a parking garage? Maybe the trucks outside are vibrating the bed? Call the front desk."

"And say my bed is vibrating? Sounds like a kid's joke." I picked up the phone and explained to the front desk clerk that I was in room 211 and a vibration was affecting my bed. I inquired as to roads, railways, or parking-garage problems.

"What did she say?" Liz asked when I hung up.

"She laughed, which I suppose means no."

We both sat and watched the bed move until five minutes later it stopped abruptly.

"That's a sign, if you ever want a sign that someone wants us to leave," Liz said. "How much clearer does it have to get? Even the furniture is trying to shake us out of here!"

I told Liz that the furniture at Clare's house had obviously performed the same service and laughed until tears ran down my cheeks like the torrential rain outside, releasing tension I'd carried with me for so long.

When the laughter subsided, silence ensued. In the dark, I could see Liz in silhouette as she lay on her back, looking up at the ceiling. "What are you thinking?" I asked quietly.

"You first."

"I'm thinking while this whole trip probably feels insane to you at this point, it feels like the only really sane thing I've done in a long time. I've spent every waking moment doing the bidding of lunatics. I risk my life flying across the country to meetings that mean nothing in the scope of time. I can't sell our series because a network elf wants to do a show about submerging a ballet troupe in a submarine-drowning incident, which is beyond meaningless. I don't know what the hell I'm doing with my life."

I was tearing up again and was glad I was in the dark. It was exhaustion—an emotional and spiritual exhaustion that I couldn't even name, let alone come to grips with. I closed my eyes to focus my mind on more temporal subjects to avoid crying.

"You okay?"

"Just tired." *Focus on the horse…a beautiful, muscular, kind, trustworthy animal.* I felt my mind growing heavy and my eyelids closing and my soul drifting off to sleep.

A woman struggles against me as I attempt to lift her dress, the fabric soft. I feel dizzy and something inside me shifts. Flashes of purple and gold, large flat stones against my back—my massive thighs clench her as they would the sides of a horse. I am physically much larger and more muscled than she, aware I could hurt her, but I choose not to, even though she struggles to be free. Unable to wait, I force my pulsating member into her small, tight center. I don't care if she fights me. This small woman with the beautiful blond hair is mine now. Mine. No one else will ever have her.

My body tenses and explodes. I climax and fall back exhausted, my heavy arm across her small chest keeping her from rising up and perhaps trying to harm me as I lie weak, overwhelmed by what I feel for her. Feelings I have never had for a woman and do not want. Women distract and weaken a warrior.

❖

I opened my eyes in surprise, blinking into the pitch dark and trying to arrange my thoughts, aware I had been out of my body in an elaborate fantasy. Strange images about lovemaking cast erotic shadows in my mind, images not of my making, at least not consciously. I wasn't attempting to create them. More troubling, I couldn't control them. I was someone else. Actually not someone else; I was myself, but I wasn't me.

"Are you all right?" Liz looked at me through a haze of sleep.

"Fine," I lied and glanced over at the clock. 1:11a.m. "Did I awaken you?" I asked apologetically.

"You were moaning."

"I'm sorry. I guess I was dreaming. The strangest flashes were going on in my head. Colors and textures. And for a moment, I thought I was someone else."

"Who were you?"

"I don't know…a man maybe," I said, self-conscious suddenly.

"What were you doing?"

"I was conquering a large fortress or compound and seizing a woman. She was beautiful, and I…I think I took her against her will." Just saying those words made me feel bad.

"That's—an unusual dream." Liz said softly.

"I've had similar dreams," I said and rolled over to go to sleep, not wanting to share any more of my mania with Liz Chase.

At that moment, my cell phone beeped from its resting place on the bedside table, and I picked it up and retrieved a message from Clare, telling me to call her, no matter how late.

Liz could easily hear Clare's plaintive tone from across the silence and offered to go into the bathroom so I could have some privacy to call her.

"No, don't go. It's too late to call. Years too late."

CHAPTER EIGHT

At dawn, the rain was still coming down and the toilet in our bedroom overflowed for no apparent reason; we packed quickly and went downstairs to use the lobby restroom. The restaurant had posted a sign that said it could not serve breakfast due to an equipment breakdown. Even *I* was beginning to see the signs. Tornados, people with Norwegian elkhound stories, vibrating beds, stopped-up toilets, and no breakfast meant someone wanted us to move along quickly. We packed the car and headed for our next horse farm in Kentucky.

The darkened old tobacco barns and rich green pastures of Kentucky began to line each side of the highway and soon gave way to mile upon mile of carefully tended three-rail horse fencing and gorgeous steeds befitting bluegrass country. The angle of the morning sun sent beams of light bouncing across the front seat of the car, making the journey seem celestial.

"Why do you suppose you dreamed of raping a woman?" Liz asked, startling me with the word and her directness.

In the light of day, the thought was even more horrible and embarrassing. "I think in those days, it wasn't rape exactly. It was more like…acquisition. Men simply acquired what they wanted and what they could afford, including women."

"Rape as acquisition? I think not!" she said, and I shot her a look that said "Let up."

"Maybe you have pent-up sexual energy."

"Look, it was a dream. I would never do that. I think you can attest to the fact that I'm pretty safe."

"Too safe, actually." She smiled.

"And what does that mean, Dr. Freud?"

"I shouldn't have said safe. I meant—"

"I'm just working out my relationship issues in my head so I don't keep repeating the same mistake. I want to have a thousand experiences once, instead of one experience a thousand times. It has nothing to do with you or your attractiveness or desirability—"

"Good," she said. Apparently picking up on my perplexed look she added, "Good that you find me attractive."

I cut my eyes at her, refusing to take the bait. *She's damned attractive and she knows it.* I glanced over at her as she put on a very racy pair of sunglasses, then leaned her head back on the seat, arching her neck and making me want to put my lips there. I turned the radio to XM and listened to Ray Stevens sing about a camel…anything to avoid thinking about Liz.

❖

We spent the night at the Marriott Griffin Gate in Lexington, a hotel that oozed old Southern charm. The lobby gift shop was filled with horse-abilia from countless Derby championships. The restaurant, in a separate colonial mansion, would have made Tara proud; the massive pillars disappeared up into the sky and framed a front porch that begged for a rocking chair and a mint julep. It was still relatively early, but we skipped dinner and fell into our soft beds, tired and happy, as if the entire trip was merely about this moment—these intimate conversations in the near dark, in beds separated by five feet of longing.

"So of the people you've lived with—the four—who made you wild with desire?" Liz asked, grinning like a teenager at a sleepover.

"That's a very odd question. Why would you want to know that?"

"I guess I was just wondering what an always-in-control, buttoned-up corporate executive likes in bed. Can't be that glued together all the time. You have to come loose somewhere."

Her tone was playful but I refused to play.

She filled the silence. "It's merely research on my part. I might meet someone in the corporate world one day and—"

"Cut it out," I said good-naturedly.

"True. Enough about you. I'll tell you what I like." She gave the topic a matter-of-fact tone. "I love kissing. Deep, sensual kissing. I could kiss—well, far longer than the average bear," she said, and I sucked the interior of my cheeks in until I was nearly biting them to avoid grinning at her and thus encouraging her.

She continued. "When I think about it I guess I'm very oral in all respects, but that makes perfect sense because I make my living with my mouth, as a broadcaster. Now, you make your living strategically with your mind, so maybe sex is all in your head—you think?"

"I think you're thinking all the time. Good night," I said and rolled over, turning my back to her to avoid temptation. I pretended the thick luxurious bedding and the silky pillow were Liz's body next to mine. Hearing her breathe across from me was sensual and disconcerting.

❖

At dawn, I bounced out of bed, energetic for no apparent reason, and commanded that we get into our riding gear and head for the small horse farm Liz had arranged for us to visit. My pants were black stretch, and after pulling them on, I was convinced I had bought a size too small, because every bulge and crease in my lower torso was visible. My new, shiny black boots seemed gigantic and had more laces and hooks than a corset.

Eying my huge black feet in the mirror, I sighed. "I look like Ronald McDonald at a clown funeral."

Liz giggled, and I was aware how much I liked hearing her laugh and how I liked being the one who evoked that laughter.

"There are no clown funerals, darling," Liz said. "Old clowns are recycled into crayons."

And this time I laughed.

We were headed for the door, bound for our big adventure, when my cell phone rang. Liz plopped down on the bed, turned on the TV, and kept it muted as I picked up to hear Walter Puckett's voice.

"Who is this Megan Stanford?" Walter Puckett boomed. My mind shifted into quick overdrive. Walter asking about a person three levels down meant, more than likely, he'd heard that Megan was Anselm's girlfriend.

"She's heading up a new area for us, strategic development," I replied calmly.

"She's a microbiologist! I think we might just be bringing our chicks into the nest." He laughed unpleasantly.

I didn't like his sneaking up on Anselm's flank; he was Anselm's peer. If he had a problem, he should confront Anselm. Furthermore, Megan now belonged to me, and although I hadn't asked for her, she was in my corporate care and would not be ambushed by CEOs with ulterior motives.

"Actually, the skill set she brings—an analytical, organizational approach to problem solving—is applicable across any business genre. And like any new hire, she's on the standard ninety-day probationary period." I spoke casually.

"So Anselm didn't hire her. You did?"

"No one hires for me," I answered obliquely.

"Well, she's cute. Maybe I should become her mentor."

"No dipping your pen in company ink," I kidded him.

"Oh, so strict. I like strict women. Enjoy your horse hunting. Maybe you'll find a stallion yet." I could hear him snickering. I wasn't about to let him get away with an insinuating reference to my sexuality without lifting the covers on his own.

"Did you hear the rumor that one of our high-level execs got a penile implant in exchange for A-Media's handling the doctor's brother's career?" That stopped him from hanging up. "How hard up does a guy have to be, so to speak?" I said, enjoying hearing him squirm.

"Ridiculous." He snorted, then quickly said good-bye.

"Fucking asshole. Maybe I'll find a stallion yet? Maybe I'll turn him into a gelding!" I said, hanging up the phone.

"You are the consummate corporate warrior." Liz smiled. "You like the battle: the sparring, the strategy, the kill."

"I *don't* like that," I defended myself.

She studied me. "A part of you does. Come on. Let's get out of here before someone else calls."

"You're wrong. I feel owned, like a leader in someone else's army, fighting someone else's war. They control where I go, what I do, how I behave. I'm tired of fighting these senseless corporate battles. That's how I feel!"

Liz dropped the subject since I was on a rant.

We drove west through richly rolling countryside to Aaron Harold's small horse farm. The moment we pulled onto the property

I felt as if I'd stepped into a centuries-old fantasy—Icelandic horses and lush green hills. All it needed was a fortress in the background. We saw a gorgeous blond mare with golden mane, a silver dapple, a liver-colored with silver mane, a snowy white one, and I knew we'd come to the right place. This felt like the land of the fairies, and if very small people suddenly pirouetted into the pasture I wouldn't have been surprised.

We strode across the open field toward the liver-colored horse, staring in amazement at the sheer beauty of her. "I wish I owned one of these horses," I told Liz.

"They're all beautiful, aren't they?" Aaron appeared out of nowhere, a young, lanky horse trainer befitting the intense beauty of the land and the beasts. He had a sweet, kind manner that put us immediately at ease. "Most of this herd belongs to a man in New York who sent them down for training. In fact, we're shipping several back tomorrow so it's good you arrived today."

And I couldn't help but think maybe that's why our hotel had seemed to be hurrying us on to our next destination.

Aaron led the way down the hill and suggested we saddle up. I followed him like a child chasing the Pied Piper, peppering him with questions about the horses. Aaron had two chestnuts saddled, one for himself and one for Liz, and a large brown and white pinto for me. My pinto's name was completely unpronounceable, while Liz's horse was Hlatur—a name that sounded like "louder" and meant "laughter" in Icelandic. Aaron said the man in New York had authorized the use of these particular horses for riding lessons.

Hlatur had a huge head, a massive mane of hair, and gorgeous big round eyes that peeked out from under his long, thick forelock. He stood quietly with his legs together and hooves aligned, his small, compact body so physically perfect that he could easily have been an artist's drawing on the side of a child's lunchbox. Liz immediately stroked his forehead and began whispering to him. Then she leaned over and gave him a slow, sweet kiss on his soft muzzle, and for a second I envied Hlatur. I wanted to ask him how those lips felt.

My horse was not at all interested in kissing me. In fact, he stomped and swished his tail and threw his head to let me know that this entire event bored the hell out of him. Unlike Liz's mount, my horse had not been trimmed for the warm weather and still sported his five inches of jaw hair, making him appear even more primitive than Hlatur. He had a look about him that said he knew a great deal more than he intended to waste time trying to communicate to me.

Aaron completed a final tack check on the three saddled horses just in time for rain to start trickling down from the sky. We insisted we could get a quick ride in before it really let loose, and we walked the horses away from the barn, then mounted. Liz's horse fell behind and refused to go with us until she leaned over and whispered to him, and suddenly, he caught up with us.

After Aaron was sure we wouldn't fall off, he led us through a narrow gulley and out into a much larger area of open land. We picked up speed and suddenly there it was, off and on for brief moments—the tolt. I felt the thrill, that smooth, effortless, bounceless moment of easy riding. Suddenly the skies opened up, and it began to pour a drenching, steady Kentucky rain that had us wet through to our underwear in a matter of minutes.

"Should we take cover?" Aaron called.

"Why? We can't get any wetter." I laughed.

"Ahhh, spoken like a true horseman," he said, and we rode on laughing and tolting, and trotting and squishing.

Liz and Aaron lagged behind. I was suddenly out in front with nothing but rolling hills in the distance. It was pure joy! But I had no connection to my horse, only the sensation of the ride. It wasn't the horse's temperament I cared about, only his ability to carry me forward. I mentally noted that this attitude wasn't at all like me. I also found myself inexplicably on guard and watchful, my eyes searching far out on the horizon. *I was looking up ahead—men were already engaged in battle.* Was I losing my mind? The images were so real. Then, in a split second, my conscious mind gave way.

The attack today on a massive castle compound, high on a promontory, its northern walls built into the rocky hills at its back and overlooking the fields below, is little different than any other raid, save the opportunity for more valuable chattel. The young aide to the redheaded warrior has already been instructed to be on the lookout for items belonging to the king that his superior might want, weaponry in particular. Inside the walls, the warriors ride across everything in their path, murdering and pillaging.

The elderly king, whose realm this was until only minutes ago, is decades older than the red-haired warrior, and he cannot personally protect his queen, who is younger and small of stature. Defying anyone to come near her, she stands her ground shouting orders as a sword-wielding invader runs her king through to the hilt. The queen is now fair game and can be slaughtered, raped, or claimed by any warrior who will have her; her outcome is not the red-haired warrior's affair.

His horse wheels in the air, and she glares up at the warrior for only a split second, to determine his advantage over her. The look in her eye is more piercing than any weapon he has ever encountered. She does not run like the other women. She stands her ground and defies him to take her life. She is both beautiful and deadly.

A soldier lunges for her, holding his sword aloft, preparing to behead her; she holds her ground and aims her sword at his groin. The red-haired warrior makes his split-second decision, leans from his horse, grasping her by the upper arm, near her barely concealed breast, and hoists her off the ground to safety.

The picture freezes there and fades, forever frozen in time—the red-haired warrior and the golden-haired queen.

Lightning strikes loudly in the distance.

Aaron shouted for us to halt. The crash, followed by the crisp tone of his voice, snapped me back to the present. I shook my head slightly and patted the neck of my horse, grateful one of us had stayed on course, and we headed back to the barn.

Since we really had no earthly idea what putting up a horse entailed, Aaron untacked them. We thanked him and paid him for allowing us to ride, then headed for our car, but the sound of thundering hooves made us turn back. Liz's small chestnut gelding careened toward us and slalomed to a halt across the fence from us, spraying turf and dirt in all directions, his head cocked quizzically as if to say, "Where are you going?" The wind blew his thick red forelock to one side, revealing a tiny starburst of white on his forehead. With those big eyes, he looked so vulnerable.

"My God, he's looking at you with so much love in those giant brown eyes. He really doesn't want you to go."

Liz walked over and spoke to him softly. "He knows he belongs to someone else." The horse leaned in and pressed his muzzle to her neck and made her giggle, living up to his name of Laughter. She kissed him and whispered to him.

"What are you telling him?"

"That I know how he feels to have to let go of someone and that I will always love him and remember him." As Liz looked at me, her voice softened. "Are you teary? You're a big softie, aren't you?"

"I think anyone would be teary who witnessed a horse crying over a lady."

❖

An hour later, out of our wet clothes and into our sweatpants, we flopped onto the big, soft hotel-room beds. Our room sported hunt décor, a bit stiff but luxurious, reminding me of the world in which hounds chased foxes and horses leapt over stone walls and banjos played. It had been the most exhilarating day of the trip: walking through a field of fabulous Icelandic horses, riding an Icelandic horse in open fields in the pouring rain, saying good-bye to an Icelandic horse who seemed to communicate with us. What a marvelously wonderful experience. Yet the images the horses evoked were hypnotic and disturbing.

"When I was riding out there I felt that I had stepped into a dream. I guess being on the descendant of a Viking horse triggered it." I tried to be offhanded about my confession, but Liz seemed to have connected to my troubling dreams and flashbacks without my having to explain myself.

"Maybe it's bringing up a past life for you. I imagine you rode the countryside lopping off heads. Fits your temperament."

"Thanks, darling," I said archly. "If that's true, why am I seeing it now, when it's over?"

"Maybe it's never over." She smiled enigmatically at me. "Speaking of never over…" she added slyly, waggling all five of her fingers, each with a small yellow sticky note attached to it.

I examined them more closely. The first read, *I will always love you*. The second, *Don't leave me!* The third *She is nothing; you are everything.* I stripped the notes off her fingers, recognizing the handwriting as Clare's.

"Where did you get these?"

"When I was putting our stuff in the closet one fell off your pants, another was on a shirt, and one was in the ice chest."

I shook my head in disbelief.

"So where are you living now?" Liz asked, pretending to change the subject.

"I really don't want to talk about it. I want to forget the whole Clare debacle."

"Hey, I'm not the one who posted your panties." She held up the most humiliating piece, my underwear with a note stuck to the crotch. Yanking off the note, she rubbed the cotton as if removing glue. "Wow, that's gonna hurt," she said, managing to maintain a straight face.

I snatched the note and my underwear from her. The note read, *I love the way you smell.*

Liz made an exaggerated display of keeping her lips pressed tightly together in a no-comment mode.

"Oh, fuck her," I said, exasperated.

"Yes, I think that's the lead story." Liz winked.

It was our last night on the road together, and being in the same bedroom with Liz had taken an emotional toll on me. I was nervous and couldn't sleep. *Why can't I just have sex with her, the way guys have relationships?* I thought. *It's healthier, actually, because it wouldn't tie me up for four goddamned years!* I clenched my thighs together as I thought about that. *If I were totally honest with myself, I would love to throw her down on the bed and go down on her! Yes, just take what I want! Case closed. God, I'm uncivilized,* I thought and went in and took a cold shower as punitive damages for base thoughts.

At breakfast in the hotel dining room, I caught Liz staring out the window admiring the green lawns and blue skies. She looked beautiful and serene, but melancholy. I was pretty sure I knew what she was thinking.

"You love that chestnut horse, don't you?" I said. "The one that belongs to the man in New York."

"You know…" She started to deny it, then gave in like someone talking about a lover. "I do love that old horse." She smiled and her face held a softness that nearly melted me. "But I'll get over it. He belongs to someone else."

"I don't recall that ever standing in your way," I said gently, and Liz blushed for the first time since I'd known her.

"The trainer said he's inseparable from the blond mare that was out in the pasture. Even if I could have him to love, it wouldn't be good to break them up. At least they get to go back to New York together," she said wistfully.

In that instant, I made my decision—as quickly as I'd purchased the toy horse in the antique store. "I'll talk the owner into selling them to us. You'll take lover boy and I'll take the mare."

Liz looked at me, apparently stunned by my suggestion. "You haven't even looked at the mare or ridden her."

"Every horse out there was gorgeous, and what good would riding her do? It would just show her that she's about to be bought by someone who doesn't know what she's doing, and what woman wants that!"

"You're doing this just because of me, when you don't even—"

"I'm doing it for Hlatur so he can live every man's fantasy—being adored by two blondes, you and his mare. Besides, I'll have someone to ride with. I'm single now, remember? Maybe I can make a relationship with this mare last longer than I have with a woman."

Liz just looked at me as if she were trying to decide what to make of me, as if for the first time since she'd met me, she didn't have me figured out.

"Look, if you believe in signs, we were literally blown down the highway and shaken out of that hotel to get us here much quicker than planned, because any later and we might never have met Hlatur. But we did, and the silly horse falls in love with you and you with him. So it's meant to be. Well, aren't you excited?"

"You haven't even talked to the man in New York. He probably won't sell them," Liz said, trying perhaps to keep herself from ultimate disappointment.

"He'll sell them. Negotiations are what I do for a living. When I go after something, it's mine. Do you want the horse?"

"Yes!" She swooned. "My God, will it cost a fortune?"

"Why is it we'll pay forty-five thousand dollars for a piece of steel to drive around, knowing it falls apart in three years, but we're worried about the cost of a furry friend for life?"

"Okay, make the deal and I'll get a loan."

"I'll take care of the money."

"No. I take care of my own business. I'll have the money…just keep it reasonable, okay?"

We shook hands. Only this time, her grip was softer, clasping me in the way she might hold a lover. I had to keep myself from sighing in public and happily contemplated long afternoon rides with Liz on our wonderfully kind Icelandic horses.

I would not have believed, even if someone had told me, that an Icelandic horse would mirror my mind and reflect my very soul. Or that what I brought to the horse would be upon me in seconds. Or that the Icelandic horse would be a vortex into an ancient past. Nor had I come upon that perplexing instruction in the *Icelandic Horse Training Manual* that said, "The best way to stop an Icelandic horse from running away with you is never to let it happen."

CHAPTER NINE

Before nine a.m., I phoned the horse farm to tell Aaron we'd like to come out and see Hlatur and his mare, only to learn that both horses had been put on a truck at dawn bound for New York. I was upset that the horses were moving in the wrong direction. If we bought them, they'd have to turn around and make the trip again, which would unnecessarily stress them. Liz looked crestfallen as she heard my side of the conversation about her beloved Hlatur being trailered away from her.

I managed in a roundabout way to learn that Hlatur's owner was a man named Furtillo, who Aaron would only say lived somewhere in upstate New York. I would locate Furtillo myself, knowing that a successful deal happened when no one was between me and the ultimate decision maker.

I rang Jane at her home, asked her to do a search on Furtillo, and she called me back in fifteen minutes, having located his number. I phoned him in Utica, New York, at his farm. His service said he was out of the country but would be calling in, and she would relay the message. I left my number.

As we loaded up the car to head home, Liz's cell phone rang. It was the station, apparently unable to wait another twenty-four hours before telling her where they wanted her to go and what they wanted accomplished.

"I did the corn festival parade last year, so that one goes to Mac." Liz lay back in the seat with her head lolling around, most likely in despair over the triviality of it all. "I'll do that one," she said in reference to another opportunity for the masses to see local TV stars live. "No, not that one," she moaned, sorting through the list. "Tell him he'll get more live cut-ins. We'll talk at the run-through tomorrow." Liz hung up and deciphered the call for me, adding that she had a new news director who wanted to beat the competition. "Which would be fine," she said, "if it were just to give the public a better product, but this guy's more like my dick's bigger than yours."

"You seem to take it all in stride."

"Because I'm not a warrior. I'm just the air-hair, remember?"

I apologized again. My remarks had obviously cut deep or she wouldn't have repeated them.

"It's okay. I *am* all about face time. The more people see me and know me and wave at me, the more viewership goes up and the more the GM loves me because I'm ratings royalty. But who I appear to be and who I am are two entirely different people."

"My point exactly. No one gets to see who you are."

"I'm only interested in letting one person see who I am," she said, and the light through the windshield splintered like diamonds onto the dashboard and the steering wheel, and refracted off Liz's sunglasses and jewelry and beautiful blond hair as if the heavens were spotlighting their own. I sighed, unable this time to conceal my reaction.

❖

The sixteen-hour drive home flew by as we, at first, fretted over Hlatur's traveling in the wrong direction, then later put a positive spin on the horses' trip to New York, saying their delayed arrival in Texas would give us time to find out what to buy them, where to board them, and when we'd ride them.

After hours of talking and laughing, Liz finally curled up and went to sleep as I drove. I thought about her and watched her occasionally out of the corner of my eye. She was a beautiful woman with full sensual lips, a narrow nose, and large blue eyes. I mentally slapped myself around; I wasn't going to start mooning over leaving her. I didn't want a relationship. Women were all great in the beginning—love was all great in the beginning—that first sexual encounter was always exciting. It was the four years I needed to remember.

"Your mind is going a hundred and ninety miles an hour." She chuckled with her eyes closed. "You think because Clare's out of the picture, and we're getting horses together, that I'm going to mistake our relationship for more than friendship and dive on you." She suddenly lunged at me like the boogeyman at a scared child, and I jumped and swerved the car.

"Damn it, are you trying to get us killed?" I said, irritated.

"Guess what, Ms. Chandler, I wouldn't jump you if you begged. So relax. Just friends." And she chuckled some more.

Liz Chase's gratitude over my plan of getting the horses certainly didn't last long, nor did any sense of being beholden to me. I didn't know what to think, but I didn't feel relaxed around her. I knew that much.

❖

Reentry was painful...sailing out of the serenity of Kentucky horse farms and blasting into the frenetic atmosphere of network and talent chaos. Jane stood in my doorway before I'd even had time to snap my laptop into its docking station.

"Hugh in legal says he's got to talk to you before lunch, but wouldn't tell me why," she said, reading from her notes and attaching people's work areas to their names as if I'd arrived from another planet and had no knowledge of the people on hers. "Jack in sales left a copy of the carriage contracts on your desk, and he didn't look happy. Maxine in talent and research says a client is suing us. One of the on-air talent was arrested for drunk driving, and there's...some other emergency!" Jane threw her hands up in the air, as if caught in a robbery in which her memory was stolen and, I assumed, to accentuate that her world had gone mad in only a few short days.

"Maxine, Hugh, Jack, Starbucks," I rattled off, prioritizing.

"Okay," she said and left.

I looked up to see Maxine in the doorway.

"Who was arrested?" I asked, my tortoise-shell reading glasses propped down on my nose.

"LaTisha. Arizona Highway Patrol."

LaTisha, whose on-air success seems to hinge on the fact that her bra size is larger than her I.Q.? I thought, but said only, "What's she doing in Arizona?"

"Vacation. Driver drinking, she wasn't. Hugh's handled. No press. My other emergency: guy in post-production beat his wife up this morning, then she tried to commit suicide. Called HR about him.

Handling the police." She spoke in a fast, cryptic fashion, aware I gravitated to executives who could cover lots of verbal landscape at a high rate of speed, pointing out the essential elements and moving on.

"Who's the wife beater?"

"Fred Davis, video editor."

"Shit. You know if this is true—" I warned, knowing I would probably lose a very creative editor.

"We know where you stand on that." Maxine gave me a big false smile. "Glad you're back?"

"Thrilled." I mirrored her smile.

She was exiting as Hugh entered my office looking like his blood pressure was spiking. For an attorney, Hugh had a nicely buffed body topped by a completely bald head that flushed pink when he was upset.

"You heard about LaTisha and Fred-with-the-wife deal?"

"Yes." I nodded, undoubtedly too calm for his liking.

"So you got the whole story?" Hugh loved to be first on the scene with shocking news.

"Yes," I said, and Hugh looked miffed.

"Seems like all your people have gone nuts!" he said, and admitted he didn't like his morning disrupted.

Since this kind of thing was in part why we employed attorneys, I was irritated that he was irritated.

"We're amateurs aspiring to the escapades of corporate—exec VP boffing a client's underage daughter, remember that one? We in programming and talent acquisition make the occasional mundane faux pas simply to get our money's worth from the allocation we take from you in legal. After all, if you had nothing to do, you could go home."

"Man, you're in a mood." He snorted as Jane plopped the Starbucks cup in front of me and my phone rang. "Might want to try to get that to her earlier, or at least before I meet with her," Hugh mumbled to Jane on his way out. "I'm going to the men's room. Shout when you're off the phone," he called over his shoulder.

It was 11:11 a.m., most of the morning gone. I grabbed the phone and Nick Furtillo said he was returning my call. Hearing what I wanted, he said he had no intention of selling the two horses. I was quite certain I'd been awake longer and had handled bigger issues this morning than Nick, so I was ready for him, inquiring about his business trip, casually communicating that I was president of a large entertainment conglomerate. I quickly pinpointed mutual acquaintances, building a bridge between us, letting him know I was more than just one lone business deal.

I left him my number, then called my bank to transfer funds to cover the horse purchase, horse insurance, transport, tack, vet checks, and other miscellaneous items. Business was something I understood. The man would sell; I could hear it in his voice. Nick was the kind of guy who already knew what he was going to do with the money he'd just turned down. He was the kind of guy who always said no first—to give himself a chance to think—and he was thinking I might be a bigger client down the road if he did this deal for me.

Jane poked her head in to say that "Hugh from legal" was back, and I grinned, thinking Jane's announcements made her sound like a courtier.

Hugh slouched down on my leather couch. "Okay, we didn't get to finish. Stinett Stone, the Olympic whatever, managed to miss his plane and therefore his gig as guest speaker for the yacht conference in Barcelona, largest gathering of private yacht manufacturers in the world." Hugh bent over the coffee table, foraging like a squirrel in my crystal candy dish. "Now in addition to being ugly, Stinett's gonna get us sued." Hugh dug for the Godivas at the bottom of the bowl.

"Worse case, negotiate our picking up part of the tab in exchange for a release," I said, not looking up from my e-mail, the possible solutions to this kind of problem not complex enough to require anyone's full attention.

"Why are we booking stars at yacht conferences?" Hugh spoke as he chewed.

"He's not a star. Does that answer your question?"

"Getting us out of this could cost a million bucks. Does that come out of *your* budget?"

"Are you trying to irritate me, because it's working," I asked. "Does our E&O insurance cover no-shows?"

"Checking."

"At the bottom of the candy bowl?" I gouged Hugh. "Alternative is to sue Stinett, but believe it or not, he's landed a supporting role in a rather large motion picture being directed by another of our clients, so that gets sticky." I finally glanced up at him.

"I never liked the guy," he muttered.

Having packed his cheeks with chocolate, he exited. Jack arrived on his heels, replacing him on my couch.

"You're out of the raspberry ones," Jack said, slopping candy out of the bowl. "You read the contract yet?"

"All eighty pages front to back three times," I said. "In fact, my office is so quiet I'm thinking of turning it into a Christian Science Reading Room."

"Good, because I've had two hours of Anselm chewin' my cheeks over this damned deal so I got to get it signed. You enjoy your vacation?"

"I loved it. Horse farms. God, it was beautiful."

"You'll probably own a horse farm one day." He stretched out on the couch. "You could strap a little mini-laptop up there on the saddle horn, ride around and do your e-mail all at the same time."

"But then I'd miss these enlightening conversations with you."

"Oh, I'd come live with you. I'd muck out the stalls…get all the horseshit out."

"Much as we try to do in our current line of work." I smiled fondly at him and he schlumped out.

I buzzed Jane, who dutifully appeared in my doorway.

"Take the candy dish out of here, will you?" I said, and Jane scrunched her face up in disapproval. "Keep the nuts at your desk."

❖

The following afternoon, I was sitting at my desk having Liz withdrawal. She'd e-mailed me a note, but other than that—nothing. I envisioned her back in her TV personality mode: client lunching, shopping with friends, having a life that didn't include me. My cell phone rang and I grabbed it, hoping it was Liz wanting to go to dinner. It was Nick Furtillo calling me twenty-four hours sooner than I'd expected. He would sell the horses provided I paid the shipping and signed a medical hold-harmless, meaning if anything happened to the horses en route or they arrived sick, their care was on my nickel, not his, and if they dropped dead I should forget phoning him. He agreed to a pre-ship vet check and I agreed to the rest.

"By the way, what's the mare's name?" I asked.

"Rune."

I Googled an Icelandic dictionary for the word "Rune" and read that it was a Viking symbol. The original word had most likely meant "secrets"—Runic symbols, drawn ten thousand years ago and found on the walls of the Trois Freres cave in France. The Runic alphabet was called the Futhark, which had contained sixteen letters in Viking times. Each rune had a name, a numerical value, and a magical use.

Rune is a secret. Maybe this horse will communicate with me and tell me why we're both here, I mused, and smiled to myself. At that moment a warm wind swirled around my neck and shoulders and rippled down my arms, sending a chill across my back and fluttering the papers stacked on my desk, causing me to glance up at the door to see if someone had opened it suddenly or if any air was coming from one of the overhead vents, but nothing seemed amiss. For a moment, I felt as if someone were present, an almost sensual feeling without a source, at least none I could identify.

Shaking off the feeling in favor of more practical endeavors, I called my bank and left word to wire Furtillo the money the following morning, then personally ordered a dozen orange roses and had them delivered to Liz Chase at the station just before the six o'clock news with a note that read *Had to take a short trip to New York, but I'm coming back to live with you in two weeks. Better find me a stall. Love, Hlatur. PS. Bringing my girlfriend Rune with me.*

Liz called at 5:45 p.m. and squealed into the phone, so excited she could barely contain herself. Her excitement fueled me; I was happy she was happy.

"How did you do it?" she demanded.

"No one can resist me when I negotiate," I said playfully, with intentional arrogance.

"You are very good," she said sweetly.

"I am, actually," I said, aware I was speaking to her in a tone I reserved for someone with whom I'd been very intimate.

"What do I owe you?"

"We'll settle up later." I was feeling rather proud of myself. Cool, confident, even cocky. I had the horses and Liz Chase was impressed. "Would you like to have a late dinner?"

"Tonight? Oh, I, uh…have dinner plans," and just the sound of her voice told me it was a personal dinner with someone.

"No problem. We'll…talk soon," I said, deflated and disappointed. I hung up and turned on the TV, tuning in to watch Liz on the six o'clock news. She was so poised. What if someone saw her and offered her a network job in New York or a cable job in Atlanta? And who was she having dinner with? *If I were Anselm, I'd just hire her to work for me so I could be around her all the time.* Morality was hell, and I wasn't sure it had much upside. When the station went to commercial break, I phoned Madge to see if she'd have dinner with me.

❖

"Let me try to work through this with you," Madge said as we ate Chinese food at a ratty little neighborhood restaurant and I sulked. "She wants you. You want her but won't go through with it because it could end in four years. She goes out with someone else and you're heartbroken."

"Hardly heartbroken," I said, trying to sound nonchalant.

"So you could just quit seeing her altogether, or you could just say what the hell, it'll be a great four years, or you could get psychiatric help."

"Oh, please!"

"Face it. You've got your gears jammed in neutral. You need a tune-up. Personally, I'd get my pipes blown out by the blonde, but for two hundred and fifty dollars an hour you can have some old broad tie your four-year fear back to the way you were breast-fed—"

"I thought you said I should stay away from Liz Chase!" I interrupted what I feared was about to become a tirade.

"That was plan A and you failed. So now we're on plan B, which is just go have sex with her and be done with it, so we can all quit hearing about it."

"Shut up and eat, will you," I said morosely.

"Dinner with you every night would be no damned picnic. I should tell her that."

❖

The following afternoon, I walked into my office to find a dozen people standing around my conference table, a cake in the center and baby shower gifts around it. I was certain I was in the wrong room. "Surprise!" they yelled in concert, and Jane giggled with glee at having stunned me. "It's a baby shower for your horse!"

I could not have come up with an event I would have disliked more than my own personal horse baby shower, unless it was a root canal without anesthesia. Baby showers were insipid enough, but baby showers for horses were completely ridiculous, and from the look on Jack's face he could not have agreed more. I swiftly went into gear, overpowering my aversion to the event and seeking to find something I could effervesce about. The cake had horses on it, the wrapping paper had horses, albeit a three-year-old's rocking horse, and the gifts were items like tiny horse blankets and tiny bowls and candy treats.

"What have you named your baby horse?" the young director of human resources, whose name escaped me and, therefore, whom I merely called HR, asked me.

"Well, my horse is five years old so she has a name—Rune."

"Ruined? Like spoiled?" HR wrinkled up her nose in displeasure.

"R-U-N-E." Jane jumped in. "But it means ruined," she said in a Shakespearian aside, the kind of sidebar that made me want to skewer her.

Guilty over that thought, I plastered a large smile on my face and tried not to say anything I hadn't edited in advance. Hugh and Jack escaped the moment a piece of cake was slung onto a napkin for them, and the rest of the crowd stayed only a polite minute more. I was relieved when it was over and Jane headed back to her desk in a euphoric state, having surprised and pleased her boss.

I sank into my chair as e-mail pinged onto my desktop. "Did you survive it?" was the only line from Liz. I dialed her on my cell phone.

"You knew in advance? Rotten of you not to warn me. Did you have a good dinner last night?"

"It was okay," she said, not offering to tell me with whom she went, or where. "I'm excited about our horses coming," she said, changing the subject. "I went to the tack store on Beauville Road today and got a few things for Hlatur. You should stop over there." I was annoyed that she'd gone without me, and she must have sensed that. "I would have bought Rune something, but I didn't know what you want for her."

"World peace," I said, and we both laughed, even though I felt like anything but laughing. Liz was separating from me. *That's an interesting thought*, I told myself, *since we've never been together.*

CHAPTER TEN

It had taken me only a few days to move into an airy new town house, spurred on by shared domesticity with Madge, whose demeanor after forty-eight hours was crocodilian. This morning I awoke to my brand-new abode, stretched out in the clean white sheets, smiled up at the big beams overhead, and luxuriated in the ceiling fan's slow breeze on my naked body like a soft summer wind, making me wonder how Liz Chase felt.

I picked up the PDA at my bedside and clicked the photo file, staring at the picture taken of Liz Chase, not asking myself why I kept her photo by my bed or why I continually looked at it, dissolving into those eyes and wondering was she deliciously soft, did she have muscle tone, or no tone, could she kiss? She advertised that she could kiss. Kissing was so critical. I couldn't remember how long it had been since I'd been met at the door with kisses. Maybe seven years ago, before Clare, with the crazy redhead who carved good-bye notes in my furniture.

The redhead's name was Rosalind. *Roz*, I thought in spite of myself. Good-looking, persistent, passionate, available. *Very similar situation,* I thought. And where had all those erotic moments led? To a threatened palimony suit, phone calls to my previous employer making me appear to be insanely gay, and to her carving her name into the bottom of all my dining-room chairs. *And Liz Chase has more chutzpah than Roz. An unhappy Liz Chase might well carve her name in my chest!* I hopped out of bed to tackle the day, delighted to have snapped myself back into reality.

I was going to get the laundry done, make phone calls, and wax my face—the latter inarguably the modern woman's most barbaric practice. Either God should have given women full facial hair, or no facial hair at all; the occasional stiff dark hair was truly a cosmic slap in the face. As much as I dreaded it, I was about to rip those hairs off in one overwhelmingly quick and painful act.

I heated the wax, hating this particular ablution, but aware every time a salon did it for me, my face broke out, convincing me bacteria lurked in their creams and waxes. Determined to be my own torturer, I sucked in my breath and wielded the spatula, spreading the thick, shiny liquid across my upper lip, down across my cheeks, and under my chin. As a drop of wax splashed into the sink basin, congealing instantly into an orange solid, I glanced up into the mirror and blinked, unbelieving. My hair, short and rumpled from bed, no makeup, sunken and tired green eyes, and now a short red beard easing up around my cheeks and over my lip revealed me unintentionally transformed. I stood transfixed, a shiver electrifying my spine as I tried not to move an inch, afraid I might break the spell. The man in my dreams, the man with the red beard—I could pass for that man!

"Move the troops around to the west wall." The phrase startled me, seeming to come from nowhere, apropos of nothing, spoken to the man in the mirror. It was completely believable. *I* would have followed me. I was aware I'd be ripping my skin off with the hair if I didn't get the wax off soon and put my hand to my face to strip away the image of the man in the mirror. The transition was seamless.

One minute I was in my bathroom mirror and the next…

I am standing over an earthen basin, rubbing my face and splashing ice-cold water on it. I am tired. My men are mopping up, tending to the wounded; the remaining women are building contained fires and cooking food. An old crone scatters her divining rocks on the stone floor and scurries across it, a pack of black wild dogs at her heels. She points her crooked index finger at the sky, shouting and cursing everyone around her and excoriating the heavens.

"Who is she?" I ask my devoted young aide.

"King's oracle," the sandy-haired boy replies. "She's cursing us for killing the king and herself for not saving him."

"I think Herlugh caused his death." I smile, thinking of the fine

young man who had delivered the most damage to the dying king. I must remember to promote him.

"Thank you for saving my life today." The young aide throws the words at me quickly, obviously embarrassed that he had needed saving.

"One day perhaps you will return the favor, saving me." I grin, doubting this eager boy will ever be in such a position. "Fetch the crone. Maybe she can tell us what the gods have in store for us."

At that moment a collective sucking of air takes place, a communal gasp. I turn in time to see the crone throw herself off a parapet to her death, her cries echoing throughout the castle, her remorse at the death of her king evidently too great for her to bear. The black dogs' cries pierce the air as they pace up and down at the spot where she had leapt.

Shaken by the bad omen of the king's oracle taking her own life, I rip the beard from my face with a sharp blade.

The stinging sensation brings me back to the present.

Peeling away the remaining wax, I saw my own reflection. For a moment, something deeply buried in my DNA had surfaced and connected me with myself in a way I still did not fully comprehend, the light of who I might have been illuminating who I was and projecting that image into the mirror.

"Maybe I do need to see a therapist," I said to Madge as I lounged on her couch, this time giving up and drinking the damned tea.

"You're feminine. You just have a large head and a strong jawline, no makeup, and of course a flare for the dramatic."

"If I had told you to take a battalion of troops over the hill looking the way I did in that mirror, you would have followed me to your death."

"Darling, I'd follow you looking just the way you do right now." Madge winked at me in her never-can-tell-who-turns-me-on kind of way. Madge was a mystery when it came to sex. She claimed to be the oldest living virgin in the country, a title most people would pay money not to hold, but for Madge it was a badge of honor. She said sex was in the head, not in the bed, and she could have head-sex while she was driving and get other things done. Bed-sex just weighed her down. "You have yet to give me a blow-by-blow of your trip with her." She raised an eyebrow.

"Nothing happened. We saw great countryside, we slept in separate beds, and we bought horses," I said, enjoying seeing her eyes fly open wide.

"You bought horses! We had dinner together and you didn't tell me that?"

"I wasn't myself."

"What kind of horses?" she demanded.

"The kind with four legs."

Madge pulled her neck back like a turtle retreating into its shell and stared at me. "What does your horse look like?"

"Don't know yet."

Madge snorted and I grinned enigmatically. For once I had rendered Madge Mahoney speechless. "Better buy some land, then." She finally found her voice. "Stop being nomadic. Despite the fact that you've made wealthy women of all your exes, you have enough money to buy a house, for God's sake, but you won't! That's irresponsible—it's un-American! You'll be boarding your horse with someone just as *you've* boarded with someone! Four someones! You won't even commit to an address of your own!"

"Are you actually shouting at me because I'm not a home owner?" I asked, bewildered.

But Madge was just shouting now to hear herself shout. I was convinced that's what lack of sex had done to her; it had culminated in verbal orgasms.

❖

It was a beautiful summer morning when Liz and I got word that Rune and Hlatur were loaded aboard the trailer in New York bound for their temporary home with us at Maynard Wilkie's farm. I'd dismissed the idea of hiring an equine transport service once I saw their route. Instead, I'd hired Maynard Wilkie, a middle-aged rancher who had hauled horses all over the country for a living. Maynard had personally agreed to drive to New York with his six-horse trailer and bring our horses home.

Friday, I took the day off so I'd be on hand no matter what time the horses arrived; Liz came over to my place right after she finished doing the morning news, and together we waited for a report of their travels. Maynard phoned to say the stable boy had told him, as they were loading, that the horses had been off their feed and not drinking water, so Maynard was keeping a close eye on them, unsure the horses were healthy.

"Looks like for all this ole boy's horse tradin' he don't take such good care of his stock," Maynard said in that flat cowboy way he had. "I can turn this rig around and dump 'em back where I got 'em and cut yer losses."

I told him to keep driving and just get them here as quickly as he could. If the horses weren't being cared for, they'd have a better life with us than with Furtillo.

By late evening, the reports were dire. Rune and Hlatur weren't eating or drinking. Maynard said he thought maybe it was the trailer movement, so he pulled into a rest area off the highway and tried to get them to eat or drink—no luck. He'd intended to get a few hours' sleep on the road; however, the horses' condition changed all that. They were stressed, he told us in his matter-of-fact way, so he was going to drive all night to get them back to his farm. Anything less and he might lose them. *Thank God I didn't use the trucking service, which would have traveled hundreds of miles out of the way to drop off other horses before finally getting to us.*

Liz fretted, wanting to know how long a horse could go without water. I dodged her question, but finally admitted a day was pushing it. She wanted to know in detail what happened after a day, but I truly didn't know. I suspected they colicked—a condition in which their intestines kinked or were obstructed.

"Horses *die* of colic," Liz said, savvier than I anticipated. "I think they flush oil through their systems to save them, but how's that going to happen on the highway going eighty miles an hour, and who's going to even know the horse has colic? If I've bought Hlatur and then caused him to die, I won't be able to stand it!"

"I may not be grace under pressure, but you are doom! Nothing is going to happen to these horses." I held her forearms to keep her from fleeing like a frightened animal. "It's going to be all right." *Do I know that or do I just want that to be the case*, I thought. But I never changed my resolute expression.

Maynard called to say he was making good time and would be pulling in around 11:00 p.m. At 10:45 p.m. on that cool summer night, we pulled onto Maynard's old, run-down farm. We saw no sign of him, but his horse trailer was parked out by the stable, the engine still running and the trailer doors open. Maynard suddenly stepped out of the small wooden farmhouse, and I strode toward him extending my hand.

"Thank you for bringing them here safely."

"Well, they still haven't taken a drink and they've got to, or they're gonna be in real trouble. I'm inside cleaning up. You all go on over to the barn, you'll spot 'em in the corral."

Maynard went back into the house and we walked toward the barn. A few hundred feet away in a small pipe enclosure, beneath the moon's celestial glow, stood two exquisite horses. Hlatur was unmistakable with his large head, massive mane, gorgeous big eyes, and beautifully formed body. He moved to the fence and nickered to Liz, she ran to him and put her cheek against his muzzle, and they cuddled together in the cool night air like long-lost lovers. I didn't recognize the beautiful little golden horse next to him.

"That's her." Liz's voice held a smile. "She's the only mare here."

I couldn't believe this gorgeous mare was mine. Flashier even than Hlatur, Rune could not have been lovelier, so elegant. Both horses stood perfectly still in the moonlight. I walked up to Rune and slowly put my arms around her neck, hugging her close. She waited for me to let go, then turned and walked toward the horse waterers...and began to drink. Hlatur followed. They knew they had reached their destination; we were the people they had come to join.

For a moment, under the moonlight, I felt a bond forging among us—the gelding, the mare, Liz, and me—two women who didn't know where this would all lead, but who were led by a force beyond understanding.

The moonlight reflected off my watch. 11:11 p.m.

CHAPTER ELEVEN

The horses awoke to an experience akin to being inducted into the army.

Dr. Brown countered suspected mild colic by pumping mineral oil down Hlatur's nose and into his stomach, a highly unpleasant experience, judging from Hlatur's attempted moonwalk out of the barn.

A large metal vise pried Rune's mouth open so shards of her teeth could be ground off, and her eyes widened as if she'd just discovered her stall was on fire.

"Gotta get 'em off, or she won't be able to chew or wear a bit," Brown shouted over the roar of the drill. "Let's give them all their shots, then have a look at Hlatur's sheath." *An odd word implying Hlatur's genitalia is his sword and the sheath its scabbard,* I thought as Brown launched into a brisk description of how in the wild a horse kept himself clean by running through streams and rivers. In captivity, the horse developed a waxy buildup in his sheath—a condition that, prior to horse ownership, I thought only happened to kitchen floors.

"You'll get so used to it, you'll think nothing of doing this yourself," Dr. Brown announced, working away with warm soap and water.

"I won't be visiting that part of his anatomy unless I've lost my diamond up there," Liz muttered.

❖

At dusk the following day, I was brushing and grooming Rune, and Liz was combing Hlatur's mane when Maynard stepped into the barn. "So have you ridden her yet?" he teased, knowing full well I had not.

"I think we should take your old quarter horse and the three of us ride out on a test drive," I replied.

"No, I'm not going out in the dark in the rain, and you shouldn't either," Liz fretted.

"It'll be fine. We won't go far."

East of the farmhouse and barn was a clearing that meandered into a thickly wooded area with trails that Maynard used to exercise his horses. I had never been back there, but I was more than willing to do it that night. I quickly saddled Rune, climbed on board—none too nimbly—and told Maynard I was ready. Liz reminded me to buckle the strap on my helmet and to take it easy. I could tell she didn't feel good about this venture, but she didn't want to send me off with any negative images. "Don't be gone long. I'll be right here," she assured me.

Had I known my horse better, I would have been able to say that Rune didn't feel too good about this either. I was still a strange woman taking her out into the dark of night through woods with wet, low-hanging tree branches, far from the little barn that contained Hlatur, her only comfort in this strange place. As Maynard and I started off into the woods, keeping our horses at a walk, I felt an immediate exhilaration. I was on board my smooth-tolting, incredibly intelligent, gentle, gorgeous Icelandic horse.

"How does she feel?" Maynard asked, obviously pleased with how things were going.

"Fabulous!"

I trailed behind him, feeling what could only be described as blissful, and after about an eighth of a mile I decided to tolt. I had dreamed of the tolt from the moment I had seen the pictures in the horse book; tolting was all I wanted to do. I wanted a horse that was a tolting machine, a horse that would continue effortlessly in that magical gait that allowed its rider to drink a stein of beer without ever spilling a drop.

"Just pull her head up a little and sit back," he said.

I obeyed awkwardly, but my mare responded like a well-tuned sports car, shifting right into gear. I experienced an absolutely phenomenal, all-time high and could have ridden forever just like that as we moved down the rough trail with celestial suspension, the wind in my hair, a broad smile on my face. Five minutes later when Maynard circled us back around to head home, I was still tolting, but at a much faster speed. I told myself to relax and just pull her in a little, but she didn't seem to respond. I sat back and pulled on the reins, then released, but she didn't slow down.

"Pull a little more firmly," Maynard said.

She was picking up more speed. I pulled on the reins again, my response reactionary. She leaned into the bit, and her tolt got faster.

"Sit back in the saddle," Maynard shouted.

My horse was no longer tolting, but had slipped a gear right past the canter and moved into a full, dead-out, panic-stricken run, as if she carried Ichabod Crane and we were being pursued by the Headless Horseman. The wet tree branches slapped against my face and body, and I squinted to avoid damaging my eyes as we careened into the darkness. I heard Maynard shouting, "Turn her head!" Then his voice fell away and I was alone on the back of my wild mare.

As Rune put distance between us and Maynard, I struggled to keep my balance and not fall over onto her neck. My upper body was rigid from fear, and my legs were weak and shaking in sheer terror; controlling this horse was impossible.

My mind projected vivid images: a friend who had broken her pelvis riding a runaway horse, her legs floating up into the air unconfined by any pelvic structure; a coworker who'd broken her pelvis when her horse completed its run by making an abrupt ninety-degree turn, sending her flying out of the saddle with bone-breaking centrifugal force. My entire thought process suddenly centered on my pelvic bone.

In an absurd inner conversation, I analyzed whether to jump from my horse. My inner voice said, "Jump or break your pelvis!" Another voice inside my head warred with it: "Jump and break your neck!" These mental images were obviously being transmitted to Rune, who must have been horrified by them and picked up speed to escape a graveyard of breaking bones.

My mind focused on the next immediate dilemma: if Rune could go this fast in the dark, slippery, tree-strewn forest, how fast would she go once we hit the clearing between the woods and the barn? Would she run full tilt up to the barn, then cut left at a tight ninety-degree angle, smashing my face up against the barn wall like a Garfield suction cup to a car window?

I could glimpse the clearing up ahead through the tree branches; time was up for decision making. Throwing the reins up in the air, I used the motion of my arms to lift myself up and out of the saddle, then flung myself off the left side of the horse away from her thundering hooves and into Rattlesnake Creek. My head hit the ground before my body, and Christopher Reeve flashed through my mind as my helmet withstood the force of the impact that could have killed or maimed me.

For a fleeting second I wondered if I could move my arms and legs, then, dazed and bruised, I staggered to my feet and listed toward the barn. Maynard circled back to ask if I was all right as I tried to put the best possible face on my embarrassing accident.

"I wouldn't want to do it again," I said, dragging myself along for a few yards, trying to decide if I had a concussion, when suddenly I looked up to see my mare standing in my path, the reins dangling to the ground in front of her. She had come back for me.

As Maynard rode on ahead to warn Liz of the vision she would see emerging from the woods, I staggered over to my horse and looked into her calm eyes. "Mare," I addressed her, stroking her beautiful face and whispering to her as she stood silent, head hanging down, "this can't happen again. You could kill me."

Rune and I walked back to the barn. In the side mirror of my parked car, I caught sight of myself, a large clump of green turf attached to the front of my helmet. I was about to pull it out when Liz spotted me trudging along.

"Oh, my God, are you okay?" Liz ran to me. "Maynard said you fell into Rattlesnake Creek. You could have been bitten by snakes!"

"At the speed I was traveling, when I hit the creek bed, I would have pulverized any snake in my way."

Maynard grinned as men in these parts did, men who figured that if I was still breathing when I got off the ground, everything was fine. "I think we'd better get you set up with a trainer and install some brakes on that mare. Green horse, green rider makes for black-and-blue."

"Let's get you home," Liz said, handing my horse over to Maynard to unsaddle and guiding me toward the car.

I sank into the car seat, in pain, thinking I had ruined my first ride with Rune; we had gotten off to a rotten start.

❖

Figuring I was in enough pain without someone in a white coat adding to it, I refused to go to the ER, whereupon Liz refused to let me stay home alone with my injuries, insisting someone should watch me overnight to make sure I didn't have a concussion. She left only long enough to grab her clothes for work, returning a half hour later to check on me. Tears in my eyes, I was standing where she'd left me, trying to get out of my shirt.

Hurrying to help me, she asked, "How hard did you hit your head?"

"Hard."

"What in hell were you trying to prove?"

"If you're staying to help me, fine—if it's to abuse me, leave."

"I don't work for you, so hush," she said gently, and I chose not to answer.

She undressed me, threw my clothes in the laundry, and heated some soup. When she came back, she ordered me into bed, but I was once again standing where she'd left me, unable to bend at the waist.

"Tried to get into bed. Can't do it. My back won't bend. Do you have pain pills?" I asked, moving only my lips.

"Do you have a doctor? Maybe we should go to the hospital."

"No. What have you got?"

"Darvocet, from when I pulled my back out a few months ago."

"Bring me one," I said as she tried to help me into bed, guiding me as I yelped. I had my arms around her and was in so much pain that I had no thought of the pleasure of being close to her, only that she was strong and smelled good. "You can't stay with me. You have to get up at dawn and go to the station," I said, every word evoking pain.

"Don't tell me what I can do! You know, while I've got you down, I think you should contemplate why you want to run. Your horse wants to run away, you want to run away. What does that mean?"

"Please don't psychoanalyze me."

"Horses get mental images, vibrations, feelings…odd that the first thing she did in your relationship is run away."

I saw a smile playing at the corner of her mouth.

❖

At dawn, it took me thirty minutes to get myself upright so I could go to the bathroom. I rolled onto my stomach and slid off the bed onto my knees, then grabbed the bedside dresser with both hands and bench-pressed my body up, trying not to spill the glass of water or knock the lamp off the table. As I hoisted myself to a full vertical stance, I yelled in response to the excruciating pain and tried to think how I would get in and out of my desk chair at the office.

I shuffled to the shower and let hot water stream across my back, feeling it loosen my muscles, counting on the "loosening" to last just long enough for me to pull on a suit for work. It took some maneuvering and a great deal of swearing to get into my socks and dress pants and slip on a pair of shoes, so I took a break before trying the bra and shirt and took geisha-girl steps to the coffee machine.

Liz had left a note propped up on a china coffee mug. "Punch button, dial office, say you can't come in, and go back to bed."

Really sweet, I thought, and picked up the remote, turning on KBUU, Liz's station.

There she stood looking elegantly perfect: big gold sculpted earrings flat against her beautifully made-up face, not a hair out of place, not an inappropriate remark on any topic, lightly laughing at just the right moment at just the right news story, so sophisticated and sexy. Turning left and right to lead into the weather or traffic, then flashing her beautiful wide smile to the camera and telling us there would be more after the break. I speed-dialed her cell phone at the two-minute break, hoping she had turned it on. She picked up immediately.

"How are you?" she asked with genuine concern.

"As you're smiling for the entire city, they would never know that you have a temporarily busted lesbian rodeo star at home in your care."

"Gotta go." She laughed and hung up. Seconds later there she was again, talking into my TV screen.

"I would love to hold you, Liz Chase," I said out loud. "I would love to make love to you—but I can't." I paused to contemplate what had just crossed my lips. *And what's stopping me?* I wondered, then let myself off the hook. *Because I can't even get my own pants off, much less yours! And just for the record, I like you better in safari pants and a white shirt.*

❖

Once inside my office, I took small steps. My head hurt and my eyesight seemed a little strange, since I'd landed on the left side of my head when I hit the creek bank. People in the hallway noticed I was walking slowly to my office rather than striding along at my usual brisk pace.

Jane greeted me with a smirk and two ibuprofen. "I heard you had a rough night."

"Hmm," I grunted, knowing that within an hour of my arrival at the office, half of the top floor would know that I'd had a horse accident.

"So Liz is phoning in and telling me to take care of you. Is she…?" Jane let it hang.

"A friend."

"Is Clare a friend, if she calls?"

"No," I said, and Jane made a little tsk-tsk sound, assuming, I suppose, that I was suffering, and she was vaguely correct. "Hugh from legal is here," she announced as I was lowering myself into my chair.

Hugh popped his head into my doorway, his buffed and balding presence a mere earpiece short of making him look like a secret service guy. I had to admit he was the closest person in the office to being a friend, and I knew he was here because he'd heard about my accident and was worried about me, something neither of us would ever have admitted or acknowledged. He was a man stripped of all pretense and so direct, it was like having a relationship with a laser beam.

"Heard you jumped off your horse. That's not true, is it? I mean, no one jumps off a horse. You were thrown, right?"

"I jumped."

"Why did you jump?" Hugh pressed.

"To avoid having her crash me into the barn and kill me. She was running like a bat out of hell, and I threw the reins up in the air and swung my body out of the saddle and over the left side of her, and landed on my head in Rattlesnake Creek."

"You swung your whole body up and out of the saddle of a runaway horse?" Hugh asked as if I was on the witness stand.

"And bounced down the goddamned creek, Your Honor."

He grinned. "You know, most people in their forties would be a little hesitant about diving off a runaway horse. You could get seriously hurt."

The age remark really riled me. "Most people in their forties can't afford a horse and a vet and a barn and a trainer and the gear so that they can have the exhilarating experience of throwing themselves off a horse." I bristled. "It was my fault." I got my anger under control. "I shouldn't have ridden at night in the rain on my first trip with her."

"Not good," he said with newly mustered sincerity.

"No, not good, but she came back for me."

"Well, *that's* good…I guess. Are you in a lot of pain?"

"No, just when I breathe or move or try to focus my left eye."

We looked at each other for a moment and burst out laughing.

"Don't make me laugh," I pleaded. "Laughing is really painful." Whereupon he laughed harder.

"Maxine from research is—" Jane tried to announce, but Maxine blew past her.

"Hey!" Maxine's large, solid frame filled the doorway, and her equally strong face, with its pageboy haircut, revealed no emotion. "Heard you had a horse accident."

"No accident. It was a planned jump off the back of a speeding horse," Hugh said, as if he were my trial attorney.

"Planned," Maxine repeated.

"Yeah, she didn't want to get hurt, so she decided to jump off while the horse was running like a bat out of hell," Hugh explained.

"I can see how that would keep you from getting hurt," Maxine said, giving Hugh a deadpan look.

Hugh's shoulders jiggled and he snorted as he tried to suppress his laughter.

"Get out!" I ordered good-naturedly but firmly. Not good to become too familiar with the troops; it weakens command, I thought.

CHAPTER TWELVE

By nightfall I was in agony, the pain so intense that tears gathered involuntarily in the corner of my eyes. I located pain pills and downed them as the doorbell rang, and I opened it to find Liz standing there with an overnight bag, asking playfully if I needed a nurse.

I replied that I did, and I wasn't kidding.

"Thought so." She walked past me, setting a sack of groceries on the kitchen counter, and put an overnight bag in the spare bedroom. "Come on, shower and bed." She addressed me as one might a six-year-old. I wanted to argue if only to save my dignity, but frankly I was amused that she could walk into my home and take over without asking and without any fear of recriminations from me, a person of great privacy. I was also relieved to know Liz would be there to call 911 if I fell over and was unable to get up.

I showered, which took a good thirty minutes longer than usual simply because leaning over to turn on the water took two or three tries, and I was too vain and too proud to allow Liz in the bathroom to see my bruised body. I studied myself in the bathroom mirror while the water was heating up. The blue-green bruise on my hip was as large as a dinner plate, and smaller silver-dollar-sized ones adorned my arm and chest. All in all, I was lucky not to have suffered broken bones. I did a haphazard job of toweling off after my shower, unable to bend much even after the blast of hot water had loosened my muscles, then pulled on a long sleep shirt and shuffled out of the bathroom.

Liz was standing outside the door. Over her shoulder I could see the bedcovers turned down, then I noticed the muscle gel in her hand.

"Lie down on your stomach."

"Can't. Won't be able to get up or turn over."

Without another word, she unceremoniously flung my nightshirt up in back and without asking permission slathered heat gel on my lower back and my shoulder muscles. I shivered as her hot hand stroked my near-naked body, causing a tingling of my nerve endings that I could feel even through the pain.

She stopped abruptly, and her teasing tone changed immediately to one of seriousness.

"Brice, how are you even moving? These are the worst bruises I've ever seen."

"No choice. I have to go to work." I kept my jaw clamped shut as she gently rubbed my body. She knew as well as I that a fortysomething woman executive had to be there, had to appear vibrant, had to be healthy and on top of her game—to avoid being replaced by a thirtysomething male who might not be any of those things.

Liz helped ease me into bed and went into the bathroom to wash the gel off her hands. A few minutes later she was standing over me with a tray of hot soup and crackers and a half sandwich.

"Really, this is far more than you should be doing. Or at least more than I deserve," I said. "It just feels—"

"Like we've been married for decades and now the only thing I rub is liniment into your back?" she said, and I didn't answer. "Okay, in that vein, do you have to go to the bathroom?"

"Do I have to report that?" I winced.

"Probably, because I don't think you're going to be able to haul yourself out of bed to get there…whiplash and any other muscle trauma is always worse on the third day, and that would be tomorrow. So you must call me in the night if you need me," she said, and went into the other bedroom.

I was staring at the ceiling, the pain pills kicking in slightly now. *Liz Chase is more caring and loving than most women I've lived with. Well, she's auditioning, that's what TV people do,* I thought. But part of me didn't really believe that. Liz Chase was just kind.

❖

Paula Zale had built a large thirty-six-stall Morton barn with indoor arena, and, as soon as I could move my body, we transported the horses there. It was new and impressive, and her Arabians were the only horses in residence. We had worn out our welcome at Maynard's farm. It was time to move our horses to their permanent location, and Paula's barn was horse heaven.

Paula was a big, bossy, heavyset woman who greeted us with a huge smile, patted our horses, and asked for their paperwork to ensure they'd had all their shots. We produced the documents and put Hlatur into a stall next to Rune at the end of the barn, excited about the possibility of training in the big arena and riding over her beautiful farm.

Paula pointed to a buxom young woman who was flapping her hands in the air. "She's not trying to fly, she's drying her nail polish. I like girls with a little class." Paula called out to her. "Floie, say hi to our new boarders, Brice and Liz and their horses Rune and Hlatur."

"Hiya!" Floie waved her red fingers at us. "You need anything, just knock on my door over there!" She pointed to the interior barn apartment.

"These ladies have Icelandics," Paula explained.

"Cool," she said, and I made a mental note that special feeding instructions or anything else relating to horse care would have to be tattooed on Floie's forehead if I expected her to remember them.

❖

I was still recovering from my accident, so riding wasn't on my immediate agenda, but I was going to the barn after work every day to pet Rune and brush her. She was a tough horse to get to know. Her eyes slanted back when she looked at me, like Norma Desmond ready for her close-up. My cuddling and cooing over her seemed to annoy her more than anything.

She was a strong horse from a barren land, a horse who had lived with male owners who no doubt left her out in all weather, fed her little, and rode the hell out of her. At least that's what I was told by Furtillo, the man Rune most likely preferred as her owner. He put her out to pasture, only hauled her up when he wanted to work her, and beyond that ignored her.

I wanted a furry friend, a virtual house pet, a position for which she had no regard. Her haughtiness told me she wanted to make it on her own, viewed fine brushes and bridles and hands-on attention as frills, the latter a sign of weakness. She was determined to have none of it. As I took her chin in my hand to brush her forelock, she yanked her head away and blew a blast of hot air on me from her flared nostrils in what could only be described as disdain.

I bent over with some physical effort, picked up her hooves each in turn, and took a hoof pick to the groove that ran along each side of the V-shaped frog. The human equivalent of cleaning toenails. The groove had a slightly unpleasant odor as I removed the dirt from it. Underneath lay a dark, mushy substance that told me she was fighting thrush…a kind of horse's athlete's foot. I painted the underside of her hoof with an antifungal, just one of the things the vet had taught me to treat.

"Your horse is a lot like you," Liz called out through the driver's side window as she put her 4Runner in park, never taking her eyes off me, watching me brush Rune's golden mane and sleek yellow body.

"How's that?" I answered happily as the sunshine warmed me and the wonderful smell of my mare lowered my heart rate. "Must be that we're both gorgeous."

Liz swung her legs out of the car, revealing her derriere in tight riding britches, and I stopped brushing Rune to stare at her.

"She's proud and she thinks she doesn't need anyone," Liz said.

"She's survived a long time alone, well, virtually alone," I said, intentionally ignoring the comparison and focusing the brush on Rune's well-muscled chest and down her long, thick neck.

"I'm predicting she'll warm up. It's only a matter of time." Liz sashayed her ass over to Hlatur, who gave her a big lip-smack through the open stall window.

"Do you see that?" I lowered my voice and spoke into Rune's fuzzy ear. "You could kiss me, even if it were just for show. It would improve my status with Liz." Rune let out a very loud snort that drew a glance from Liz. "Forget I asked!" I said to my difficult mare. I stroked her long, golden mane and her short, sleek yellow coat and led her back to her stall.

She flatly refused to enter it, digging in, then at the last minute taking two small, dainty side steps and leaning her full weight against me, pressing me into the stall wall like a cockroach. I buckled at the knees, moaned, then staggered to my feet, yanked on her lead rope, and tried to pull her into her stall.

"I can tell you one thing for sure." I grunted as Liz came over to help. "If you get a freaking horse, you're looking for ways to resolve issues no human can touch."

"What's she doing?" Liz asked, taking the lead rope from me and quietly walking Rune into her stall, making me look like an incompetent fool.

"Why in the fucking hell did I ever think I needed a horse? I'm afraid of heights and speed, and I have control issues! What is this mare but control issues tackled at uncomfortable heights at a high rate of speed?"

I knew once I started something with my horse I had to finish it kindly, with patience, and in the way I'd like it to end, because horses have amazing memories, and what Rune would remember today was that she was able to crush me, then avoid exiting or entering her stall.

I clamped my jaw shut and circled Rune around in the stall, leading her out, then back in again, praising her afterward. *I'm exhausted and in pain, and I've done nothing more than untack her. It isn't like I'm not showing this horse a lot of attention! I've adjusted the fit of her tack, changed her bit to give her a copper ball to roll around on her tongue for relaxation, bought toys to entertain her in the pasture, special treats from the tack shop, and massaged and groomed her. My reward is no love, no riding pleasure, and big expenses.*

"Respect from the horse!" Paula boomed loudly as she passed the stall, jarring me out of my mental monologue. "You don't think you can control this eight-hundred-pound animal with little leather straps for reins or that little lead rope. You and the horse must have respect for one another."

She was right, but I didn't like hearing it. *I'm not building any trust with her; she hates me,* I thought. Managing to kneel down in Rune's stall, I looked her in the eyes. *You're sweating around your eyebrows and you look worried. Are you afraid I'll sell you, or beat you, or even eat you?*

Suddenly I felt an intense wave of sadness wash over me. It was her sadness as well as my own. I looked up at my recalcitrant mare and began apologizing, as tears ran down my cheeks.

"I know I took you away from your owner. I know you're sad. I am so sorry."

Rune stopped eating her hay and took a few steps toward me. I was no longer afraid she would crush me; I was too sad to care. She lowered her head slowly until it rested on mine, and I didn't move as she placed her big rough lips on top of my head then slowly, her warm breath creating a trail, slid her lips down onto my forehead and let them rest there for over a minute, breathing softly on my skin, calming me as she might have calmed her foal.

I sat still on the stall floor, not wanting her rough lips and silky soft muzzle to move from my forehead, and closed my eyes. The images appeared.

The blond queen is behind me, astride my horse, her arms wrapped around me. I'm fighting her people, killing them as she screams in terror but clings to me. Then chaos—my horse is confused, my own men are clawing at us, wanting the woman, wanting to kill the last vestige of this realm she represents. A soldier slices at her leg, and I swing my sword and block the blow, and in that instant, he is beheaded by the enemy. In saving this woman I have caused the death of one of my own men. I should throw her to them—but I cannot.

I move my horse farther up the ramp and take a position on the wall and watch my men dispatch what is left of the enemy. I retreat to an inner part of the compound, dragging the woman with me. She stands, defying me to touch her. I pull her clothes from her. Naked, beautiful beyond all imagining, she glares at me. I push her down on the straw pallet. Her legs radiate heat, my thighs wrap around her, and her breasts pressed so tightly to my chest cannot muffle the beating of her heart. I climax in no time and take myself from her.

My aide is in the doorway; some of the troublemakers among my soldiers have my horse and are threatening to kill my mount and leave me afoot. I pull the queen to her feet and, with the help of my aide, exit down a small stone tunnel where another of my men has rescued my horse. I hoist the woman up onto the horse's back and see in the animal's eyes absolute terror that the men who have walked beside her are now trying to slash at her throat and kill her.

I shout to the woman, "You belong to me! Go into the hills and wait. You are not safe from either side now. My men want to kill you, and yours would give you up to die to save their own necks. I will come for you." Ripping the leather cord and stone symbol from my neck, I thrust it into the woman's hand, allowing her a fleeting glimpse into my heart, aflame as surely as this compound is on fire. Angry over my inability to control my emotions, I shout at the horse to run, slap the nervous animal on the buttocks, and watch as it takes off, heading for the faraway hills, abandoned, with a strange woman as its charge.

"Get up before your legs cramp." Liz stood over me in the stall and her voice caressed my heart in the way Rune's lips caressed my forehead.

I got to my feet unsteadily and looked into my mare's face, her eyes soft for the first time, looking deeply into me. "It's different now. It's safe," I said to Rune.

Liz looked at me as if to inquire of my sanity.

"This horse put her lips to my forehead, and suddenly I was in another place, another time. I had taken the queen by force, then put her on my horse and sent her into the hills because my men wanted to kill her."

"Well, that would explain why you're having so many issues with men in this lifetime—and maybe why it's hard for you to get a date," she said impishly. "So this queen—she's there fighting alongside you?" Liz stopped joking.

"Apparently I gave up war for her."

"I'm more interested in why you keep getting back on this horse— you could permanently injure yourself."

"I get back on because nothing beats me." Even as I said it, I realized the insanity of getting back on an animal who obviously didn't want me on her, in order to prove I could control her.

"I think this horse is here to help you work on that issue. You got this horse because of me, not for you. You and the horse had no attraction, nothing in common—a lot like the women you've chosen. But women can walk away. This horse has nowhere else to go. You're going to have to build a relationship, Brice. She knows you didn't pick her because you love her."

I looked over at Rune, who was eating prairie hay from a corner of the stall, seemingly uninterested now in whether I loved her or not, so long as I left her alone.

Chapter Thirteen

I heard the commotion in the hallway before I ever saw Jack's face, or his nervous secretary with the odd hairnet hair, or Megan Stanford. I couldn't imagine what topic they all had in common until Megan spoke. "Brice, a woman's out on the eighteenth-floor ledge, and she's threatening to jump."

"You called 911 and HR?" I asked, my heart suddenly double-timing.

"Yes, but you need to come," Megan said. And I deserted my desk and followed her and the others down the hallway and into the elevator.

"Is it an employee?" I asked as we waited for the slow transfer of bodies up to eighteen.

"Zane Stephens," Jack said, and images of the heavy-set, mid-thirties woman in the mailroom filled my head. Zane rolled her wire cart up and down the hallway every day delivering letters and magazines and useless flyers to every office in the building. Most of the people who talked to her were secretaries, but all of us knew her. Why a woman in her thirties would be satisfied pushing packages down corridors every day of her life was too depressing for me to contemplate. And today, apparently Zane felt the same.

The elevator doors opened to reveal a dozen people in the eighteenth-floor lobby circling the reception desk and strung down the hallway toward an office that overlooked the avenue below and was where all the action seemed to be centered.

"Who's talking to her?" I asked Jack.

"I don't know, but not the right person or she wouldn't still be out on the ledge. You need to talk to her. You could relate to her."

"To a gay woman on a ledge?" I asked reproachfully.

He gave Megan a look that seemed to say he'd anticipated that kind of response and worse.

As we parted the sea of bodies to get into the room and over to the open window where one wide and battered black tennis shoe was visible at windowsill height about ten feet away, I cut the rest of my comments short.

"Where are the police?" I asked Megan.

"On the way. Special suicide unit. Deals with edge-of-the-ledge people," Megan said in the cryptic briefing style I preferred, having obviously learned it from Maxine.

I nodded, acknowledging her comments. I hated heights, so I clung to the window molding as if it were a winning lotto ticket and leaned out to assess Zane's resolve. She was wearing a sleeveless white shirt, and her bare arm bore a large tattoo with the word "Mary" on it. Her heavyset body, clad in black men's pants and a worn belt, was pressed up against the wall of the building. Her straight brown hair, maybe five inches long in all directions, blew in the wind as she struggled to keep her balance, her chin jammed back against her throat as if her body had decided it didn't want to follow her mind to its death.

"Zane, it's Brice Chandler. Can you move carefully over here, just a few feet, so we can talk?"

She hesitated, then slowly slid her left foot toward me. *That was easier than I thought.* After a few cautious sideways steps she loosened a tiny piece of the ledge with her foot, and it crumbled and tumbled over the side, falling eighteen stories, as everyone near the window gasped.

The collective intake of air seemed to make Zane nervous. "Tell them I'm not a sideshow!" she ordered.

"I will. Just relax a second." I leaned back inside the room and addressed the crowd for Zane's benefit. "Ladies and gentlemen, Zane would like for all of you to know that she doesn't have your fucking mail! So go back to your desks and wait until she gets to each of you. Thank you and good-bye."

People around me looked startled as I waved them off, and Jack and Megan jumped in to help clear the room. Now, with just a handful of us left, the real work was at hand. I grabbed the window trim and leaned back outside to report the exodus to Zane in my role as the Christiane Amanpour to the suicidal.

"Done," I said, my head once again hanging out of the window. My stomach lurched as I glanced down.

"Who was in the room?" Zane asked, which I took as a good sign. People seriously about to jump probably don't care what's happening back inside, I reasoned.

"Damn near everybody in the building. You have quite a following," I lied.

Zane let me know she wasn't going to be won over with that kind of BS, then added that she cared about only one thing.

"What's that?" I asked.

"Ending it," she said, and her tone was flat and tired and laced with anger, and I worried I'd misread her and maybe she was going over the side despite everything.

I launched into a litany of questions—the kind I could get into when time was ticking and I was about to lose my audience over a ledge. I asked who had upset her: was it work, was it her family, was it someone at home? What could I do to change things, who did she want us to call and let her talk to, all while I wondered where in the hell the damned police were.

My neck was cramping from the odd angle of hanging my head out the window, and I was running out of topics when she finally said, "There's no one at home anymore."

"You were living with someone and now…you're not."

"We broke up," she said, and looked down.

Finally I had it. I knew why we were all out on the ledge. "Who is she?" I asked, one hundred percent sure I had the gender right.

"Mary. Mary left me."

Of course! The name Mary is tattooed on her arm, for God's sake! Why didn't I figure that out?

"You can't know what that means," she said. "You can never know how that feels." Zane suddenly launched all her anger and venom and what felt like her resentment of a lifetime at me—*me, the only life form currently hanging out on the ledge to save her silly ass.*

That thought made me realize how quickly my sympathy could shift when people irritated me and my neck hurt. I was probably not the best person to be talking someone off a ledge.

As I contemplated that fact, Zane yelled, "You don't get it! My lover just left me!"

"Mine did too. For someone who looks like you!" I shouted back.

A pause, then Zane chuckled. "Don't fuck with me."

"I'm not fucking with you. In fact, if you throw your ass off this ledge no one will ever fuck with you again." I gave her a moment to consider that double entendre. "There are other fish, dear."

"Yeah, well, you know how important this was to me. Do you see my arm?"

"Yes, well, it *is* more challenging when you've given a woman top billing on your bicep. Tattoo 'Proud' in front of it, and people will think you're a Tina Turner fan. Or 'Poppins' after it—"

"And people will think I'm a fruitcake."

"Or simply add another 'r' and the word 'me,' and it's 'Marry me'!"

I could hear Jack saying, "I think she just proposed to her." I made a mental note to kill Jack, if I ever got my head back inside and the kink out of my neck.

"Come on, Zane, you've got a sense of humor. Years from now you'll find humor in this. Come in, please, for me."

It seemed like minutes. Silence. Zane was obviously thinking it over. Slowly she edged toward me, and when she got within reach, I told her that a couple of men were going to help her inside so she would get in safely. By now two police officers were in the room, and they got her by the arm and one leg and hoisted her to safety.

Suddenly my heart raced and my body ached and I had to sit down. Zane looked at me as they led her away, and I gave her a thumbs-up. Who knew what was going to happen to her now. I asked HR to stay with her and report back on whether she had family or someone to take her in.

"Man," Jack almost whispered. "You were somethin' else! Brilliant saying your girlfriend left you for someone who looks like her."

"She did," I said, and gave him a look that dared him to continue.

"You're killin' me!" he said.

"I'd like to," I said. "Get out, will you."

The room was nearly clear now, everyone following the woman in crisis, each with his own role to play. I looked up to see Megan Stanford observing me steadily from a few feet away.

"What?" I asked testily, sensing she was holding something back.

"That was the best thing I've ever seen anyone do."

"Well, then, you need to get out more," I said, letting her know I wasn't up for any adolescent sentiment. But she was undeterred by my sarcasm and gave me an admiring grin before leaving.

How fragile we are, I thought, often tethered to this earth by a single soul who becomes the string that keeps us from floating away. And when that tie is cut, we want to leave like a balloon ascending into the heavens in search of our soul's connection. I was sweating, having just connected with the thought that Zane could have actually chosen to jump.

My adrenaline finally ebbing, I pulled myself together to walk back to my office and suddenly they appeared: a cameraman and a news anchor—*omigod, it's Liz,* my mind registered.

Liz's expression conveyed that she knew she might be in uncertain waters. "Brice, I understand there was a suicide attempt. My news director asked me to go live from the scene—"

"There'll be no live-from-the-scene," I said decisively, leaving no room for discussion.

She checked her watch, apparently under time pressure to make the cut-in for the noon news, then made her decision. "Get word to the booth, no cut-in," she told the cameraman, and he used his cell phone to call.

"Can I tape, then?"

"Not really," I said, my mind flashing with anger. I felt ambushed, invaded, taken advantage of. A million things I could not articulate. And all by Liz Chase, who had used her relationship with me to somehow get into the building and up to this floor.

"This is an important story, Brice." Liz's voice was quiet.

"I'm sure it is. But it's another woman's story, not yours, and she may not want to share it with the world," I said, angry over the invasion of privacy.

"I have to get something while I'm here." She looked resolute. "Roll tape," she said, turning to the cameraman and speaking into the lens the moment the red light signaled her that the camera was on. "This is Liz Chase live on the scene at A-Media Entertainment, where today a woman tried to take her own life by jumping off the eighteenth-floor ledge of this building. I'm standing here with Brice Chandler, division president, who reportedly was on the scene and talked the employee off the ledge. Ms. Chandler, can you tell us what happened?" Liz implored, and I said nothing, merely staring at her.

"What did you say to her?" Liz probed.

"Don't jump," I said, staring coldly at Liz.

"Did she tell you why she was jumping?" Liz asked, and that was the last invasive question I could handle.

I put my hand over the lens to end any visuals and made a silent cut sign across my throat, wishing it were the cameraman's.

He looked at Liz, who nodded her okay.

When the light went off, I said, "Perhaps to avoid the invasiveness of the press," and walked out.

Liz caught up with me. "You couldn't give me a single sentence?"

"Don't ever pull something like that again!"

"I didn't pull it on you. I called, and your HR department and your secretary approved my showing up. They thought what you did was heroic, and they thought it would be fine to get it on tape."

"Well, they thought wrong. Someone's life about to end is not cause for the circus to show up and pry into her despair." I bit the words off.

"I suppose TV cameras are a circus to someone who doesn't want anyone to get too close." Liz turned and walked away.

How dare she use our relationship to get the story she wants. "Oh, no, you're not getting away with that!" I said, catching her by the arm and stopping her. "Why would you do this to me?"

"This isn't about you! Stories like this one get tagged with suicide-prevention hotline numbers and places where people can get help. It's not about just one woman on a ledge, Brice. It's about a lot more who are thinking about stepping out on it."

"These are my employees, not docudrama subject matter, and my employees don't affect you!"

"Really? Your employee who recently abused his wife is Fred Davis. His wife who then, in despair, stayed home and tried to take her own life is Toni Davis, my former college roommate. So I guess your employees do affect me." And Liz Chase exited, leaving me stunned.

"Shit," I said quietly to the world at large.

CHAPTER FOURTEEN

I lectured Jane and the HR woman on the liabilities and lawsuits associated with allowing unescorted news crews into the building to invade the privacy of our employees. I might as well have been trying to teach pigs to sing. Jane kept saying she thought Liz and I were friends, unable to comprehend ethics over friendship.

She spent the rest of the day storming past me like a cloud of condemnation, and I finally understood why men hired secretarial eye candy whose greatest concern was whether or not they'd chipped a nail. *If I have to tolerate a head full of irrational thoughts, I'd far rather have that head sitting atop a nice set of breasts*, I thought as I caught sight of Jane's electroshock hairdo and mummified knockers flying by. I put my head in my hands in a weary state of contrition. *I am thinking far too much like a man.*

That night, at the barn, I apologized to Liz for insulting her profession by calling it a circus, but I still believed that I was correct in wanting to block press from sensitive internal issues—adding that whoever ended up on camera in a situation like the one we had today had better handle the sound bite right.

"That's why I put the president on camera."

"And that worked out well, didn't it?"

She shrugged.

We were a bit wary of one another. My anger had startled and hurt her. She obviously felt what she was doing was for the greater good, but her uninvited invasion of my world for personal gain had made me question if I could trust her.

"How's your friend, your ex-college—"

"Like all abused women, believing it's her fault, fearful and ashamed that her own suicide attempt might cost her husband his job. She can't even connect with a solution like leaving him. It all makes me so angry. All my news director can say is that he wishes we had some footage of her right after the attempt. Close-up of some slashed wrists, maybe?"

"I could demand that in order for her husband to keep his job, he has to stay in counseling," I offered as Liz entered Hlatur's stall. Suddenly all office conversation ended.

Hlatur was bathed in sweat, his chest and flanks wet, and he wasn't eating, his hay untouched on the floor. Liz felt the top of his hooves for heat, a sign of fever. His head hung low, and, although stoic like all Icelandics, even he could not hide the fact that he was ill. Liz lifted Hlatur's reddish tail and stroked the smooth, silky red cheeks of his muscular butt to let him know where she was and what she was doing as she took his temperature. He hadn't been his usual outgoing self for several days and she'd taken his temp a couple of times, but it had been normal. Tonight was a different matter.

"Call the vet!" she said, her voice rising in alarm, and I grabbed my cell phone.

Twenty minutes later, Dr. Brown, our silver-haired cowboy vet, sailed into the barn bellowing out his usual, "How we doin'?"

I wasn't very jovial in return. "He's sweating his head off, and he's got a temperature of 103.5," I said quickly, knowing 101 was normal and 103–104 was an emergency.

"He does look a little wet. What's the matter with you, fella?" Dr. Brown looked into Hlatur's soft fawn eyes as if he expected an answer. In fact, I think that's how Dr. Brown got his answers about horses; he asked them. "Let's take a listen," he said, putting his head down against the horse's belly rather than using his stethoscope.

"Let's give him something for the fever and calm him down." He gave him a shot of Banamine and prepared to take blood as Hlatur pulled back, showing the whites of his eyes, and we held him and talked to him. Dr. Brown hit the vein in his neck with one deft poke, for which I was grateful. "We'll run a blood profile. Call me if his temp spikes again." He took the needle out, I let my breath out, and Liz showed Dr. Brown out.

Liz rubbed the spot where the needle had been and hugged Hlatur, her arms barely reaching around his massive red neck. He blinked slowly as she consoled him and waited to make sure he was cooling down. I was nervous and used the time to lead Rune in and out of the stall a couple of times, with and without her halter. She was obeying me with hand signals now, which meant she was at least acknowledging moments when I was in charge.

After that, I swept the floor around Hlatur's stall, wondering why it was taking so long for the Banamine to take effect and lower his fever. I had loaded the last poop from Rune's stall into the muck buckets and turned out one bank of overhead lights, when I heard Liz's panicked voice.

"Brice! Help me!"

I ran to Hlatur's stall. Water was visible on the shavings at his feet; he was so wet that without thinking I glanced overhead to see if water was coming from the ceiling. His orange-red coat that always glistened in the barn lights was so wet it looked chocolate brown. I phoned Dr. Brown again and left a message on his cell. Ten long minutes went by. My phone rang.

Dr. Brown was less jovial this time. "What's going on?"

"He's wringing wet. Water's dripping off every hair of his body and falling at his feet. He's very sick."

"I'm about fifteen minutes away," he said and hung up.

Liz held Hlatur's big hairy head up, supporting it in her arms as he swayed slightly. It appeared that the weight of his head and big massive jaw would otherwise sag to the ground. She kissed his forehead over the white starburst under his forelock and massaged his ears with the large mass of fuzzy hair in them, looking up at the ceiling every few minutes as if she might find God there…someone to save her poor horse.

The door on Hlatur's stall was ajar, and he pushed it open with the tip of his nose and staggered slowly past Liz out to the concrete apron in front of the barn and stood there to meet the vet. He apparently knew he needed help, and this was the man who could get it for him.

Brown pulled into the driveway, got out, looked at the horse, and listened to his belly again. "Let's get a tube down his stomach. I don't hear anything moving."

I assisted by applying the twitch—a crude device that twisted Hlatur's velvety lip into a knot, making any sudden move painful and thereby immobilizing him for safe treatment—as Dr. Brown put the long plastic tube down Hlatur's nose and carefully moved it into his stomach, bypassing his lungs, since a tube mistakenly placed in the lungs could kill a horse. He pumped mineral oil down the tube and then, after what seemed an eternity, pulled the tube out. He gave Hlatur antibiotics and God knows what else.

Finally Brown said he thought we had a handle on it now and told us to watch him for a couple of hours.

Shaken and tired, we plopped down on the tack trunk across from Hlatur's stall where we could watch him.

"Thank you," Liz said weakly, then suddenly laid her head on my chest. Liz was as damp as Hlatur, so upset over her horse that she too had broken out in a sweat. "What's wrong with him?" she whispered.

"We'll find out." I held her close, feeling how small and vulnerable she was underneath the competent exterior and momentarily forgetting all that had happened between us.

She glanced over at her horse. "He's going down!" she said, jumping up.

I dialed Brown again, saying we were in real trouble this time. Without waiting for his return call, I called Maynard; I knew we needed to get Hlatur to a hospital.

"You've got to get up, Hlatur," Liz pleaded. "Please, honey, come on. Come on, up!"

Hlatur slowly rose to his feet, off balance and swaying unsteadily, as Maynard's truck entered the front gates. When Maynard opened the back door to his trailer, Hlatur staggered out to board it as if he knew this was his ambulance and time was critical.

We followed Maynard, peering over the hood of our car to see Hlatur's body swaying in the horse trailer in front of us and praying to God that Hlatur wasn't dying. This time I wasn't so sure. I knew he was a very sick horse, and no one seemed to know what was wrong with him.

❖

Hospitals of any kind are scary places late at night on emergency runs, but horse hospitals, in most parts of the world, are scarier, lacking comforting colorful décor and people in starched uniforms to signal that patients are in professional hands. Mostly horse hospitals look like the inside of an old concrete garage, where someone's installed a set of horse stocks that keeps the horse from bolting and leaving. All the equipment looks primitive and, at best, like something that might be used under the hood of a car.

Dr. Brown, in blue jeans and an old shirt, said we'd better do a belly tap, and without further discussion, he began shaving the underside of Hlatur's furry red tummy.

"What do you think it is?" I tried to sound calm for Liz's sake.

"That's what we're trying to find out."

"What will the belly tap tell you?" I persisted.

"What's going on in this guy—infection, parasites, something." I sucked in my breath when the unimaginably long needle went into Hlatur's sweet belly, and I let it out minutes later when the needle came out.

Liz had her arms around Hlatur's big neck and her head buried in his thick mane, silent tears running down her cheeks. Perhaps she was trying to console him, but she also couldn't bring herself to watch her precious horse's belly being prodded with a needle as long as a sword.

"Okay." Brown pulled back from his work. "We're going to put him on IVs and watch him around the clock. I'll let you know what the tests show tomorrow."

"Is he in danger…?" I didn't want to say of dying, but I knew Dr. Brown could finish the sentence.

"He's a pretty sick boy. We'll just have to take it a day at a time and see what happens."

A wiry vet tech in her fifties, wearing faded blue jeans and a dirty work shirt, came out of the office and led Hlatur out of the garage-like examining room across a driveway and into a large open barn containing several oversized stalls in the middle of a dirt arena. The sides of the stalls were nothing more than rough wooden slats running from the floor to a height of seven feet, but there was plenty of soft bedding on the floor and fresh water.

"He's so ill," I said, following close behind her as a wind kicked up, swirling a fine, soft dust around our ankles, and for a moment the fragrant, balmy air that seemed to come from nowhere lifted my heart and gave me inexplicable hope.

She looked at me over her shoulder, acknowledging my concern. "He is what you see," she said, and while I thought her remark cold,

I noticed her eyes were warm and as clear as crystals, and she had a gentleness about her that made me believe she would take care of poor Hlatur, whom she led into his hospital stall.

Overhead a pulley system held the hookups for large IV bags that would dangle above him out of his reach. The IV line and needle extended out of the sky and found its mark in his neck. I hadn't stopped to analyze how horses have fluids administered through their necks. I would have thought Hlatur would have pulled the line out or that he would have flopped down and rolled on it, but he seemed to know it needed to stay in him, and he stood quietly.

I had to demand that Liz leave her horse alone that night, so I engaged the help of the vet tech, who assured Liz she would watch over Hlatur and that he couldn't rest if Liz was in the stall with him, and I was again struck by her ethereal eyes and wondered how she had ended up with this mundane job. We kissed Hlatur good night and told him he must get well, we needed him—Liz, me, and Rune—we all needed him. Then I drove Liz home with me as she protested.

She sat on the couch, by the phone, for an hour, saying the vet tech watching Hlatur might call and praying Hlatur would survive, while I fixed dinner and thought about how tired I was. Late nights with the horses and early mornings at work were taking their toll.

And then there was the stress of Liz. I stayed in a state of heightened nervous energy whenever she was around, and she was around me every day. *Maybe that energy's the only thing keeping me on my feet now,* I thought. *Maybe she's just a sexual battery to keep me charged. And why do I still have it when we both know there's a barrier between us? She knows I have a quick temper and a sharp tongue, for one thing. And I know she's stubborn.*

Liz pushed her food around forlornly and stared at her plate.

"The vet tech said something strange about Hlatur. She said, 'He is what you see.' I was too upset to process that remark at the time, but I think she meant that what you see is what he'll be. Believe he's going to get well, and he'll believe that too. And stop pushing your food around like a three-year-old. I don't cook for everyone." *I'm beginning to have the hostess manners of Madge!* I thought. *That must be what living alone does to you.*

For a moment the look on her face signaled we might have war, but she finally bent over her food and began to eat.

The phone rang, and I picked up the handset while we were at the table. It was Madge. I told her I was just thinking of her but couldn't talk right now.

"She's there, isn't she?" Madge asked. "I just tune in to those kinds of things. Knew she was there!"

"I moved into a two-bedroom condo, remember?" I answered her unasked question obliquely. "Liz's horse has been terribly ill, and we've been up with him for hours. But I know he's going to recover."

"And how about you?" Madge asked, completely unconnected from animals and the way their illnesses could tear at the heartstrings. "Sounds like you've recovered. Ain't life grand?" She gave the phrase a hillbilly twang and told me to call her later.

"Gay friend wanting to know if we're sleeping together?" Liz said in a matter-of-fact tone.

"Asexual friend wanting to know if anyone's sleeping with anyone. I've put fresh towels in your room and clean sheets on the bed. You need to get some sleep. Your horse will live, Liz, I know that."

When I got up to go to the bathroom, the clock read 1:11 a.m. *Do I only look at the clock when it's one eleven, or is it always one eleven?* I thought I heard Liz crying in the next room and walked down the hallway, hesitating, before opening the door to tap lightly on it. She sniffed and tried to conceal the fact that she was upset, drying her eyes quickly in the dark.

I crossed the room and sat down on the edge of her bed, putting my hand on her forehead and pushing back her curly locks. "Hi."

She blinked and wiped more tears from her eyes with the sheet, and I handed her a tissue.

"I'm sorry about invading your office. I let the story get personal, and I didn't respect your wishes because I knew you—which means, basically, I suck as a reporter."

"I would never agree with that assessment," I said, and looked into her teary blue eyes. I don't know what caused it: the childlike vulnerability, my guilt over having yelled at her, the fact that I just wanted to touch her so badly I couldn't sleep, but I found my lips speaking the words, "Come on." I took her hand in mine and hoisted us both out of the bed. "Follow me," I said, leading her down the hallway and entering my bedroom.

"Climb in," I said, indicating the bed as she gave me an odd look. "If I had a teddy bear, I would have just tossed it in there to you—but I don't, so you're going to stop crying over Hlatur and get some sleep. It's all going to be okay, I promise."

Liz wrapped herself around me, let out a sound somewhere between a sob and a sigh, and fell asleep almost immediately.

I, on the other hand, was now wide-awake. Liz Chase's body seemed a natural fit, curving into mine as if we had once been molded of a single piece and had somehow become separated. And she smelled heavenly, damp tears and all. At this moment, I began to wonder if four years with Liz Chase wasn't better than forty years with someone else. I buried my lips in her hair much as Rune had put hers in mine, and I comforted Liz Chase like a mare might comfort a frightened foal.

❖

Liz was up and dressed when I awoke. We had slept together— that intimacy made me feel awkward and exhilarated. When I stumbled into the kitchen, she handed me coffee as she dialed the vet.

A male technician said Hlatur looked about the same, reportedly didn't move much all night, but at the moment was eating a little hay and grain. We took his improved appetite as a much better sign than I'm sure it was. Liz called in to the station and arranged for someone else to anchor, saying her eyes were so swollen no makeup would cover the damage. I had to go to work.

"Thanks," she said, and ducked her head. "You're definitely a full-service friend."

I wanted to tell her I would enjoy rendering services beyond those already delivered but clamped my lips shut, merely smiling and nodding.

❖

I arrived at the office and moved quickly through the roster of issues Jane outlined for me. I took four meetings, rifled through research papers on audience numbers, and returned calls. I was operating at a heightened level of efficiency while being virtually out of my body.

How could horse ownership transition from being such a great experience to being such a nightmare? Hlatur's illness and possible death made everything at the office seem even more ridiculous.

I was aware from Jane's questioning that she was trying to be sympathetic but even she thought my anxiety over a horse a bit excessive. When I turned down an invitation to have dinner at Anselm's home, she looked at me with furrowed brow, as if to say I was putting both of our livelihoods at risk since executive admins are often buried with their dead leaders.

But I knew Anselm wasn't asking me to dine because he enjoyed the pleasure of my company. He wanted hours of uninterrupted time to probe me on areas of the company with which he'd been out of touch, or to get the inside scoop on certain employees, or even more importantly, to find out what Walter Puckett was up to. Best case, Anselm would confide in me about whether we were being corporately merged or purged. Whatever the evening might hold, it was meaningless in the scope of time. *Meaningless.*

"Please tell him I feel bad about having to decline, but that one of my horses is very ill and could even…die. If I were to attend the dinner, my mind would be elsewhere and I wouldn't be good company."

Jane took on the look of an executive secretary who had been briefed sufficiently to understand the issue, absorb it, empathize with it, and relay it in the most poignant of terms.

"He'll understand," she cooed. "It's like having a baby who's ill."

"It is," I said, hoping this epiphany wouldn't launch her into ideas of get-well horse showers.

I realized, as Jane turned to leave, that a change had taken place at the center of my being. In that instant, I had chosen something else over the corporation to which I had always pledged my allegiance. I had chosen the horse—a horse that was not even mine—a horse that belonged to a woman who was not even mine. I wondered what that decision might mean for my future.

❖

After work I pulled into the vet clinic driveway, bringing Liz something to eat, and received the latest medical reports. Hlatur's white count was still high; his T cells were off; his temperature flared.

Liz stood in his hospital stall and stroked his tortured neck, whispering quiet words of encouragement into his big, fuzzy ear.

I knew she was begging him to live. I assumed she was telling him again that Rune was waiting for him if he would only get well. Hlatur looked at her with faraway eyes, and neither of us knew whether he wanted to leave this earth or stay.

Wanting reassurance about the condition of Liz's horse, I sought out the woman tech who'd cared for Hlatur. A vet assistant told me she wasn't here; in fact, he'd never met her personally, their schedules just didn't seem to cross, but occasionally clients would tell him that she'd saved their horse's life, so she must be good.

On that note, Hlatur suddenly pulled away and slammed his body into the stall wall, yanking out his IV, blood trickling down his thick neck as he paced around in a nervous state. After Liz opened the stall gate to run for help, I shouted for her to watch out as Hlatur bolted past her into the parking lot. Two attendants joined us as we attempted to circle him, arms widespread trying to divert him from the busy highway only a few hundred feet away.

Hlatur reared up and spun around and threatened to run over us, and I made up my mind that I would be hospitalized before I would let Liz's horse die on the freeway behind me. Liz screamed as he headed for it; I could hear semis whizzing past, but I stayed focused on him. *Is this horse trying to commit suicide, unable to withstand the indignity of capture and incarceration?*

An attendant ran inside the building and returned with a lariat. Hlatur whirled, bucked, snorted, and came to a complete stop, just as the cowboy was getting ready to lasso him. We hadn't seen him show that much energy or interest in days.

Liz approached him slowly and stroked his neck, then slid a halter onto him and led him back to his hospital stall, his sides like bellows and his nostrils flared.

"That's a good sign." The attendant beamed. "He's trying to leave. Your horse is feeling better!"

Liz and I got Hlatur settled down before heading to the car, where we sank into the cushy leather seats. I let out a long sigh, my heart still pounding.

"It's just every fucking thing every fucking minute. I am so fucking *tired* of life being so damned hard." I came close to whining.

"Do you know how many times you've said 'fucking'?" Liz smiled slightly.

I sighed philosophically. "'Fuck' is an interesting word. We're all trained to recoil when someone says that word, but legend has it 'Fuck' is an acronym meaning Fornicate Under Command of the King. It was an order to procreate. The king could have commanded that everyone engage in Conjugal Licentiousness Under Command of the King and the acronym would have been 'Cluck.' Then we'd be going around saying, well, they were caught clucking in the back of his car. She was just clucking her brains out. Well, clucking A! He's a complete cluckhead. Cluck cluck cluck—"

"Brice." Liz patted my leg. "You just need rest, that's all."

Chapter Fifteen

The vets had finally reached a diagnosis. Their best guess was peritonitis—the deadly inflammation of the stomach lining that Hlatur had most likely had for some time and which had lain relatively dormant until this episode that had nearly killed him.

Now having it under control, they pronounced Hlatur a candidate for home care, as long as he rested and stayed destressed. His white count was still up and, as the doctors would continually repeat, he wasn't out of the woods by a long shot, but they felt that part of his healing would involve getting back to his normal routine and his mare.

When Liz met me at the barn the following afternoon, I was still in my office attire. Nowadays my Amalfis always had mysterious pieces of hay wedged inside them, and the pockets of my business suits held horse cookie crumbs. I was a double agent, living a corporate life with country longings.

"Hlatur, you're home!" I exclaimed. "Give me a kiss."

Hlatur puckered his upper lip and punched it up against mine.

I laughed.

"Don't kiss him on the mouth!" Liz giggled. "We don't know for sure what he has."

"What he has is great lips, don't you, big guy?"

Hlatur nodded his head up and down vigorously, and Liz giggled more.

"He knows everything you're saying. He's the smartest horse," she exclaimed.

"Do you hear that, mare?" I opened Rune's stall. "*You're* the most intelligent horse on the planet. Women are always brighter. That's why smart horsemen always leave a mare in charge of the herd." I whispered to her as I stroked her long nose. "If there's danger, the mare will get them out of it."

I could stay only a few moments longer because I had to race back to the office, gather up my laptop and briefcase, and meet the car that was picking me up to take me to the airport. I had to be in L.A. that night for the grand opening of our new studios.

"So you're leaving shortly," Liz stated quietly.

"I am."

"We'll all miss you. Please fly safely." She turned and walked away, neither of us knowing how to say good-bye.

❖

I got back to the office in time to learn that a rumor had leaked to the press that A-Media Entertainment was being sold to Baron, Inc. The proposed name change from A-Media Entertainment to Baron Entertainment, Inc. generated much discussion.

"Brilliant, we sound like a dried-up company unable to conceive," I remarked to Hugh.

"Did you see it?" Hugh asked in disgust, referring to the press release in the morning paper and displacing Jane as he paced up and down in my office, not unlike Hlatur on his IV line.

"Did you know this was coming?" I countered.

"There's been talk about it for months, but I didn't think it was anything serious. Half a dozen companies have wanted to buy us."

"So if the deal goes through, our new board of directors, according to the trade press, will include an Austrian banker and someone from Madrid? Well, they can't be worse than a guy who spends every waking hour figuring out how his direct reports can help get him laid."

"Walter asked you to get him laid? I didn't know that." He paused. "You suppose he scores?"

"He's got teenage hormones and middle-aged money—every young girl's dream."

"Well, at least they're getting something out of it," Hugh said. "That's gotta make you feel better."

"Makes me feel swell," I said sarcastically. "Gotta catch a plane. See you in L.A. tonight."

❖

The grand opening of A-Media's new studios in Los Angeles was a gala event designed by a huge corporate-events team. Months of corporate-wide planning and arguing and budgeting had served up this delectable night, billed as *All Eyes on A-Media.*

Celebrity ice carvings and twenty-thousand-dollar gift baskets were themed with eyes. John Wayne had been overdubbed to make it appear that he was saying, "The Eyes of Texas are upon you, A-Media. Congratulations," from a giant LCD screen. Tight shots of Bette Davis's face slashed across the screen in time to "She's Got A-Media Eyes." KISS's famous tongue shot had been cleverly reanimated to make it appear that the lead singer's eye, and not his tongue, flew into the lens, intercut with Roger Rabbit's eyeball-out-of-socket animation, all rocking to a new rapper track.

Guests ate sushi hors d'oeuvres made to look like eyelashes and stared down into their soup at crystal paperweight eyeballs that stared back at them, and starlets dropped their evening shawls to reveal eyeballs tattooed down the prominent bones of their spines. It was the kind of bacchanalian orgy that did Walter Puckett proud.

Although Robert Baron was scheduled to take over, this was Walter Puckett's night—he was still very much in the game and on the court, having managed to secure a place on the board, to the chagrin of many board members—in particular, Michael Kaloff. While Walter Puckett would no longer be CEO, he would still hold sway. He was so ecstatic this evening that he was hitting on LaTisha, our T&A talent, in full view of the press.

We watched as Walter danced the lithe and beautiful LaTisha over to the buffet table within a shish kabob's length of us.

"How are you, my dear?" He blew kisses at me. "I have talent!" He giggled and pointed to LaTisha with one hand while pinching her buttock with the other.

She jumped but kept her smile intact.

"As a newly appointed board member, remember all eyes are on you," I quipped as a shutter flashed and we were digitally dogged by the press.

"Then they'll get an eyeful, won't they?" And he rolled his eyes up in his head in a mock scandalous gesture and danced off with her.

Maxine shook her head. "He's something else."

"Are they *all* sleeping with him?" I inquired.

"Only the ones he asks." Maxine shrugged. "They're young and want to get ahead and, let's face it, he can take them places."

Like the hospital, I thought, but didn't say it. Michael Kaloff had confided in me earlier in the evening, after enough stiff martinis that he wouldn't have been able to distinguish me from a Rottweiler, that Walter had once tried to slam-dunk his girlfriend through a car window. I spent the evening talking to clients and well-wishers, everyone happily heralding the beautiful new studios and state-of-the-art postproduction facilities that spoke to our commitment to our networks. I didn't get back to the hotel lobby until almost one in the morning, heading for the elevators to my room.

Hugh slid across the marble lobby floors, skidding to a stop in front of me. "He is in trouble up to his thematic *eyeballs*."

"*He* he?" I said, making sure we were talking about Walter Puckett.

"Yeah. A guy in the hotel has digital pics of Walter in bed with two hookers—maybe double-teaming or, hey, rim shots. They're all naked from the waist down, but from the waist up they're wearing T-shirts that say A-Media Entertainment. If one of those photos gets into the tabloids, it's all over!"

I couldn't stop laughing. "Omigod, who took the photos?"

"A disgruntled husband, we think."

Maybe Walter had groped his wife and he was taking revenge. It wouldn't be hard to get two hookers to trick Walter into putting on the T-shirt, then arranging for someone to burst into the room. Whoever did it had struck with the precision of the Israeli army.

But somewhere in the back of my mind was the not-altogether-unpleasant thought that Anselm had trapped Walter Puckett like a lizard traps a fly—silently outwaiting the Megan Stanford inquisition, patiently setting the trap at this Hollywood gala—then, with the speed of a lizard's tongue, snatched Walter Puckett right out of his board seat.

I went to my room giggling over the image of Walter, the two women in corporate T-shirts having sex with him, and the photographer in the doorway.

Standing by the bedside table, I stared at the phone, wanting to call Liz. We'd spent so many nights together, been through so much—

It's natural that I miss talking to her, and I need to check on Rune and Hlatur. I nervously dialed her, which I'd never done on a business trip. Suddenly I realized that for Liz it was three a.m., but I wasn't able to hang up before she answered.

"I'm sorry, I woke you," I said, somewhat embarrassed over having done it.

"You can wake me any time."

Her voice was so soothing I thought I could fall asleep on it. I just sat still, enjoying that response. What a contrast to my calls to Clare. *But then my calls to Clare had been an interruption to Clare's infidelity.*

"Are you awake?" Liz teased the silence.

"I am. I called to tell you a funny story. First you must swear it's off the record, since it would make a great news story," I said, and she swore.

With every image of Walter and the hookers, Liz laughed louder and begged me to fill in the details. Who caught him, where, when, what was said, who'd reported it? We fantasized about all the delicious possibilities that could come as a result: published Internet photos, blackmail, his having to resign from the board days after being appointed.

Our prurient interests spent, silence finally ensued.

"Isn't this a bizarre way to while away my life—watching assholes like Walter Fuck-it get themselves in trouble for boffing young women?" I sighed, then Liz sighed empathetically. "So how are the horses?" I finally asked.

"I gave them a big hug for you. They miss you already. Do you have a nice room?"

"I do. Room 1111. So weird. I notice that all the time—everything has ones in it. I wish I knew what it meant—maybe just that I'm crazy."

"What are you doing right now?" she asked, ignoring the ones in favor of just the two of us, her voice changing to sultry.

"Getting ready for bed."

"If I was there, and you were as mellow as you sound, I'm betting you'd be coming on to me right now," she whispered.

"I think you have us confused." I was smiling and couldn't help myself.

"Since you're safely a thousand miles out of my reach, is it okay for me to say I've been thinking of you tonight?" Liz's voice was so soft it was creating twinges of electrical current from my heart down to my groin and up to my brain, then repeating that circular pathway until I reverberated.

"You haven't been thinking about me. You've been in bed asleep." I tried to change her mood.

"Especially when I'm in bed. Are you still bent on never having a relationship with me? Because I would love to have you calling me at night saying sexy things."

"Oh, Liz, if we have a relationship, then I lose a lover and a friend. My track record is four years…that's all. The chase, the catch, the finding a way to fit into each other's lives, homes, work, the distancing, the end. I call it finding, fooling, fucking, forgetting, and it's guaranteed 'over with' in four years."

"I have a different program. It's called the wild attraction, the consummation, the laughter, longing, loving, the merging, the forever."

"I can't have one more relationship that goes south."

"Maybe your relationships go south because you pick people already headed in that direction," Liz said. "You don't want to let your lover in, so you pick a lover who doesn't want to get in. I want in, Brice. I want to be your lover. I *am* your lover. You know it in your heart."

"I'm working on it."

"In this lifetime?" Liz prodded lightly, then told me good night and hung up.

I threw myself backward onto the bed moaning. I couldn't remember any of my other relationships ever driving me to this kind of distraction. In fact, I hadn't really been physically attracted to anyone like I was to Liz, and now I was in a state of constant arousal. I loved her voice, and her looks, and the way she was built, and the way she smelled, and the way she moved, and even the way she flared up and got mad at me.

But I would never let Liz see that in me. Just as I'd kept corporate America from ever seeing under my strong veneer. Just as Rune kept me from ever seeing a soft, loving look in her eye. She and I were all business.

I picked up the phone and rang Madge.

"She's been thinking about me," I said sullenly.

"Well, now I am too. Thinking why in the hell you're waking

me up in the middle of the damned night. It's nearly four a.m. Are we talking about Liz Chase? You can run a great big corporation and you can't outrun one little blond woman."

"Go to sleep," I said and hung up, wide-awake now, alert with the alcohol wearing off. In all my life, I couldn't remember Madge ever being so unhelpful.

CHAPTER SIXTEEN

The next morning as everyone slept in, nursing their hangovers, I got up early and decided to take in the JP Getty Museum.

I hadn't slept well. Liz was on my mind. I could envision her soft, blond head of curls on the pillow next to me and imagine how good she felt. *To wrap around that small waist with one arm and slide my hand down...* I squeezed my eyes shut and clamped my knees together, warding off this thought. *I need to get out of this bed, out of this hotel, perhaps even out of my own skin.*

I slung the covers back, hurried into the bathroom, and took a cool shower. I dried off, blow-dried my hair, threw on some makeup and a pair of slacks with a nice shirt and a loose sweater, and caught a cab, sinking back into the thin, torn black leather seats, for the first time in my life not telling the cab driver the route to take or to slow down. An hour later, I was wandering through the echoing corridors of the museum soaking in the artifacts and artwork.

At the end of the last corridor, as I rounded the gargantuan arches leading into a dimly lit room, a massive painting overpowered the wall, and me. The canvas perhaps twenty feet long and twelve feet high, an elaborate battle scene, gripped me with a force that obliterated the paint and brushstrokes of the castle compound and made the painting real, as real as the clan of men who beckoned me now to take up arms and fight.

In the foreground, elevated above the rabble, was the huge image of a red-bearded warrior, hoisting a blond queen up behind him on his horse. Other horses trailed behind him, the whites of their eyes wild in terror, as men, hundreds of them in great detail, battled among the fires and flames. I was as frozen in time as the image on the wall, the adrenaline from a thousand years of warring still pumping in my chest, as I struggled to whisper, "Oh, my God, it's real!"

I walked up to the painting in disbelief and read the plaque beside it: "*The Battle*. Painted in 1642 in Iceland by the last living Mistress of the Runes. Donated to the museum by Edward S. Samuels, San Francisco."

The name that was on the postcard given to me by the woman at the Yakima River! *How can that be? It's too bizarre to be a coincidence. So I've been dreaming about a painting that actually exists? Maybe I saw it years ago and it stuck in my mind.* I sat down on the bench in front of the painting. It was early morning and the room was empty. *I know the feel of the folds of the woman's garment, like the down of a bird's breast or a mare's soothing breath. Does the painting convey that to me or did I touch that fabric, run my hand across it, hold it between my fingers, and lift it to caress what was beneath?*

I rose and approached the painting, getting as close to the image as possible. The red-bearded warrior: muscles taut, brow furrowed, sweat beading on the tan, rugged skin of his neck where the leather cord with the stone hung, and a symbol that looked like the letter "M" carved in it. The warrior looked exactly as I had dreamed him, and his queen, blond and blue-eyed, looked exactly like…Liz Chase. Goose bumps raced up my arms, over my shoulders, and down my spine. What was I looking at? What did this mean?

I don't know how long I stood there soaking in the painting. It was a religious experience—an awakening—a realization that life embodied some sort of continuity, some pattern or cycle or rhythm that couldn't be summed up in a banal paragraph about joining God in heaven. Something or someone larger than myself existed out there— *Who can paint!* I joked in my head to keep myself from falling to my knees and sobbing.

Leaving the room silently as if from a chapel service, I maneuvered the length of the museum to the gift shop to inquire about a copy of the painting. The woman behind the counter ran a search based on title and said they didn't have a painting by that name.

I found a docent outside the gift shop, a tiny, wiry, frail old lady who looked like she was asleep on the bench outside the glass door. *Should be called a doze-nt,* I thought as I bent over to ask her if she could get someone to take a digital photo of the painting, or if someone in the building knew more about it. She was unable to recall the painting and walked back down the corridor with me to the room.

I rounded the huge support arches and entered the gallery where across the room, on the wall, hung a totally different painting, this one of a massive forest filled with large old fir trees and pine-needle trails that wound through them. The canvas was the same size and in the same frame, but it wasn't *The Battle*.

"This is the room, but this wasn't here," I explained to the docent as I pointed at the large expanse of forest. I was confused now; where was the painting?

"We do change the artwork around from time to time," she said kindly. "How long ago were you here?"

"Twenty minutes."

"Oh! Well, I can assure you that the room hasn't been changed over the last twenty minutes!" And she laughed lightly. "Is it necessary to find just that painting? Or would you be interested in looking at others of that period?"

"No, it has to be that painting. It's, uh…"

"Your dream painting?" She filled in the sentence. "Yes, people fall in love with certain works of art. Well, I know you'll find what you're looking for, if you just keep searching. And I would be more than happy to help you." She had a lilt to her voice, and she cocked her head and stared at me with piercing blue eyes.

"I…just need to see that painting."

"Would you like to leave an address, in case I come upon it?"

I hesitated, then thought why not. "Okay." I took a card out of my wallet and handed it to her.

"So you're a corporate…" She tried to read my title.

"Warrior," I said without thinking, and wondered where that word had come from. It had been resounding in my head for some time, but I'd never spoken it aloud before. It crystallized who I was—living in a different world now still filled with kings and killing, in the context of well-defined corporate rules.

The docent laughed. "Of course, warrior. Plenty of battles still to fight, aren't there?"

Her eyes twinkled at me, but I was ignoring her. My mind was processing in terabytes. *How could the painting just disappear?* I turned my back on the docent and retraced my steps a corridor at a time, scouring the museum, looking in every room, down every possible wing; but the painting was gone.

I saw it! I pleaded with myself. *So where is it?*

"You're asking questions I can't answer right now."

The docent was still at my side, and somewhere in the back of my mind it registered that she was answering questions I hadn't yet verbalized, but had only thought.

"But continue to ask. Answers do materialize, I will say that. But twenty minutes, you say…" She seemed to be musing over something. "Of course, suppose there's no time, because of course time is man-made. Then if there's no time, there's no distance, because getting from here to there no longer takes time. And if there's no time or distance, then everything 'there' is here and everything 'then' is now, including your painting. So it simply must be here!"

"If there's no time or distance, then we have no ancestors," I said in a rather condescending tone, irritated at her and the museum for losing track of the painting.

"Unless we are our own ancestors!" she chirped. "Suppose every historical age is like a large theatrical production, and all of life is happening under a big tent, many tents, and the performances are going on simultaneously. We don't think so, because we can't see out of our own tent.

"But just occasionally, someone lifts the flap and escapes and raises a flap on another tent and looks in, and perhaps sees a show with different costumes, but the script is universal: it's about love and lust and loss and success and failure."

I felt like I was in college again, only this time on drugs. I stopped and whirled on her. "I was in a painting that was on your wall! A painting made centuries ago. So how was I able to be the red-bearded warrior on horseback from centuries ago and also be me, Brice Chandler, today?" If this woman wanted to play psychological games, let her deal with that.

"Maybe the soul has so much energy that it multitasks?" she said, undeterred by my tone.

"Well, a lot of multitasking has obviously taken place, because my friend was with me in that painting."

"Sounds as if she's more than a friend, in that case." The woman smiled benevolently.

How does she know my friend is a she? I wondered, but focused instead on our debate. "I admit, what you propose in your simultaneous performances all under different tents does skip a lot of death and dying. The downside would be that when we die *simultaneously*, that's the end of everyone, forever."

"Or it means that we never die...the show always goes on!" She grinned impishly, apparently delighted at having stirred me up. "You have so many questions, and you will find the answers. Never stop seeking the answers."

I looked at her as if she'd lost her mind and decided to speed-dial Liz and tell her about the painting. The answering machine message began, so I hung up and turned back to the docent, but she was gone. *Where did she go?* For someone who seemed elderly and frail she could appear and disappear faster than anyone I'd ever seen. I hit redial and this time when Liz answered, I told her about the entire bizarre experience.

"It was you," I said breathlessly.

"So you and I were together in another lifetime and we're together again." A long pause. "Come home to me, Brice," she said, not seeming to care about the painting, but only about us.

"I can't. I mean..." I let out a long sigh. "Just because I think you look like a woman in a painting...we can't have a relationship based on that."

Another pause. I knew that I'd stepped over the line in the offhanded way I'd dismissed her.

"Then I won't keep bothering you about it," she said quietly. "I believe in living life fully and embracing love completely, Brice. I believe this is our sign. Have you thought about that? Have you thought about us together at all?"

I heard her struggling with the next few words, then I thought she might be crying. The line went dead.

I went dead. How can I be this old and be this goddamned confused? Not confused, conflicted. All right, scared. Scared and tired. Tired of starting over.

CHAPTER SEVENTEEN

I was in L.A. for the remainder of the week in meetings, but I managed to get home Friday night, a full twenty-four hours early. By Saturday morning, despite the rainy weather, I wanted to see my horse, and I wanted to see Liz. We'd planned to go to the barn together on Sunday, but I decided to stop by and see if she would change her plans and go early.

I whipped into her driveway and set the parking brake in one swift motion, then jumped out to find Liz standing on her front porch with a woman who was leaning against the porch rail in what looked like an ownership stance, her leg up on the step, her body draped over the banister. *Who the hell's that? Cocky stance like she thinks she owns the building and everyone in it,* I thought.

She wore spike heels and a tight skirt, and her body was buffed like she worked out. She certainly didn't own the house, so my guess was she thought she owned Liz. As I was trying to unravel that thought, Liz caught sight of me over the woman's shoulder. The woman started to leave, then turned back and planted a very long, deep kiss on Liz's lips, waved, and jumped in her car and drove away.

Liz walked slowly down the steps toward me as my heart sank, and I realized of course the woman had most likely spent the night with Liz. My mind replayed my surprising Clare by coming home early from a trip, and now here it was again.

"Hi!" Liz said, seemingly unembarrassed. "Sorry, I would have introduced you."

"No need. We didn't have an appointment. Tomorrow's our day.

I just had the urge to go out to the barn and thought I'd stop by and see…but you're busy, so we'll do it tomorrow as planned."

"I've just started seeing someone," she said softly. "She's been asking me out for a while, and I've said no."

"Well, looks like yes to me."

"I need to fill in some blanks for you so you can stop judging me, which I'm pretty sure you're doing."

I could have landed right in the middle of that remark with a few of my own, but I decided silence might serve me better at this point because I was too hurt and too angry to really formulate my thoughts. So I let Liz have the floor.

"After my college roommate, I haven't had any real relationships with women and damned few with men. That's why no one in town knows I'm gay—because I barely know. Recently I got into therapy and finally figured out that I like the way women look, smell, and feel, but obviously not just any women because I'm wasting my time on you. I have to quit that. I need to make my life happen, Brice, instead of letting life happen to me. I can't wait any longer."

"Then it wasn't worth waiting for. What does she do?"

"Owns a construction firm."

"So did she…add onto your bedroom?" I said lightly, but with dark intent.

"Actually, she hasn't worked on my house. But she's not afraid to have a relationship, which is a real plus when you're attracted to someone," Liz said, adding her own false brightness.

"Well, congratulations!" I headed back to the car.

"Hold on, I'm going with you!" Liz dashed up the porch steps, grabbed her purse and keys off the hall table, and locked the front door, getting into the car with me before I had time to protest. Nearly volcanic, I slammed the gearshift into reverse and barreled out of the driveway, ignoring pedestrians in my path.

"Careful! You're getting really close to people!" Liz warned.

"Apparently not!"

"Brice, you can't have it both ways." Her voice was quiet.

"I never said I wanted to have it at all," I bit back at her.

"That's precisely my point. You can't begrudge someone else finding pleasure in someone you've decided you don't want."

Lightning suddenly crashed down around our car in jagged

streaks as we drove; it was so close and so loud that my heart jumped involuntarily as I raced through the storm in silence.

Twenty-five silent minutes later, I punched our code in at Paula's farm gate, careening down the elegant drive toward the barn. There in the large south paddock Hlatur and Rune, drenched, lightning crashing around them, were running up and down the pasture by the fence, squealing to one another in obvious stark terror.

"Let's go!" I shouted, and we jumped out of the car and grabbed the halters off their stall doors like relay runners. We were inside the pasture in seconds, but the horses had worked themselves up into such a frenzy we couldn't reason with them. They were running away from us, not to us. Our panic, and my residual anger, apparently made us appear to be in the same dilemma they were, and they weren't following people more crazed than themselves. *A horse trait that executives should master,* I thought.

In a matter of seconds we were soaked through to our skin, our hair matted, and our voices barely audible above the thunder and lightning.

"Don't touch the metal building!" Liz screamed as lightning struck nearby.

"Rune!" I called. "Rune, here, girl, come on!" I called again as Rune circled me, her head held high, her whinnying sounding more like a scream with every new lightning strike.

"We can't stay here!" Liz screamed to me. "We're going to be hit!"

At that very moment, Rune passed close enough for me to get my hand on her mane, and I grabbed it firmly, with authority, and said calmly, "Whoa, easy, easy, easy…" As I slipped the halter over her head I could see her shoulders and sides shaking. "It's okay, it's okay."

The lightning strike of all lightning strikes slammed out of the heavens and pierced the ground a few feet from us. I couldn't see for a second but heard Liz scream again and thought she'd been hit. My heart almost leapt out of my chest. She was crying. I knew, in her hysteria, she would never be able to catch Hlatur; their fear would feed off each other.

"Take Rune inside and get her in her stall. I'll get Hlatur."

"No!"

"I need you to get her out of here. Go! We're right behind you."

Liz jogged off in the rain with Rune in tow. Hlatur and I, of course, were not behind her. He took one look at me and bolted, in an apparent terror fit at seeing his mare leave him. The thunderclaps were coming in waves. I trailed after Hlatur, trying to seem nonchalant, as nonchalant as a person can be in a lightning storm. I was sodden, and my clothes were so heavy they were difficult to move in.

The pasture was a rectangular three acres. The horse and I were up at the narrow, western end of the pasture, nearest the barn, but all the horse had to do was turn east and take off and I would have to cover the seemingly endless span of ground on foot to get him, and most likely never would. I stopped chasing him.

"Hlatur, come on. I'm going to get you out of this storm. Come on, boy. Come on." I moved slowly toward him and he snorted, whirled, and ran. I approached again, trying to focus only on the ground around him and not look him in the eye, ignoring the raging waters and lightning strikes. "Hlatur, come here." I crouched down, as I'd been taught, to look uninterested and less threatening.

Another lightning strike and he took off. The light was intense and terrifying; the hair stood up on my neck. It struck so close to me that my legs were shaking. I held my arms out and tried to wave him into a corner. Liz had nearly lost Hlatur to peritonitis, and now if this crazy horse got hit by lightning or died from pneumonia I didn't know what she'd do, but I'd seen lightning kill horses and cattle, and I didn't want it killing us both.

The more I intensified my efforts to get him, the more he intensified his efforts to avoid me. A double whammy of lightning bolts hit so close to me that I felt the electricity in the air and a tingling sensation ripple through my ears.

"Damn it, horse, I'm leaving you! I'm not going to get killed for you, and you're going to die if you keep this shit up!" I turned and ran toward the gate. As I put my hand on the latch, I felt a heavy breath on my shoulder, then Hlatur's head and soft wet lips pressed up against my ear. *Of course!* I thought. *The only thing a herd animal fears more than being caught is being deserted by the herd; and I'm the last of the herd in this field.*

"Good choice, guy." I slid his halter on and slapped the strap over the top of his head and through the buckle. Liz was crossing the arena at a jog when I entered with Hlatur in tow.

"Oh, my God, you're my hero!"

Liz had an endearing little-girl quality that surfaced on those rare occasions when she was upset and had been rescued all in the same moment, and to hear that I was a "hero" made me laugh in spite of the conditions.

"The lightning was horrendous, and I was leaving him when he caught up with me."

"Oh, Hlatur, you could have been killed."

She hugged his big neck, then flung herself on mine. *She feels so damn good pressed up against me, I could fucking faint if I weren't ready to kill her for sleeping with that bitch.* I broke away to put Hlatur in his stall, then the two of us stood shivering, her arm around me, staring out of the barn doors into the raging darkness. I didn't want her ever standing like this with anyone else. In fact, I wanted to murder anyone who ever tried to stand with her like this. And if I thought about that woman kissing her on the porch, I could go insane.

Floie, the barn manager, came dashing into the barn from her interior barn apartment. "Oh, wow, I had no idea it was raining! I was taking a bath."

I stared at this vapid girl who was now all pressed and perfumed while I, the person paying hundreds of dollars a month to have my horse cared for, stood soaking wet and freezing cold, my life just recently in peril.

From past experience, Liz knew an eruption on my part was entirely possible, and she didn't want harsh words with a barn manager who could mistreat our horses in order to get back at us, not an uncommon cowboy trick. She pinched me, warning me to think before I spoke, so I paused to carefully phrase my response.

"You shouldn't take a bath while it's lightning. If the lightning had struck a plumbing pipe, you would have been killed." I smiled as if the idea were a pleasant one. "By the way, the horses are terrified of lightning, because it's rare in Iceland, so it would be great if, the next time it storms, you could either grab them in advance or call us so we can get here in time."

"Oh, sure," she said, missing the point.

I kissed the horses and sloshed out to the car, sneezing along the way. "I can't go on like this. I need my own ranch." I sneezed again.

"You're not getting sick, are you?"

"I don't know the answer to that."

"Let's get you some Nyquil. You need a good night's sleep."

❖

"I'm perfectly capable of taking care of myself. Go back to your construction worker," I said as we sloshed through Walgreens picking up a few over-the-counter cold remedies. I no longer cared that I looked like a drowned rat. I was depressed and tired and obviously coming down with something.

At the checkout counter the jovial clerk who rang us up sang out, "How you ladies doing this evening?"

"Fine, thanks," I lied flatly and handed him two twenty-dollar bills.

"You two sisters?" He withheld our change pending an answer.

"No," Liz said quickly.

"Well, you sure do look like sisters. I'd swear you were sisters."

I snatched the bag from him and headed for the car, leaving Liz to get the change.

As she climbed into the car, I seethed. "Why in hell do people think we're sisters? We look nothing alike."

Liz patted me in that calming way I'd patted my own hysterical mare caught in the lightning.

"I might as well have found another guy in the store and said, 'Hey, are you two brothers? Well, you sure do look alike.' People should stop that are-you-two-sisters shit," I groused.

"He was trying to strike up a friendly conversation and didn't know what to say." Liz took up for him.

"Then he should just give me my change and say nothing." I was still fuming over Liz's houseguest. *She seems perfectly acceptable, if that's what Liz wants in life. Someone to pick out her flooring and landscape her patio.* "I don't see what you have in common. But if it works for you, go for it!"

"Me and the guy in the pharmacy? What are you talking about? Do you have a fever?"

I ignored the question, because I *did* have a fever, and it wasn't brought on by my cold.

How did I get to this point? Angsting over, mooning about, and craving a woman I've lost! And the idea that she would just randomly pick a construction worker is unbelievable. That has to be the person she was having dinner with the night I phoned her to say the horses were ours. This has probably been going on forever...

"Behind my back." The words came out accidentally.

"That's where it's hurting?"

"It hurts everywhere," I said. And I meant it.

CHAPTER EIGHTEEN

The following Monday at precisely eleven o'clock, roughly seventy executives from various divisions of the company gathered in the corporate auditorium to lay eyes on the man who, virtually overnight and in complete stealth mode, had purchased controlling interest in A-Media. CEO Anselm Radar, or Darth Rader, as the staff had now dubbed him, bounced up to the microphone looking veritably pumped full of joy and enthusiasm.

"*This* is a great day for our company! For a long time A-Media has been looking for the right partner to help us take our business to the next level, and after months of negotiations and meetings about our company's culture and people, we have decided that Robert Baron is the man who can lead us into the next millennium!

"Robert, as you know, doesn't come from the entertainment world, which is a good thing." He laughed, and a polite ripple of laughter followed in his lame-joke wake. "And he's going to bring some much-needed strategic planning and forward thinking to this company, while cutting costs and shoring up our business units."

Robert Baron was a short, gray man in his mid-fifties who looked a bit like Mickey Rooney, if Mickey Rooney was having an incredible gas attack at this very moment. When he came to the microphone, Robert Baron contorted his face into several different, and completely unique, facial expressions, none of which were emotionally relevant to the moment. "Hello." He stopped to make another gaseous expression for dramatic emphasis.

"Before coming here to join you, I was at the NSSGA, which is the National Stone, Sand, and Gravel Association."

I heard two audible giggles before the audience realized Robert Baron wasn't kidding.

"These are the industries I'm most familiar with, so you will certainly have a lot to teach me in the coming months. Nonetheless, I think we have common ground…"

I shot Hugh a look, and he averted his head and tightened his lips. I panned the room to get the reactions of my jaded compatriots, who were gaping in stunned amazement at their new leader.

"Our slogan was 'Paving the Way to Success,' and we did that in a very logical and organized way: through predictive maintenance tests, damage-failure control, and motivating workers. I expect some of these things would be applicable to the media industry, and although I don't understand broadcast and publishing and the various things that you do, you probably don't know what a Ringfeder Shrink Disc shaft-hub locking device is."

He laughed, and a few people in the audience did too, but it was a faint laugh that acknowledged that we were all screwed.

"Over the next several weeks, I'll be meeting with each of the presidents and vice presidents of your divisions to create an open door of learning and cooperation. My secretary, Bambi, will be getting with you to schedule some time."

Hearing the name Bambi, Jack leered at me and I smiled in spite of myself. "Meanwhile, if you have any questions, please drop them in the question boxes I've asked be located at the exits. Just keep doing what you're doing, and we'll look for smooth roads ahead. And I want to say I'm very proud to be part of the great organization you've helped create. Thank you."

Applause and then Anselm and Robert left the stage and the room. Maxine charged past me like a bull. "His expertise is *gravel*?"

"Well, what do you think?" Hugh asked slyly.

"I'm thrilled. *Finally* someone who knows how to fix my driveway."

"You know we're ruined." He became serious.

"The wonderful thing about change is it never stops. This guy is temporary, guarantee you."

"You know what they call him in the sand and gravel biz? *Robber* Baron."

"I love the way you withhold salient points until just the right moment," I said. But beneath the bravado I knew that this man would cripple our company—ruin any chance of our ever breaking ahead of the competition. Gravel. Whoever hired him had rocks in his head.

Leaving the assembly of staffers, I headed across the wide expanse of offices and cubes separating the workers from the executives. A bank of TVs, mounted high above the lunch atrium, caught my eye because Liz Chase was on camera. I stopped to look. She was talking about suicide and the statistics in our city, then they cut to me on camera saying I told the woman not to jump. I noticed several employees had stopped to catch the news story.

The editor cut back to Liz, who told her personal story about her college roommate who had almost committed suicide. "Weeks earlier, she called me telling me she and her husband were having a lot of trouble, and she asked me if we could have lunch. I told her I had a busy day at work. I didn't realize her call was a cry for help." Liz ended by asking people to be aware of depression, fear, changes in behavior, and she gave the hotline and counseling numbers. I walked back to my office while dialing her cell phone.

"Saw your story on suicide. Very nicely done. And I'm sorry about everything."

"Even though you were totally uncooperative, I managed to make you look good in the edit, don't you think?"

"You did a great job. Just wanted to tell you," I said and hung up.

I went out to the barn and into Rune's stall and stroked her forehead, then put my arms around her neck, having begun to look forward to hugging this huge furry neck after work every night. Her almond eyes were now big and round and soft, and she nuzzled my neck and left her lips there, breathing on me. I realized she knew my smell and liked it and was comforted by it. Maybe we were starting to bond, this contrary mare and I.

"I told you I will never give up on you. You are one gorgeous mare." Tears were running down my cheeks.

I didn't see Liz in the barn until she stepped into the stall with me and took my hand and held it entwined in hers. "Underneath all that fury is a very loving woman," Liz said to Rune. "And I think, horse, you're starting to bring that love out in her."

The mare let out a great sigh that indicated she knew that. I let my breath out with a sigh as well and was silent, collapsing back into the stall wall. Liz took my hand and massaged the bones inside my wrist, and my entire body loosened up from my back to my groin, and my head became light. Then she massaged every finger of that hand, sliding her fingers along each knuckle.

"Lotta stress in those hands," she said, holding her hands out for my other wrist and massaging it. "There you go, Ms. Chandler," she said in a seductive tone. "That's all the tension I can release under the circumstances."

I felt myself leaning into her, unable to stop, and I put my forehead on hers, not unlike Rune, communicating deeply with her soul.

A horn blast nearly startled my heart out of my chest, and I snapped my head up to see a strange car light shining down the barn aisle.

"Hellooo!" someone yelled, and I recognized the construction woman.

"Thinking of adding a wing to Hlatur's stall?" I asked without a trace of venom as Liz's construction woman swung her high heels out of the car and onto the gravel.

Liz gave me a look that begged me to wait, but I wouldn't.

The woman was approaching, all teeth and tits. "I came to see your horse!" she called out.

"Don't introduce me," I said with great sadness, collecting myself, kissing my mare good night, and walking from the barn past the woman. *Hate her cologne*, I thought idly as I backed out of the driveway, throwing gravel four feet into the air, allowing me to truly leave in a cloud of dust.

❖

I pulled into my driveway feeling sadly alone—not just alone, but alone without Liz. As I climbed out of the car, I could barely make out the person whose silhouette was outlined on the wall adjacent to my front door—Clare, standing in the shadows on my front porch. I got out of the car and locked it.

"What are you doing here?" I asked.

"I want to talk to you. Is that allowed?" It was a conciliatory phrase delivered in a slightly mocking tone.

I found myself wanting to keep my distance as I asked her to step aside so I could unlock the front door.

Inside, I flipped on the lights and realized I still missed Odin after all these years. He had always been there to greet me whenever I came home, no matter where home was. Now even Clare was more welcome than the silence. She looked good in that New England *Town and Country* way.

We said nothing as I made coffee, knowing that's what she would want, while she found a spot in the corner of the leather sectional and lounged back on it with her arms resting atop either side, waiting for me to set the coffee down in front of her.

Then she leaned forward, catching my wrist and holding me there. "I made a mistake," she said, looking directly into my eyes.

"A mistake—you mean like a typo, or a missed question on an exam?" I extricated myself from her grip and took a seat in the rocking chair across from the couch.

"I want you back, Brice," she said, and she sounded as if I were an object she'd loaned out and needed returned.

She was wearing a tight, low-cut blouse, and it dawned on me that she had come to seduce me, to seal the deal with sex. Clare and I hadn't made love in months before I'd left her, and I'd been away from her many more months. *So sex for the sheer sensation shouldn't be completely off my dance card,* I thought, but I knew it was. Liz had now ruined even sport sex for me, which made me even more critical of Clare's venture into that arena.

"Why did you sleep with that woman?"

"Her name is—" Clare began.

"I don't really care what her name is. Well, I guess I do. What's her name?"

"Elsie."

"Elsie?" I felt the corners of my mouth tilt up involuntarily. "Like Elsie the cow?"

"The cow joke has been overplayed, don't you think." Clare frowned in disdain.

"You mean milked? Well, not for me. I can get endless hours of joy out of it, and especially now, thinking I was cuckolded by Elsie the cow. Was she good in the hay or just an udder delight?"

Clare got up and paced, I presumed to repress her irritation. "I had an affair with her because she was there—"

"Like Mount Everest?" I quipped, as the doorbell rang. I answered it without even bothering to look through the peephole first, not caring who was on the other side and certainly not expecting Liz Chase.

"Can I come in?" Liz looked a bit sheepish.

It was bad timing, but nothing could be done about that at this point. I gave Liz a look that said I was glad she was here and hoped she would remember that look once she found out who was in my living room. Then I stepped back and let her enter.

"Liz, this is Clare."

Liz looked like she'd been nailed to the floor at the front door, and her face held a moment of surprise, then hurt. I suspected it mirrored my own face when I'd driven up to her house that Saturday to find the construction woman kissing her.

"Liz Chase, the TV anchor?" Clare asked, approaching her and extending her hand. "Well, Brice, that must be how you got that sound bite on the news about suicide prevention. You know people in the right places."

"She got it because she was the person who talked that woman off the ledge." Liz smiled and faced me, the sorrow perfectly visible in her deep blue eyes. "You left something at the barn, but you...probably don't need it now." Somehow I knew she was referring to herself.

"Liz, please stay."

"No, you're busy. Looks like you're having a little construction work done too. Good-bye, Clare," Liz said and left.

"What does she mean, construction work?" When I didn't answer, Clare reached for me, saying, "I want to stay over, Brice."

"No," I said flatly.

"No?" Her voice was amused. "Don't tell me you're after the TV anchor." Clare seemed to find the possibility more humorous than problematic. "We have great jobs, money, friends. We can have great sex—it's a nice package, Brice," she said seductively, putting her breasts against mine.

I was still for a moment, struck by the realization that being this close to Clare didn't arouse the slightest desire in me, while merely thinking of Liz set me on fire.

"It *is* a nice package," I said, backing away from her, "unfortunately, delivered to the wrong address." I opened the door for her.

Clare paused as if trying to decide what to say, then left, miffed, which was as close to pissed as she could muster.

I thought about phoning Liz on her cell phone, but what could I say? *Besides, Clare's being in my home doesn't erase the construction worker's being in Liz's bed—hardly the same thing.* I turned out the lights and fell forlornly into my own bed.

The next day the senior executive team gathered in the conference room around the large custom-made, polished marble conference table to give Robert Baron our state-of-the-business overview. He was obviously a man used to striding through caverns of rock and shale and shouting above the clang of heavy equipment at union men in hard hats, so sitting for three hours in a plush conference room had him twitching. I could relate.

As he listened to Hugh talk about capital expenditures, Baron lowered his eye to the table's edge and stared across the stone. He rubbed his hands across it lovingly, then caught himself and tried to pay closer attention; but the lure of the iridescent blue marble, with its splash of black ore, was too great for him, and he tore the edges off his documents, rolled them into little balls, and popped them back and forth between his palms across the gleaming marble surface. In fact, I was beginning to believe that this marble table was his favorite part of the company.

"So, any questions, Mr. Baron?" Hugh wound up his presentation.

Robert Baron glided back into his body like a time traveler. "No!" he said loudly. "Can we take a break?"

"Why don't we all meet back here in fifteen minutes," I suggested.

The entire room exhaled and fled the conference room like rats leaving an airless ship.

As Baron and I continued the discussion, he acknowledged that we'd covered most of the material on employee-incentives: stock options, insta-bonuses for exceptional work above and beyond, and recognition for invention and innovation, but he was squirming.

"I was thinking more along the lines of actual plaques, you know, awards versus money. And I don't want to leave out the little guy. One that always works is an award for safety," he said, frowning perhaps to emphasize thought.

"Safety," I repeated.

"Safety in the workplace is one of the biggest problems any major corporation has. People could fall right through the plate glass in this conference room or down those stairs, for that matter!"

His excitement over physical accidents was amazing to watch. I wanted to tell him that, in my experience, media people were in danger of being *thrown* through the conference-room plate glass or *hurled* down the stairs, but not of falling through or down them.

"None of our employees really carry anything heavy or work around equipment that blocks their view, so I don't think safety—"

"You see, that's where you have to open your mind. If you asked these hundreds of folks out there to put their minds to it, I'll bet they could come up with some knock-your-pants-off safety solutions. Let's give it a try, what do you say?" He was buoyed by his own idea, as evidenced by the excitement in his voice.

"Sure," I said, knowing I was now reporting to a very basic man: a man who saw things in black and white; a man who liked to simplify; a man who wanted our complex media conglomerate to look, sound, and function like a rock quarry.

When the staff reassembled in the conference room, I reiterated Robert Baron's plan. "And so Robert would like to have our entire staff, down to the level of administrative assistants, put together their ideas on safety."

"We'll have a safety suggestion box and we'll have a safety award," he boomed at all the blank faces in the conference room.

"Mr. Baron?" HR spoke.

"Don't call me Mr. Baron. Call me RB."

"RB," she said, "I think that's a wonderful idea."

He beamed at her, and we ended the meeting on that happy note.

I bumped into Maxine in the ladies' room after the meeting. "So how do you like him?" she asked, giving me a mischievous grin.

"What's not to like?" I smirked.

"Well, I've got to get back to my unit and determine whether my research analysts need to be outfitted with steel reinforced boots. People step on our toes all the time."

❖

Hugh plopped into a chair in my office twenty-four hours post-RB. "We're an entertainment company."

"You don't find RB entertaining?" I asked dryly, and Hugh smiled.

"We need every staffer focused on talent deals and programming and marketing and deal making, and this entire building is running around filling suggestion boxes." He yanked some small squares of paper out of his pocket.

"Have you been robbing the suggestion box?"

Hugh read, "'The towel dispensers in the bathroom jut out and are too close to the door. If we moved them back about six inches, no one would ever scrape their arm.' 'The handrails on the staircase are metal, and on cold mornings you don't want to touch them, so you walk without holding on. Maybe we could change them out for wood.' 'It would be really nice if we could have a picnic once a month on our lunch hour, so we could all get to know each other better.'"

"That's out," I said happily. "It's technically not about safety."

"That was HR's suggestion."

"We've got to let her go."

"We can't let her go. She's sleeping with RB," Hugh stated flatly.

I paused for a long ten seconds. "Robert Baron has only been in this building twenty-four hours."

Hugh shrugged. "And that's about how long it takes."

Everyone in this company is screwing someone on the spur of the moment, without any internal turmoil about ownership, fidelity, or longevity. So what the fuck is wrong with me? Damn it, Liz Chase!

"What are you thinking?" Hugh interrupted my mental digression.

"I'm thinking that as chief legal counsel, you are the person who should intervene with Robert Baron regarding the sexual harassment lawsuit he might cause us as a result of his boffing, of all people, HR!"

"What happened to the candy bowl?" Hugh complained, and it was apparent to me that male executives were basically nonconfrontational animals who, far more than women, preferred sex and candy.

❖

I went to see Madge, who stared at me so long over the top of her glasses that I began to squirm. "What are you doing?" she inquired accusatorily.

"I'm trying to sort things out! I'm struggling with who I am and why I'm here, and then I find this painting of Liz and me that was apparently painted in the 1600s of the two of us when we were other people living about a thousand years before that, and now the damned painting is here and it's been donated to a museum in L.A. by a man who became a ferryboat captain in San Francisco and whose great-great-granddaughter I met down by the Yakima River."

"You'll never sort that out. That kind of thing is pure coincidence," Madge said, and I looked at her as if she might be out of her mind. "All very interesting, but it has nothing to do with your life. And you can use it as an excuse not to focus on your life, because God knows you look for excuses at every turn—"

"I'll leave if you start this."

"Proving my point! I am asking you what you are doing inside yourself. At the most basic level, you and this Liz Chase person—"

"Why can't you just call her Liz?"

"Because you have never brought her here, nor have you introduced us, so to me she is that Liz Chase person on TV, and you have been seeing each other for months, and—"

"We're not seeing each other. She's seeing another woman."

"And it's driving you insane?" Madge raised her eyebrow like an antenna.

"I'm fine with it!"

"Do you want to sleep with her?"

"Madge, really, there are plenty of women—"

"Answer the question!" she said like a sexual magistrate.

"Yes! Damn it, I do! I think about it all the time. I want to murder that other goddamned woman with the heels and tits."

"Then why don't you negotiate with yourself, since that's what you do best. Why don't you tell yourself that you want to be with her for a weekend and get it out of your system? She can go back to her construction worker, and you can concentrate on more important things," Madge said, and I felt like she was gently poking fun at me, but somehow it sounded like a completely intelligent idea.

"So not a relationship, but more like a contractor arrangement versus full time?" It seemed like a reasonable solution. In fact, it seemed like the smartest idea I'd ever heard.

Chapter Nineteen

Having Jonathon King and Michael Kaloff place a call to me from the same office was akin to two jackals deciding to share a carcass without a fight.

"Brice, I've got Jonathon King with me," Kaloff boomed.

"Hi there, Brice!" King hailed me in a vocal tone I thought should be reserved for having just struck oil.

"Need your help as we move into the next phase of our company's unscrambling of bad leadership." They both chortled, then did a bit of jocular sparring back and forth about who liked who and what wasn't true. It seemed that neither of them was claiming Anselm or Puckett at this point. They were aligned now for the sole purpose of ousting Robert Baron.

I pondered that possibility. When Puckett got caught in the hooker deal, King no longer had a man, which gave Kaloff and Anselm added power. So obviously, King had to balance things out by finding himself a new knight. I was still unclear who that might be and why Kaloff would agree to King's choice.

"He's gone. Out. Finished," Kaloff said, as if he'd personally thrown Robert Baron out the door. "That little safety-in-the-workplace deal showed what a shallow guy we had on our hands. Didn't think we'd heard about the safety speech, did you?" he said, seeming quite pleased with himself and letting me know there were spies in our midst.

"Last time I checked, you can't be fired for safety reasons," I said.

"Hey, that's why we pay two floors of attorneys," Kaloff said. "To look for the hook, the deal breaker. Busted his contract for health reasons—at his request, of course."

"It was brilliant," Jonathon King said. "Not safe to be unhealthy!" The two of them burst into laughter again.

"So who's the new guy?" I asked, knowing they were leading up to something.

"Well, we had to do some horse-trading to get some of these board members to stomach the breakup and potentially bad press…it's Carlton Daniels. You know, Chester Daniels's son?" Kaloff said, taking the lead and not waiting for my response. "I know he's young, but you can help him get through the waters down there when he shows up. It would be a personal favor if you'd kind of take him under your wing."

"What experience does he have running large corporations?" I asked calmly, knowing the answer.

"I don't think that's the question." Kaloff's jovial tone chilled. "I think the question is does this company need a rejuvenation. A youthfulness. A born-again-ness. That's the question."

I took a deep breath. "I've always supported the board's decisions, but for my money this is a big mistake."

"Well, the board doesn't think so," Kaloff said. "You wait until you meet him, and you'll change your mind."

When I hung up I knew two things: I didn't need to meet Carlton Daniels in person to know his appointment was a colossal mistake, and my unwillingness to embrace Carlton Daniels's rising star could very well put mine in decline.

Contemplating Kaloff and King's ousting of Robert Baron, I realized that planning for the future was a waste of time if the future was in anyone's hands but my own. After all, Robert Baron had done nothing more than be the man they'd hired, yet his personal stock had skyrocketed, then plummeted virtually overnight.

His demise made me want more security in my own life—a place for my horses, something more than a rent receipt; I wasn't waiting any longer. I picked up the phone and called the realtor I'd known for years and told her I was finally ready to make a move.

It had been forty-eight hours since I'd talked to Liz or seen her, having e-mailed and called but gotten no response. I was beginning to think that maybe she and construction girl had gone away for a few days, a thought that ate away at me.

I went out to the barn after work to train Rune in the round pen, a circular metal corral in which the horse learns to work by hand signal and to stop when asked, a way of helping the horse hook up with the rider. We worked for about fifteen minutes and Rune was perfection, keeping one eye on me as she ran, turning abruptly when I extended my arm and backed away from her. When I lowered my voice to a soft whoa, she slowed, then turned in to face me, licking her lips to let me know she acknowledged my being in charge. I approached her and patted her and thanked her.

As I led Rune back to the barn, I spotted Liz down the aisle putting Hlatur in his stall, and my heart leapt. She smiled as I approached and pulled something out of her pocket.

"The money for Hlatur," she said, handing over a certified check. "I told you I'd pay you back. And thank you."

It felt to me like the final payoff, the last piece she'd been waiting to deliver to be free and clear of me. I tried not to take the check, but she wouldn't hear of it. "He's my horse and I want to pay for him."

"Guess we're both into big purchases, then. Want to see the ranch land I'm about to close on?"

"You're buying land? Why didn't you tell me, not that it's any of my business?"

I enjoyed seeing the surprised look on her face and said, as I put Rune into her stall and gave her a horse cookie, "I've wanted to own this particular land for years, but I'd given up on the dream. Come on." I indicated I would drive her there. We left the barn and approached my vehicle.

"Climb in," I said, thinking the last time I'd asked her to climb in was when I was putting her in bed with me.

"What's this?" she asked with a slight smile.

"I sold my Jag."

"And bought a truck?"

"Girls can drive trucks. What kind of chauvinist are you?" I asked and Liz chuckled. "What?" I dared her to say something.

"Nothing. I was just thinking I could get you a gun rack for Christmas."

"And it might surprise you to know that I'd like that." I smiled just looking at her beautiful face.

"You're full of surprises," she said.

And I thought that she had no idea how full.

❖

Liz and I drove out of Dallas heading east for forty minutes until rolling hills suddenly came into view and wrapped their warm bulges around the one hundred and sixty acres of flat fields and ponds and woods that seemed to stretch forever. No car horns, no people, no city sounds of any kind—just cows lowing in the nearby fields and coyotes howling.

"Oh, Brice, I've never seen anything so beautiful," she sighed.

"Prettiest piece of land in the county, little lady." I pulled the truck off the road, and the tires bounced over the uneven pasture until I came to a stop in the field. I climbed out and lay down on my back, arms outstretched in a hugging of the earth, staring up at the clouds and the stars, oblivious to whatever varmints might be crawling around me, and marveling that this piece of earth would be mine for a while. This was as close as a person could get to heaven: a place away from people and noises and lights, just the sounds of animals and the wind and the smell of the clean, clear air.

"Come lie down on the grass," I said dreamily.

"I want to see everything from here," she said, sitting on the tailgate of the truck.

"You're just afraid of lying on a red-ant hill." I grinned.

"It doesn't matter. I even love your red ants." She held her hands out and I pulled her down onto the ground. "I can't believe you did it." A long pause. "So does Clare approve?"

"There is no Clare. I sent her away. Didn't even kiss her, unlike Miss T&A, who was lip-locked on you—"

"There is no one, I promise you," and we were silent for a long while just listening to the cicadas and the wind.

"This is the first real homesite I've ever bought, and it's because of you," I said as she lay so close her body seemed to make the sky twirl like a Tilt-A-Whirl spinning and revolving around me in a dizzying effect.

"You make me so emotionally nervous that I can't concentrate—"

"Oh, Brice, do you hear yourself? Don't you realize…look, I don't know how to get through to you, so I'm just going to say it. When I'm around you, I am so wet for you," she whispered. "Make love to me."

I was so surprised by her words that I snapped my head back, nearly knocking myself out on the hard-packed earth.

"Let go, Brice." Liz rolled over on her side to face me and her lips roamed across my lips in a hauntingly beautiful moment that held so many memories my mind was flooded with them.

I pulled her to me with the strength from another dimension and crushed her mouth beneath mine. Realizing I could be hurting her, I loosened my grip and was more careful, my tongue moving inside her molten mouth with care and longing.

She pulled away completely undone, I could see it in her eyes. She was on fire and I was a pool of desire.

"I want you," she whispered. "I've wanted you for so long. I only know that we're soul mates." She slipped her fingers through my hair and pulled my head down to kiss me again with a passion born of eons.

Swirling around in my head was the black Viking horse, but then Hlatur and Rune; a small ranch house, but then castle walls and musky stone rooms; a fire pit on the ground where we lay, but a large fireplace and the earth of this ranch beneath us as we rolled on animal skins on the floor and made love by the fire in the brutally cold winter.

I unbuttoned her blouse, loosening one of her breasts from its resting place, putting my mouth on her.

She moaned and pulled away. "You're not making love to me here. I'm not going to have bug bites all over my private parts. No." She pushed me away, smiling at my insistence.

I was panting when she let me go and literally staggered to my feet as she giggled over my sexual state of imbalance.

As we started to get back in the truck, I spotted a person fishing on the bank of the pond in the dark. I told Liz we'd need to post signs once we moved out here, aware I had just assumed we'd move together.

The pronoun wasn't lost on Liz, who looked up and smiled, taking my hand as we strolled over to the person on the embankment. She looked to be an old Indian woman, but as she tilted her head to acknowledge me, her light blue eyes caught the moonlight.

"Hello," she greeted us happily, as if we were on her property rather than her on mine. "So you are here now."

"Yes, I just bought this land—I own it."

"Buying and owning," she said. "Using and repairing—those are better words. The land outlives us, so who owns who? The land is the teacher. The user is the student."

"That's a beautiful thought," Liz said. "What is your name?"

"I am the woman who knows if you love the land, the land will love you. You bring horses to the land. Your horse shares your spirit." She smiled knowingly at Liz before packing up her fishing pole and waddling off down the dirt road.

"That sounded wonderful about the horse sharing my spirit."

"How did she know we have horses?" I asked.

"I don't know, but she had the most beautiful blue eyes, like reflections off the pond. Do you suppose she's one of the neighbors?"

Before I could answer, Liz suddenly backed me up against a giant oak tree near the pond's bank, pulling me in to her and kissing me.

"Hey, what about the neighbors," I protested, looking to see who might be watching.

"Sorry, I don't do the neighbors," she murmured and ran her hand down the waistband of my pants, sliding her fingers between my legs. "I think you want me." She smiled and I almost blacked out, two bodies of water flowing side by side.

I had to force myself to pull away and drag her back into my truck and head for town, Liz leaning way over onto my side, her hand lying in my lap. I was nearly too weak to drive.

"We rode these Viking horses centuries ago, you and I. That's why we became obsessed with them the minute we saw them," she said.

"Well, if we rode Viking horses eons ago, we're not doing such a good job now. I in particular have lost my touch."

I pulled up in front of her house and she tried to drag me inside with her, but I refused, saying I was catching a flight in only three hours. This wasn't the time. But I promised I would pick up where we left off—promised. *I have to pull myself together,* I thought. *I have to get my bearings.*

❖

I was glad to be leaving on a flight the next morning. It was a quick overnight to Chicago for a client meeting, but it got me out of town before I could get myself into any more trouble. Despite only two fitful hours of sleep, I felt exhilarated. The limo driver pulled up to my door, loaded my luggage, and held the car door for me. This trip I was determined to be more tolerant of any idle conversation, but ironically the driver didn't say a word as we drove. My head was a Cuisinart of last night's events. My cell phone rang, startling me.

"You're involved with her," Madge accused me.

"A car is taking me to the airport," I said, trying to sound like a buttoned-up executive.

"Did you kiss her?" When I didn't immediately respond, she said, "You did! Did you sleep with her?"

"For someone who claims to be totally disinterested in this topic in general, you have a rather salacious appetite for detail."

"Call me when you dump the goon in the cap!" she demanded, insulting all uniformed employees, and hung up.

I leaned back in the seat and looked out at the scenery. I knew I was on the precipice. Could I actually make the leap? And if I leapt would I be sorry in four years?

I text-messaged Hugh about my arrival time and told him to meet me at the Royal Bar & Grill not too far from the hotel where we were staying. I'd traveled enough by now that I had my haunts in almost every city.

"How was your flight?" I asked as I approached Hugh's table.

"You wouldn't have liked it. The seat belt sign was on the entire time. What do you want to drink? You look pretty—hot." He scanned my slimmer frame and dreamy eyes. "What's up with you?"

"Nothing," I smiled, embarrassed that lust and love were apparently running across my face like a giant billboard. "Wine spritzer. I'm about drunk out. My plane ride was so damned scary I tried to borrow a lady's rosary. When she wouldn't give it up, I counted olives instead."

"So why are we rendezvousing away from the public pond?" Hugh liked to drink in the hotel bar wherever we stayed so everyone would spot him and ask if they could join the table. That's how he got his information, and that's why I didn't want to tell him this news at the hotel.

"Robert Baron, CEO of safety, is gone. We have a new leader," I said. He cocked an eyebrow in doubt. "I have my board sources."

"Baron just got here. We don't have a new leader." Hugh blew me off with such disdain I knew I would have a grand time walking him through this update.

"Deal fell through," I said nonchalantly, knowing that would get a rise out of him because he was a corporate attorney and should know about all deals wrapping up or falling through.

"Why don't I know that?"

"Because they don't want you to know…or any other attorney inside legal. They're going to spin it that he has health problems and had to back out."

"What kind of health problems?" Hugh asked, behaving like an attorney.

"The kind that occur when the board wants your ass out and you don't want to go."

"So there's a new guy? Who is it?" He demanded.

"It's a man—of course a man. Good news is he has media experience: talent agency, publishing, and music, but not *much* experience because he's twenty-six years old."

"Twenty-six!" Hugh was forty-nine, so this struck a chord.

"Yes, our networks were on air many years prior to his birth. In fact, they were on air before anyone even considered that birthing him might be a good and pleasant experience."

"Twenty-six!" Hugh uttered again. "Who is he?"

"Son of one of our most influential board members…" I dragged it out for him to guess.

"You're not telling me it's Chester Daniels's son?"

"That would be the kid."

"You're putting me on. Carlton Daniels? Carlton Daniels is a complete idiot, a buffoon. His own father thinks he's an idiot! Why would they name him head of *anything,* much less this whole freaking company?"

"Well, if you're the board, it's hard to top yourself after hiring a womanizing ex-basketball star and a gravel guy, unless, of course, it's a twenty-six-year-old buffoon."

"I think you're wrong. I think someone's pulling your chain."

"You're taking this pretty hard. You don't even know Carlton. Maybe you'll grow to like him, even love him."

"I fired him at the last place I worked—he was eighteen." Hugh looked like a deer in the proverbial headlights.

"You fired the kid who's going to be our new leader?"

"He was an incompetent, arrogant little jackass."

We looked at each other for a beat and both burst out laughing,

"You're so fucked," I said.

❖

I arrived home twenty-four hours later, threw my luggage into the hallway, grabbed my car keys, and headed for the barn, where Liz had promised to meet me. Not seeing her immediately, I hugged the horses, greeting them with kisses. Rune's soft golden muzzle nestled into my neck, and she let out a deep, breathless nicker that sounded sensual in its welcome. "I think you missed me," I said to the mare, but my eyes caressed Liz, who had suddenly appeared in front of me. Seeing her made me think about kissing her, and for a moment I stepped back against the stall door and just stared at her.

"Welcome home," she said. I thought I saw her catch her breath. "Check out the goats," Liz said in a sultry voice that made me let my breath out laughing. Only Liz could couple an erotic moment with the presence of goats. "Paula says goats have a calming effect."

"Then I should have packed one in my luggage, because I've been anything but calm," I said, staring into her eyes.

"Really?" she said, smiling and obviously pleased with herself.

I watched as the larger-than-average goats roamed through the barn chomping on everything in sight; they didn't look like much of a sedative to me.

Paula, the barn owner, rounded a corner, forcing Liz and me to focus on Hlatur and Rune rather than each other. We took the horses out of their stalls and groomed them while Paula asked about my trip.

One goat walked right up to Hlatur and casually took several large bites of chest hair out of the poor horse. The goat had apparently been at this all day because so much chest hair was missing from Hlatur's front that he looked like a moth-eaten raccoon coat.

"Goat, stop that!" I said sternly.

"Hlatur likes it," Paula said placidly before Liz could speak.

I knew Hlatur didn't like it, but that was the problem with being a renter: anyone could be evicted at a moment's notice, which created tension in me about how to respond. As this thought ran through my head, the goat again gnawed away nonstop on Hlatur's chest hair. The sight was distracting, to say the least.

"I don't want Hlatur to hurt the goat," Liz said. "And look what the goat is doing to Hlatur's hair."

"I think they're okay," Paula said nonchalantly, which was her way of letting us know that as far as she was concerned the goat could do whatever it wanted.

At that moment, a loud crunch was followed by several slow crunches. Right before our eyes, Hlatur had casually leaned over the hair-hungry goat and bitten off the end of his horn. Now Hlatur was chewing it up as if it were a giant waffle cone. Crunch. Crunch. Crunch.

I was frozen. Paula looked utterly shocked. Liz was silent.

"I think they grow back," I said deadpan.

Paula whirled and left the barn. Liz and I giggled uncontrollably.

"Your horse has the funniest sense of humor!" I said, and then just as suddenly I added, "I missed you. I missed laughing with you."

"Me too," she said. I pulled her out of the main aisle into a side aisle and pushed her up against the exterior stall walls, kissing her madly. She wrapped her leg around mine and clung to me like Velcro. We were both breathing so heavily I didn't know where we were going to take this on the cement in a horse barn, when I heard heels clacking along the floor and caught sight of the tip of Floie's head coming toward us. She had obviously seen two people in very close contact. I pushed on Liz's shoulder and she slid down the stall wall to the floor, giggling.

"Something wrong?" Floie kept approaching, and I wondered how disheveled I was and how much of Liz's lipstick I had on my face.

"Could you stop right there!" I said with firm authority. Floie stopped. "To your left, back a little, right there, could you duck into that feed room for me and hand me Rune's new halter. You'll see it on the cabinet or the wall. I forget where I put it."

"Why would it be in the feed room?" Floie looked confused.

"Because that's where I left it."

When Floie ducked into the feed room, I gave Liz her signal to make a dash for her car. She disappeared out of the barn as Floie came back with the news that there was no halter in the feed room.

Pointing to the stall door, I said, "You're right, sorry. Forgot I put it back where it belongs."

I stepped into Rune's stall and gave her a big hug, wiping my face and lips on her mane, and Rune cut her eyes at me as if to say she knew what I was doing and didn't appreciate being used as a napkin. "You owe me," I told her and kissed her genuinely on her big jaw.

❖

When Floie went back to her apartment I rang Liz, who was safely driving home in her car.

"I've saved a TV personality from scandal."

"Come to my house tonight," she said, her voice sensual.

"Now that would be scandalous. Can't."

"Won't," she said. "You can't hold out forever. I will have you, Brice Chandler."

"You have a problem—you have a construction worker."

"I told you, I don't."

"Could you elaborate?"

"I had a lot of dinners, she kissed me…we never slept together."

"I don't believe that. She looked like a woman who had been slept with."

"Not by me."

"I have a proposition for you. The next time I see you, we'll discuss it."

"I hope it's a sexual proposition."

"Actually—it is." I broke out in a large smile.

"You kissed her?" Madge asked, lighting a cigarette, which she only did when things were making her so nervous it was that or bite her nails off up to the elbow.

"I did," I said in the same tone someone would use in admitting they'd run a red light.

"And…?" The question hung in the air like the anticipation of Christmas.

"It was fucking phenomenal!" I squealed and fell backward onto her couch, hugging the couch pillow to me.

"I warned you. I warned you, I war—"

"It was a kiss, that's all."

"If you sleep with that woman, you'd better plan to stay for life because you'll never get away from her." Madge lifted a finger towards the heavens.

"And what if I don't want to get away?"

"Ring me in four years when she's throwing shoes at you—you know, right now you're still getting pelted with Donald Pliners. You're getting to the age when it'll soon be orthopedic oxfords. You want to stop before that happens."

"You think she's a four-year deal?" I sighed.

"I think she's a deal—make it experimental. Break the fever, for God's sake. You're wearing me out."

CHAPTER TWENTY

The next afternoon, we drove out to the barn together, Liz and I, and the entire vehicle was filled with her perfume and a sea of hormones that almost made me dizzy. I pulled onto the dirt parking area next to the barn, noting Paula's truck was gone, as was Floie's car, and it appeared we were the only people within miles.

Liz unsnapped her seat belt and wrapped her arms around me, pinning me back in my seat and kissing me. Her mouth moved across my lips as if it longed for something and then found it in the swaying of my body, the tilting of my hips, the moaning of my soul, and the surrendering of my entire being to hers.

I pushed her away finally, realizing there was nothing I wouldn't do in public if she stayed in my mouth one more second.

"Doesn't someone like you, who can kiss like that, miss being kissed like that every morning and night?" she breathed into my mouth, and I unsnapped my belt, grabbed the door handle, and bolted out of the car.

"You've got to stop that or I will shred your clothes right here," I said, and headed for my horse.

"Or we can just take them off." She wrapped her arms around me from behind and unzipped my riding pants, slipping her hand down the front.

I whirled away from her and redressed myself while jumping into the horse stall with my mare, putting her between us, giggling over literally being chased by Liz. "You're not molesting me in the barn!" I said, insisting she occupy her time with her horse and get ready to ride.

"Only if you swear you and I will spend the night together after we ride," she said, blocking the stall door. I looked into those fabulous blue eyes and melted into a pool of hopelessness. I stared at her breasts. *I really want this woman.* And like someone who'd been too long on a strict diet, I succumbed to chocolate.

"I'm waiting for your answer," she said, interrupting my erotic thoughts.

"Yes," I said and smiled at her.

"Yeees," she sighed and gave me an absolutely sizzling smile. And with the bargain struck, we both returned to our horses.

❖

Rune stood perfectly still while I saddled her and whispered to her that I was about to get involved with Liz Chase. While appearing exceedingly bored by that piece of information, Rune nonetheless indicated she might tolerate my riding her by further standing still as I climbed on board and shifted in my seat.

Liz was riding ahead of me as I gave Rune the signal to walk. She loved to walk out fast, which I liked about her, but quickly the walk turned into a tolt that was a little too fast. I slowed her down, but she was go-ey and irritable. In fact, Rune always felt like a revving engine under me, an engine that wanted to shift into a higher gear.

We headed toward the west end of the paddock at a walk, and when I said a low "whoa," she came to a full stop. I relaxed, rocking back slightly in the saddle, and dropped my hands to my lap. As the white paddock gate swung open just slightly in the wind, I felt Rune tense up, then her back end rolled up under her, and she sprang forward.

I gathered myself up in an instant and pulled back on the reins, but she jolted forward, then reared up with eyes wild and mouth open. She was no sooner up in the air than she was down again, taking a sharp right. I pulled her head toward her flank to keep her from taking off down the long pasture, but she spun in the direction I pulled, and the centrifugal force of her turn threw me off her left side. I heard Liz scream as I fell to the ground with a body slam that knocked me out.

I vaguely remember the excruciating pain on the left side under my arm. I remember the sound of Rune's breathing as she stood over me for a brief second, her fit momentarily subsided, and Liz screaming my name. I was semiconscious on the ground.

Heal my horse, I ask as I lie injured, not knowing if I will live or die. The golden animal lies beside me, having nearly run herself to death to keep us both out of the hands of my enemies, but they overtook us. The queen is safely away, but I am pierced through my chest, my horse injured beside me. The woman in the white robe has come out of nowhere to minister to me. She lays her hands on my horse and the horse's breathing becomes normal. And the horse stands up and shakes itself and is healed. My own fate still lies in the balance.

"Brice, can you move?" I could hear the terror in Liz's voice, which sounded muffled and far away.

"Just leave me here a minute," I whispered.

She disappeared and returned with ice packs, sliding them under my back.

I lay there until that part of my body numbed, and I could hear her dialing my chiropractor on her cell phone. I don't know how I got up. I was having trouble breathing, just like the horse in my dream. When I took in a breath, a sharp pain exploded on the left side of my chest. I crawled to the paddock fence on my knees, unable to use my left arm to pull myself up, and Liz tried to find a place where she could hold on to me without my screaming.

Once up, I dragged myself to the car and she loaded me in. Every little bump in the road was like a knife in my body, and by the time we'd made the forty-minute trip to the doctor's office, my body had taken on the shape of the front seat. Straightening out and walking was excruciating, but I finally made it through the office doors and to his chiropractic table.

"Don't try to lie down," he said. "We need to X-ray your chest."

My ribs hurt so badly that I was almost oblivious to the pain in my back and neck and hip, the large gash on my shoulder, and the fact that my head was ringing. My theory was that if my lung were punctured, I wouldn't be breathing well, and my breathing was getting better. I was going home, not to the ER, and the chest X-rays confirmed that my ribs were not broken.

"I won't ride that mare again," I said, choking tearfully on the words and my physical pain. "It's not worth it."

A part of me wondered about the timing. Did I do this on purpose? This accident definitely postpones a physical relationship with Liz. But why would I want to do that? Why does Rune do what she does—to avoid being ridden, to avoid being controlled by someone?

I spent the night staring at the ceiling moaning in pain and thinking. *You can't swim across the ocean if you won't let go of the dock. So why won't I let go? Be honest with yourself!* I demanded when I felt myself drifting away from the issue. *What are you so fucking afraid of?* I asked of the bedroom walls.

In the silence, I thought I heard my own voice say to me, Liz is so perfect. To have a relationship with her and then to have it fail—that would be different than all the other relationships. That would be— heartbreaking—and the heart would be mine. I felt a tear gathering at the edge of my eye. There, goddamn it, I've said it.

After work the following night I went out to the barn and had Liz saddle Rune for me, though she protested mightily. My ribs hurt so badly I couldn't lift a blanket, much less a saddle, but I was determined to settle something in my mind.

"You can't live alone out on the prairie, you'd kill yourself," she said, girthing up my mare. "You shouldn't be doing this. You're on pain pills. You hurt so badly you can't sleep, and you're out here acting like you think you're a PBR champion!"

"Life is short, horse," I said to Rune, ignoring Liz. "I own ranch land now and I want to ride my horse across my land and return in one piece. I don't know if that's what you want, Rune, but I'm going to get on you. And if you don't want me to ride you, throw my ass down in the dirt, and that will be my sign that you'll just live out your life as a brood mare or as a hood ornament. Otherwise, ride me well and that will let me know that you want to be my horse. It's up to you."

"Good God, what are you doing, Brice!" Liz wailed as I hauled myself up into the saddle, silent tears streaming down my cheeks from the pain of the effort.

I lay across Rune's neck at first, having to gather the strength to sit upright, then caught my breath and tried to relax, waiting for Rune's answer, as I pointed her toward the end of the small outdoor arena. I knew one thing: whatever happened, I couldn't be in more physical or emotional pain. Rune moved with grace and poise, one ear back listening to me.

When I lowered my voice and whispered, "Whoa," she stopped without so much as a tug on the reins. It was an absolutely beautiful ride, and she signaled me with every careful step that she didn't want to do anything that would upset me. She wanted me to know that she wanted to be my mare. We had the beginnings of a new relationship.

It worked because I stopped trying to control her by force. I did it through mutual understanding and cooperation. I realized in that moment that Paula was right. I had been the problem all along: not illness, lameness, or poor barn help. It all boiled down to respect and trust. Did my horse respect me and trust me, and did I respect and trust my horse, because that's what steered and stopped an eight-hundred-pound horse, not two little leather reins that could snap in a heartbeat. Respect and trust came only if we were in sync—heart to heart, and mind to mind.

"Will you please get off, Brice," Liz pleaded as I pulled up in front of her, smiling, as if this horse and I had just waged war and conquered an unspeakable enemy.

"Yes," I said and slid down, nearly passing out from the pain.

Bending to look into my mare's eyes, I started to thank her for the wonderful ride when I saw something deep inside her steady gaze. A chill ran up my entire body, making me shake as I remained locked in her look. The horse was clearly communicating with me, telling me I was starting to understand. I blinked and she ducked her head as if refusing to tell me more, leaving me wondering if she had really told me anything at all or if I had imagined it. I slowly patted her neck and kissed her soft muzzle, sagging against the fence rail in agony as Liz approached to lead her away and put her up for me.

"Brice Chandler, you are the most stubborn damn woman I know!" I could hear Liz shouting, but I didn't care. I was happy.

I thought I heard her mutter, "At least there's one female she'll go to any length to ride."

I had to have imagined that.

Carlton Daniels, kid CEO, could have been my son, had I allowed him to live to be twenty-six, which I would not have, had I known he would grow up to be Carlton. He rented a cherry red convertible Maserati a week before his arrival and had it delivered from Houston, a city over two hundred miles away, for his big entrance as our new leader. He wore a leather bomber jacket, fighter-pilot shades, jeans with holes in the knees, and a fifty-thousand-dollar wristwatch. Every secretary in the place swooned, and every male executive over forty analyzed what in his wardrobe would ever again be cool enough to wear to the office.

Carlton came to town to meet with engineering because the tech-world was his love, and by noon on his first day, a swarm of men in short-sleeved shirts with pocket protectors surrounded him. It was like watching Tom Cruise signing autographs at a backhoe convention.

When he finished parading through the building, he joined Jack, Hugh, me, and several other key execs in the conference room.

"Hey, what's up?" Carlton asked, slouching into his chair.

"Looks like you're up, buddy." Jack slouched as well, like the sales chameleon he was.

"Cool," Carlton said.

I introduced myself, as did others around the table. When he came to Hugh, he grinned. "I know you. Some of you probably don't know that Hugh here actually fired me. No, it's okay. It was a long time ago and I needed firing—but I'll be watching legal closely," he joked. "I just wanted us all to club a minute…kind of set the tone for where I think we should be headed.

"You know, I drove the Maserati in here, not because I drive Maseratis—in fact, my dad would probably kill me if he knew, so don't tell"—he delivered the line in a cornball conspiratorial tone—"but to make a point. If we're going to stay ahead of the pack, we need to create a certain hipness to who we are. Do the unexpected.

"You know, in L.A., it's not exactly hip to have your operation in Texas, and, let's face it, the media industry is in L.A. and most of the people we want to impress are there, so here is simply not hip. In fact, traveling to Dallas is not hip, and I want to turn that around. I want everyone in L.A. wanting to come here to see *you* because *you're* what's happening."

"Carlton—" Jack began.

"Just call me C."

"C, we have a contract controversy going on regarding our latest client agreements," Jack began again. "Are you on board for refereeing that so—"

"So no, not my focus. You guys are big enough to battle that out amongst yourselves. I care more about image. When you have the look, they want to be with you. For example, your entire conference area—your walls, your floors, they're blue. Blue is like…blue. It's not hot. It's cool but not *cool,* cool. It's stay-away-from-me cool. I want something that says let's get it on. I want to bump up the lights and hump up the color."

I couldn't restrain a large grin.

"And I want to hire more young people," he continued.

"Carlton, if you're twenty-six and you're referring to young people, then you're referring to embryos. Why don't we shoot for competent people regardless of age?" I smiled at him, trying not to move my body even a centimeter, since I was still experiencing excruciating pain from my horse injury.

"Goes without saying, but we give the hot, hip, happening honeys a little face time before we go to the grandma-garage."

He smiled in a way that made me wonder if he knew he was insulting me and everyone in the room, or if he was just stupid.

"How does that work legally, Hugh? Can we do that?" I asked innocently, hoping Hugh would set him straight about discrimination, but Hugh had already suffered one near-death experience in having once fired Carlton, and he wasn't walking into any shrapnel on this fight.

"Probably a way to work around it."

"We could make bench-pressing a hundred pounds a prerequisite for secretarial jobs," I said dryly.

"Exactly," Carlton said. "Because a lot of secretarial work involves lifting fax machines and boxes of files, and older women couldn't do that, and it's an insurance risk or whatever. I want to talk to you about programming too, Brice. I'm thinking we need to get some e-squeeze going on our nets. Do you watch that show where they have a celebrity walk up and down the beach and ask guys if they'll do crazy things for money, like one guy had to drop his pants and propose to another guy, but he didn't have on any briefs?" Carlton paused to chuckle and chortle, as if he were seeing it again at that very moment. "Another one had to let them put shaving cream on his chest and let a duck eat it off. It's just wacko stuff, but it's major eye blog. Let's set up a meeting to talk that."

He left an hour later for L.A., asking Jane to return his rental car. We gathered in the conference room again, this time feeling more threatened than usual.

"He's going to knock every one of us off," Hugh said. "That's his MO. He visits and does his hot and happening thing, and then he brings in a bunch of twenty-two-year-old kids and it's like the halcyon days of the Internet bubble, when twenty-year-olds were making a million dollars going to work in their socks and T-shirts and playing basketball in their offices."

"What do you think, Brice?" Jack looked concerned.

"Anything happening here will be filtered through the eyes of a hopped-up, barely post-teen, testosterone-driven male."

"I gotta get him laid. Young guys are all about gettin' laid," Jack said, having reached a decision on how to handle him.

I studied Jack for the first time. He was wearing tie-dyed and stonewashed jeans, punked hair, and bad posture.

"I'll bet you wore that to the beach when you were eighteen. Who would ever have guessed you could recycle it into office attire thirty years later," I needled him.

"Check this out. It's a prototype, and Carlton's going to flip over it. It's a music chip embedded in my sunglasses." He rubbed the edge of his glasses and began grooving to a sound only he could hear. "Want to try them on?"

"No thanks, I already have voices in my head," I said, and sank back into one of the rich blue leather chairs as everyone else vacated the conference room.

❖

Horses and employees get spooked when they don't trust the intelligence of their leader, and within days our offices were full of spooked people. We'd suffered poor leadership before, left in the hands of number crunchers and deal makers, generals claiming they wanted peace when war was all they knew. They did deals in secret and kept employees in the dark. People and horses are jumpy in the dark.

But now the staff was beyond merely jumpy; like any herd of horses they assessed their new leader, and it appeared that he was frightened or perhaps crazy or maybe just plain dumb. The horses knew they were in trouble; the herd had no leader. Oh, there was Carlton, the board-appointed twenty-six-year-old CEO—but no herd of horses is going to follow a colt.

CHAPTER TWENTY-ONE

Bull riders who taped their ribs and climbed back on another bull were either insane or had access to better drugs, because I couldn't even sit up without shrieking. Liz stayed with me a good deal of the time and put up with my occasional lashing out at her like a wounded animal.

I began four weeks of agony, the kind of agony that wouldn't allow me to lie in my bed in any comfortable position. I rarely slept more than two hours a night; I was unable to turn on either side or breathe well, unable to live my dream and unsure what my dream was anymore.

But each morning I dragged myself to work without the benefit of pain pills. I wouldn't let anyone at the office know how injured I was. I had never shared my personal life—I didn't want to get too close to people at work, certainly not to less strategic warriors who could get me killed in a corporate battle, or to weaker ones who under pressure might betray me. I kept my distance.

By nightfall I was on pain pills and feeling like I might pass out. To occupy my downtime, I lay around the townhouse and reworked ranch-house blueprints—making the barn part of the house. I'd become more emotionally attached to my mare, watching and talking to her, and I wanted her under the same roof with me.

I was getting hooked on the fact that I could communicate with her and she seemed to understand—the way she looked at me, or made a sound, or tilted her head. Maybe I was wrong, but I thought it was possible that this amazing animal could know what I was thinking and maybe even teach me something, if she didn't kill me in the process.

The house I had designed centered around one large thirty-by-thirty-foot room that combined kitchen, living area, dining area, and office. The proposed fourteen-foot ceilings would lift the spirits and make that space seem less confining. A large master bedroom, walk-in closet, and bath adjoined the north end of the main room. Off the southeast end, separated by a breezeway and tack room, lay the barn aisle with two horse stalls across from a deep basin sink and a wash area for horses. Adjacent to that, a sliding door led to a feed room and workshop. A firewall running east and west separated the breezeway, garage, and tack room from the rest of the house. Everything was compact and efficient.

"So you've already started construction, you're changing the house plans, and you're doing it all without consulting me?" Liz said, and I checked her expression to see if she was kidding.

"Yes, but I'm completely open to input, if anyone is interested."

"No hallways?" Liz asked, looking at the drawing.

"No. Every room opens off the main room like a cabin."

"But hallways—"

"Separate people from each other. I haven't had good experiences with hallways. I've vacuumed them, shouted down them, asked myself if that cold draft lingering at the end of one might be a spirit. Hallways are unsettling and cost money."

"You have a strong opinion on every piece of trivia in the world, don't you?"

"Hallways are anything but trivia. Hallways are tunnels. Tunnels are nothing more than mini-corridors. And corridors ultimately result in concourses where people are lost forever."

"That's a very odd but interesting way to look at things." She put her arm around me and her nearness felt confirming, accepting, and something more. It felt sexy. "You promised me, before you threw your body under your horse for the umpteenth time, that you and I were going to have a talk about the next step in our relationship. The proposition, remember?" And she kissed me sweetly, her lips lingering on mine, creating that swaying effect again as if my gyroscope was malfunctioning and allowing me to float without bodily orientation to the earth.

"Okay, here's the proposition," I said, trying to breathe. "I want you more than I've ever wanted anyone in my life. You are driving every molecule in my body insane, but I refuse to allow my physical desires to overwhelm my basic intelligence—"

"This started off nicely, but it seems to be headed in the wrong direction," Liz said while kissing the back of my neck and edging up to my ear. I knew I needed to blurt this out while I could still think.

"I have to get you out of my system. Now wait a minute. Don't get upset and whirl on me," I began, catching her by the arm. "If I could just get physically used to you, my mind could catch up."

"What are you suggesting? That you want to have a one-nighter with me?" She looked at me, clearly puzzled, then started laughing.

"I don't think one night would do it."

"You are priceless! You think like a man!"

Liz marched off, and I could tell Madge's idea wasn't as smart as I'd thought.

❖

"So how did you bring it up to her?" Madge asked later that evening while I slumped on her couch. As I walked through the entire scene with her, Madge's chuckle progressed to out-and-out laughter, followed by guffaws. "That is the worst presentation of a great idea I've ever heard. You did it off the cuff, out in the open, on the spur of the moment like she was a hooker on a street corner. You are priceless, Brice."

"That's seems to be the consensus."

"I'm surprised she didn't hit you." Madge grinned.

"Lately your advice sucks." As I stalked out I could still hear Madge laughing in the background.

❖

I rang Liz at the station before the sun was up to apologize and asked her if we could meet for breakfast and talk.

"Have you thought about seeing a counselor? Might do you more good than an omelet," she said with a lilt in her voice.

"I'm seeing a sexy TV anchor and I'm incapable of two relationships at one time."

"Good to know." Her voice softened. "Let's do seven fifteen after my show."

I hung up and checked my watch. It was five a.m. and I was standing in the middle of my one hundred and sixty acres in the dark with one ungloved, frozen hand wrapped around a paper cup filled with coffee, waiting for the sun to come up and the crew to drive in. I believed if I was going to prove I was on top of every construction issue, I'd better be on-site ahead of the workers long before I was due in my own office.

One of the problems with driving from town to the ranch construction site was that by the time I got there, I inevitably had to go to the bathroom. I shifted my weight and tried to think about something else, but it was a losing battle. I was going to have to use the portable potty.

I stomped across the cold, hard ground remembering how I used to be afraid of this expanse of land; it had seemed so far away, so big and so barren, as if I could get lost out here and no one would find me. Now I prowled around in the predawn dark energized. I pried open the big plastic door on the portable toilet and braced myself against the cold wind as the thirty-mile-an-hour gusts flapped the door like a skiff sail.

As soon as I lifted the potty lid I slammed it back down. A pile of human waste was stacked so high inside the cavernous hole that it left the toilet lid smeared with feces. I gagged and backed out of the john, then jotted down the phone number stenciled on its plastic door.

"Pretty rank, huh?" It was the crew boss, and I was startled at the way he'd appeared out of nowhere, his advancing sounds muffled by the intense wind and the wide-open prairie.

"Gotten to where I'd rather drive down to Buford's Store than do my business here," he continued, with what was clearly a sharing violation.

"Ever think about just calling the number on the side of this unit and asking them to change it out for a new one?" I shouted above the high winds as I placed the call and left word on their answering machine.

The crew boss glared at me in the same way Hugh did whenever I suggested tidying up one of his legal documents, and it dawned on me that complaining about shit rather than cleaning shit up might actually be a gene on the Y chromosome.

Changing the subject, I asked him for an update on the work they'd complete today.

He grudgingly gave it to me, construction workers having an aversion to estrogen on the job site.

I headed for the new horse stalls that we'd finished the day before. Since the barn two-by-fours were already up and the stalls already bolted into place, the area was inaccessible by large dump trunks; therefore, dirt had to be brought in on a truck, loaded into wheelbarrows, and pushed into the barn and over the stall lip before it could be dumped.

Heavy equipment the workers used for tamping down the stall floors wouldn't fit through the finished stall doors, so they had to tamp the dirt with a handheld pneumatic device. A fine layer of rock screenings made its way into the stalls via wheelbarrow load, until it was just a cushy rubber mat's height away from being flush with the aisle. The horse shavings would bring the entire stall up to the one-by-four edging. The dirt work complete and screenings in place, it looked beautiful, and I could only imagine how happy the horses would be.

I stopped at Buford's Store before heading off to my breakfast with Liz. Several men in cowboy hats and tight Wranglers eyed me as I ducked into the ladies' room. When I emerged a big fellow in farmer overalls said, "You the one bought the hundred and sixty acres?"

"I'm the one using it for a while," I said, suddenly thinking of the blue-eyed Indian woman and wondering vaguely why all of the interesting women I'd seen over the last few months had blue eyes. *Or maybe Liz's gorgeous blue eyes are just making me aware of blue eyes in general*, I reasoned happily.

The man eyed me unabashedly as I left the store, and one of the tall lankier guys packed his jaw with a chaw of tobacco and climbed into the beat-up pickup parked next to mine.

"Like that truck?" he asked.

"Love it."

He nodded and we both drove off.

I smiled, thinking if I were straight I could pick up guys with my pickup. *Maybe that's why they're called pickup lines. Men stare at trucks with more longing than cleavage.* I checked myself in the rearview mirror as I drove, noticing I was so cold my nose looked like I drank my breakfast under a bridge. *That's attractive,* I thought.

Thirty minutes later I pulled into a small caboose-shaped diner and saw Liz was standing out front waiting for me, looking celebrity-fabulous even in a parka. Passersby were waving to her and saying how much they enjoyed watching her on TV.

"Hi," I said and leaned in and kissed her on the cheek, moving slightly closer to her mouth as I pulled away. She sighed and I put my arm around her. I didn't notice where we sat or who served us or what we ate. I never took my eyes off Liz, determining how to begin this conversation without having her rocket out of the seat and leave.

"You look beautiful," I began and she thanked me. "While I was out freezing my ass on the building site this morning in the dark, I was thinking of you, as I seem to do nonstop."

"Now these are the kinds of conversations I love," she said, drinking her orange juice.

"Good," I said and paused to breathe. "I was thinking that our… relationship…is more loving than I've ever experienced, even when I was living with someone, and I just don't want to do anything but make that better."

"What are you asking me?" Liz was cutting into her waffle now, obviously enjoying my inability to eat and my fairly nervous condition.

"Well, most likely a lot of things…later. But right now, at this moment, at breakfast, I'm asking if you would think about sharing the ranch with me." I paused to take a breath and sip my coffee.

"Share, as an investment? Or are you asking me to live with you?"

She knew full well what I was asking.

"This is the first time I've ever suggested living with someone with whom I haven't slept, but I've tried it the other way around and the results haven't been spectacular."

"We'll see," she said.

I could tell Liz was amused, just by the sound of her voice.

"We'll see? And what, exactly, will be the determining factor?"

"How I'm treated. I'm not a one-night stand. I'm a full-time partner: at work, at play, on the ranch, in your head, in your bed. That kind of partner. And when you're ready for that, I'm ready for the ranch."

She stood up, put ten dollars on the table, kissed me on the cheek, and left me to contemplate partnerships. Liz's style of negotiating seemed to consist of a list of demands delivered upon exit.

❖

I left for the office, put in a long day to keep from thinking about what Liz had said, then drove back out to the construction site to check their progress, as I did every night. Liz surprised me, pulling up a few minutes after I arrived bearing sandwiches.

I walked toward her vehicle, grateful she was here. *But how long would she stay with me?*

As she got out of the car I began in the middle of the conversation I was having with myself. "Am I driving you crazy?" I blurted out.

"Yes."

"So it would be better for you—"

"If you would just come over to my house and get in my bed, damn it!"

She pushed me back against my car, and I glanced around to make sure all the workers were safely out of sight.

"Don't look around for cover. I know you want me. You're the biggest damned chicken I've ever met in my life, Brice Chandler. You're an emotional coward. And I have really had about enough!"

Why the hell did I think I needed to bring up the subject in order to let her beat me to death with it? Because what you're doing to her isn't fair, I thought.

Liz pushed her pelvis up against mine as if welding herself to me and kissed me with a mouth hotter than a branding iron.

"If you took me by force in our last lifetime, then it seems to me that you owe me. And it's time you paid up."

"All kidding aside, if we both truly believe I took you by force, then why do you want me now? Why aren't you tracking me down with a butcher knife for a little quick karma…cutting my balls off, figuratively speaking?"

"That's one kind of lesson. Maybe I'm here to help you with a less painful one—how to have a mutual relationship with a woman in which power is shared." She smiled, watching the look on my face. "I think that scares you more than a woman with a hatchet."

"Do you have to attack me in the middle of a field?" I pulled away. "So what if we do this thing…"

"Make love," she corrected me.

"…and I'm insane about you and then you find out that the reason my relationships last four years is me…I'm the problem. And then you leave me."

"You're already insane about me, and we already know you're the problem." She kissed me teasingly. "And I'm a stayer. It's hard for me to even take the trash out because I don't want to part with it. Lighten up, you're a woman in love, and soon you're going to realize that, and won't that be fun."

She slapped one of the sandwiches into my hand. "Chicken," she said in a tone that sounded more accusatory than descriptive and sashayed over to her car, got in, started the engine, and left.

CHAPTER TWENTY-TWO

I was beginning to appreciate men on the ranch construction site more than I did men in the office. The men on the construction site were crude, rough, and crazy, but whatever they were, they were without pretense. At the office all that crudeness, roughness, and craziness was concealed, until just occasionally it would pop up like a beach ball held too long underwater. When someone on the work site did something crazy, he acknowledged it. When someone at the office did something crazy, he denied it. In fact, even the sane among us now seemed to accept acts of craziness.

"We just bought a guitar factory," Hugh said, plopping down on my couch.

"We who?"

"We the A-Media conglomerate led by Carlton Daniels."

"Why?" I faced him, letting the word string out into a long and disgusted question mark.

"He wants to be in the guitar-manufacturing business. Guitars are his passion. In fact, this particular plant made a very expensive guitar he's been trying to get his hands on, and they keep it in their offices housed in a glass case like a museum piece. So in order to get it, he bought the company. Thought I'd let you know because now, in addition to promoting talent, rumor has it you'll be marketing guitars."

"How did the board let this happen?" I asked, exasperated.

"He convinced them it positioned the company as cutting edge—and he got them each a pair of Super Bowl tickets and an invitation to the players' party. He's not as dumb as I originally thought."

❖

How could I support Carlton Daniels? I didn't share any of Carlton's beliefs; in fact, I wasn't sure he had any beliefs, other than if he could hang on for two years, he'd be rich. If left unchecked he would, I predicted, run the entire corporation into a wall, and the board of directors would be left with no choice but to sell off the parts at salvage. But right now the board had taken leave of its senses. They were having a collective midlife crisis—breathing the virile exhaust from their young CEO.

Carlton's corporate arrival had put a new set of rules into play: results were not as important as shared ideology, the litmus test a leader falls back on when he doesn't understand his business well enough to defend his own views. Once understanding the business falls by the wayside and shared ideology becomes the sole criterion, completely incompetent executives readily rise to the top and stay afloat, simply by assuring their leader that he's as infallible as the pope. In common vernacular, it's called sucking up.

"Right now we want to market them as the hottest guitars on record," Mahiserat, a dark-haired, dark-skinned man, ordered. He seemed to be Carlton's corporate swami, risen to power via the roommate resume, having shared a dorm room with Carlton—or so it was rumored by jealous executives whose college roommates had proved far less useful. Beyond that, none of us knew Mahiserat's title or role in the company, a fact that seemed irrelevant to Carlton who, I assumed wickedly, traveled with Mahiserat only because his name sounded like an Italian sports car.

"And we're footing the bill to retool the factory to make guitars, but only for left-handed musicians. Is that what you're saying?" I ventured.

Mahiserat made eye contact with Carlton. "Correct. To cut costs. No more right-handed ones," he said, doodling on a pad with his left hand and making no fiscal sense.

"How many left-handed guitar players are there in the world willing to pay a hundred thousand dollars for a guitar?" I asked.

Then I made eye contact with Jack and Hugh across the table, signaling them to jump in and utter a thought or ask a question, but I was in this fight alone and weary. The battles were too numerous of late, the foe not even worthy of killing; there was nothing to be gained from thrust and parry with a sparrow.

"I think we've got it," Carlton said in an upbeat tone and beamed at Mahiserat, which I knew was corporate code for she doesn't get it.

"Good," Mahiserat said and beamed back at Carlton, who beamed at Mahiserat. "We'll see you all in Boston, then, at the annual meeting."

"So, how did you think it went?" Hugh asked after Carlton was safely out of earshot.

"We are being jerked off by a prepubescent jerk."

"I agree. It went well," he said, with upbeat sarcasm.

❖

Tuesday, Liz had to leave town for two days on a shoot for the station—original local programming to air during sweeps week. I phoned to tell her that by the time she got back I would be on my way to Boston, but I couldn't reach her and had to leave the message on her cell phone.

Wednesday afternoon my plane touched down in Boston, along with a hollow gnawing in the pit of my stomach, eating away at my soul, as I tried to ignore the stupidity of this constant, senseless drill of traveling thousands of miles to hear new leaders' visionless visions, running up hundreds of thousands of dollars in meeting expenses, then coming home to cut more line items in the budget to make up for these unnecessary expenditures.

The Boston event was surreal: a corporate nature film of rival animals gathering for the first time at a coveted watering hole to clap eyes on Carlton, the virulent young stallion who would lead the herd. The older stallions watched from afar, not wanting to confront him, jealous of the host of giddy fillies sidling up to him. Older mares watched him out of the corner of their eyes, while wolves patrolled the outskirts waiting for opportunities that might be afforded them without much effort. There was circling and snarling, and mating late at night, under cover of darkness, and then there was me—the Boss Mare, the one they counted on to lower her head, extend her neck, lock eyes with this young, mannerless stud, and drive him back outside the circle of influence, letting him back in only if he exhibited good behavior.

But I had temporarily and inexplicably lost the desire to do battle with young stallions. I watched the entire event as if I were watching a film shot through a heavy gauze filter—detached, emotionless, knowing suddenly, but assuredly, only one thing: I wanted more out of life than to be part of this herd. I wanted to go home to my ranch and to Liz.

I packed up and left the conference early, aware my leaving would not go unnoticed and not caring. Like a migrating bird that gives no real thought to its flight path but navigates solely on instinctual DNA, I drove without thinking, straight from the airport to Liz's house, and banged on her door.

When she opened it, she looked gorgeous in white drawstring pants and a loose shirt. I was tired, but I still knew gorgeous when I saw it. I looked into her deep blue eyes and said softly, "I'm only good for four years."

Liz pulled me into her hallway and began undressing me as she led me upstairs.

Between kisses I murmured, "It's not worth it, I'm warning you. It's like getting a degree in something you'll never use. It'll ruin our friendship."

"I'm taking you up on your offer. Two days with you. Just two days—and if you're still uncertain that we're soul mates after that, then we'll call it off."

"I don't believe you."

She stopped abruptly and pulled back, apparently fed up with my vacillating, and buttoned my shirt up in a businesslike manner. "You don't think I can give you up? Go!"

And I knew she meant it.

"Damn!" The pain in my groin outweighed any shred of common sense I had left. I grabbed my recently rebuttoned shirt and, in an external exhibition of my internal rending, ripped it off my own body, the buttons flying. Then I grabbed this insanely, infuriatingly beautiful woman and nearly lifted her up the final steps to the bedroom where the pent-up sexual desire of months and months erupted.

I was so charged up I was almost unable to breathe as we both fell onto the bed, unable to tear one another's clothes off fast enough. Every muscle in my body, every ounce of strength in me was alive with wanting her.

I closed my eyes and slid my hands around her bare breasts and let out an involuntary sigh, caressing every inch of her skin, firm and supple and exciting, the velvet softness igniting an ancient longing locked in my soul—a wanting that was endless, fathomless, beyond all sense and senses. Her neck was bathed in that perfume, that scent that had wafted over me the first night I'd met her and had tantalized me again and again whenever the wind shifted in the night air at the barn or she sat next to me in the car. It was a scent reminiscent of fragrant spring flowers mingled with the sweat of nighttime passion, a scent that was ever changing as her body writhed in excitement and my mouth trailed down her belly and into the small golden canyon between her thighs. My lips covered that hallowed space, hot from my wanting her, and wet heat erupted and flowed over me and into me, my own sacred stream.

A tingling began at the base of my neck and rippled down my back like a mare's soft, warm breath and bound me to this lover I had known for eons—and whose comfort I had sought in every time and place, her soul my soul, her heart my heart—and once more I was enfolded in her love. I wanted to be in her and with her and around her and on her forever…four years forgotten.

Two days went by without our ever going outside or taking a call. Liz Chase made love to me as no one ever had, and now no one else could ever touch me. She erased every sexual experience from my past as mere dalliance and became the erotic fixation for all my fantasies, her senses emblazoned on my heart, my soul, and every portion of my anatomy that might possibly be aroused. She wasted no time talking, since we'd been talking for months. Instead, she made love to me so many times in so many ways that I was virtually senseless. I finally understood that fucking someone's brains out was an actual medical condition. I was ruined. Liz Chase had me, and she seemed no worse for wear.

"So now," she said, kissing me, "do you want to forget all this or are we having a relationship?"

"We're definitely having a relationship—an exclusive, soul-mate kind of forever-after relationship," I breathed as she entered me again, pleased with how my body had become her own private river.

❖

My office bordered on insanity. I carried the memories of lovemaking with Liz to the office with me like a soldier carries a keepsake off to war.

But I relegated even Liz to the back of my mind as I battled my way through the bullshit. Projects were on hold pending budgeting, rebudgeting, budget cuts, and zero-based budgets. Moles in corporate were feeding back to me that Carlton was funding a large launch of his guitar company and a national rock concert tour on the backs of the core business units' P&L.

Our employees were showing signs of fatigue and stress, but another more insidious undercurrent had surfaced—an internal, unspoken us and them. The "us" contingent consisted of those people who catered to Carlton's whims, told him his plans were on target, and held secret meetings to show him their ideas, circumventing normal channels and unwary bosses. They were like the hyenas in *The Lion King*, emboldened by the possibility that an overthrow was in the making and people who had yanked them up or dressed them down would now be ousted.

It wasn't long after that Mahiserat, visiting Dallas on his way to New York, invited me to lunch. He kissed me hello on the cheek, settled in with his brisket, and told me quickly what a wonderful job Carlton thought I was doing for the company, but that my services were no longer needed. My mind flashed on some of the great men I'd worked for, and how this man who wanted me gone was definitely not one of them.

"And I'm being asked to go because I'm doing such a wonderful job?" I asked pointedly.

"It *is* an irony, is it not?" He slowly chewed the rich, fatty pile of beef. "I know this is fresh news to you—what has happened. Carlton wants to see a new look, a new feel, a new life, that is all. The young, you know, they are not so serious, so investigative, so driven. It is a new way to look at the world, I guess."

"So my fatal flaw was bringing too large a flashlight to the frat party?"

"Aptly put." He daubed his face delicately with his napkin, checked his watch, and pushed back his chair to leave. "I will see you in meetings later today, and we will keep this between us until all is finalized on paper."

And just like that I was off my horse.

CHAPTER TWENTY-THREE

I dialed Liz as I drove toward the office, telling her what had just happened. I was in shock and angry.

"Come home to me," Liz said. "It's all right." She seemed to find a calm spot inside her. "I guess I knew deep down this was coming."

"How did you know?" I asked, dazed.

"When you told me that you'd put your feet in the Yakima River that night after I left you at the restaurant, I thought, she's washing all those people away."

I was depressed, interspersed with panic over the speed with which it had happened, not allowing me time to plan my transition. Much like the Cro-Magnon woman in *Clan of the Cave Bear*, I was stripped of all trappings related to the tribe, and now they would look right through me, refusing to recognize my existence. To them I was dead.

"Of all times to be with you," I moaned into the phone. "This is no way for our relationship to begin."

"Our relationship began over a year ago. You just weren't aware of it. And it's perfect timing. Now you'll know I didn't go after you for power or money. I just fell for *you*."

I hung up only when I pulled into the driveway and fell into her arms. We curled up on the couch and she kissed my neck.

"What kind of cosmic timing is this!" I wailed. "I should be having the most wonderful, sexy relationship and I'm unemployed!"

Liz diverted my attention to the small package on her hall table along with the rest of the mail. Surprisingly, it was addressed to me— surprising because I didn't live here and no one else knew I was even seeing Liz. I unwrapped the package with near-lifeless hands. Inside lay a single small oblong stone.

"How did someone know to send this package to your address?"

"Don't know. It's a runestone, shaped like an arrow pointed toward the heavens," Liz said and went to her computer to search for the symbol. "Teiwaz, the Viking Rune of the Warrior. Maybe it's a message from your horse," Liz said, trying to lighten the mood.

I dug around in the package trying to locate a note or name but found nothing. The package had been mailed from an address in San Francisco on Telegraph Hill, but without an occupant's name.

"Maybe it's from that docent at the museum. I left her my card."

"Not unless she's moved to San Francisco," Liz quipped.

"Wherever she is, I'd like for her to find the painting." I tossed the package back onto the table, too depressed to be interested in it.

❖

That night, Liz wrapped around me, cradling me in her arms, and I fell asleep and dreamed I was on a mountaintop with my horse.

Injured in a skirmish, I retreat to rest. My wounds are infected; I have a high fever, and in the night I writhe in delirium and, half asleep, roll into a ravine, too weak and fatigued to crawl out. Depressed, I make up my mind not to try to save myself. I close my eyes, awaiting my fate, and see the queen waiting for me, no doubt wondering where I am.

I hear the sound of small rocks crumbling on the hilltop above me; then the rocks tumble down the steep slope, sliding over and around me. I look up to see my horse, slowly picking her way down the hillside toward me.

"You can't save me, go back!" I signal her, but she will not cease her precipitous descent until her soft muzzle comes to rest on my forehead. Certain I am breathing, she looks about, seeming to assess our situation.

"Now we're both in trouble," I say. "You can't get me out, mare, or yourself back up, and there's nothing for you to eat down here."

But the horse has other ideas. She takes the back of my tunic in her teeth and slowly drags me farther down the hill, at one point rolling me as I moan in pain. Farther she drags me until I can see the edge of a small riverbed.

She tows me into the water, deeper and deeper, until I am floating at the level of her back. With great effort, I pull myself shivering onto her, and she swims downstream a kilometer, maybe more, until the land flattens out and she can ride me to safety. The horse has saved me—not fighting the mountain but embracing the stream.

I awoke murmuring, "Embrace the stream. Embrace the stream." I was out of breath and covered in sweat, but had a new acceptance of what had happened to me.

Every day the herd wakes up and decides who will be boss; it's a title that's constantly earned between sunrise and sunset. Unlike weak-kneed boards of directors, horses never designate committees to run the herd. Only one stallion leads the way. Of course, on any given day, without so much as a voting quorum, the number-two horse can sense a fatal sign of weakness or lack of desire and seize the opportunity to take over, and then the corporate and horse worlds merge again, as blind obedience to the new leader ensures everyone's survival.

Most likely many of my peers had been forewarned that my lunch with Mahiserat was the end for me. Most likely Hugh knew, and Jack, certainly Anselm and Kaloff and King knew, and perhaps even my senior staff. None had chosen to warn me; they were looking to their own survival and to which of them might become number one.

Madge gasped when she opened her front door and I told her before even entering that I'd lost my job. "Lost" was an odd euphemism for a firing. Maybe it referred to the loss one felt at no longer belonging.

She snapped me up by the scruff of my self-pity. "Well, good! You weren't using any of your creative talents!" She headed for the kitchen to get me tea and most likely to collect her thoughts.

"It was an entertainment conglomerate! How much more creative could a business be?"

"It was a boys' club, and nothing creative could get past the parties and pussies and pitiful profits!" she shouted at me while alliterating.

"I heard from Maxine and Hugh, both of whom seemed genuinely sorry I was canned, but their sympathy will wear off if they get my office or my leather furniture."

"That's a pretty callous thought." Madge frowned.

"Whoever your leaders kill is the enemy. If you spend too much time mourning the dead, you're a traitor."

"What about your secretary?"

"She probably hasn't noticed I'm gone." I smirked. "But I got a nice voice mail from Zane Stephens, upset over my leaving."

"I should hope so. You saved her life."

"We're all on the ledge at one time or another. No tea. I just wanted to stop by and show you what somebody mailed me." I showed her the runestone, both of us knowing it was just an excuse for me to come by and talk to her.

"A rock with arrows on it? Who sent you that?"

"Hell, I don't know. Could have fallen out of my own head. I've got to go meet Liz." I sighed and kissed her on the cheek.

She snorted like my mare at the show of attention. "Liz is still with you, is she? That's the only thing you should care about right now. Focus on the two of you. This corporate thing isn't real."

And I saw more warmth in her translucent blue eyes than I'd seen in years. "Thanks, Madge."

"Get out of here. And don't get maudlin on me. You know I won't put up with that."

❖

Liz spent so much time at my place that she was almost living with me. We were even discussing putting her house up for sale. I was passionate about her and could not let her out of my sight.

Tonight we were settled in on the couch researching Samuels and the ferryboat operation as I ran my hand idly up the inside of her thigh and she kissed me so passionately I was instantly light-headed and pushed her back onto the couch, untying the ribbon at the top of her cotton slacks.

She giggled and redirected my hands to the day's mail on the coffee table. "Can't I just kiss you without it turning into something else?"

"Not like that. That was a come-fuck-me kiss and you know it," I said, smiling and only half focused on the reply to my letter to the San Francisco Historical Society. Opening it, I found a response to my inquiry: a picture of an older, portly man with white hair and beard, looking like a rich merchant of the 1800s. The short paragraph below it said that this was Edward Samuels who, during his lifetime, had a commercial ferryboat operation and lived in a three-story flat on Telegraph Hill, now listed in the historical registry.

I looked at the address sticker more closely, then jumped up and ran to retrieve the package the runestone had arrived in. I compared the two addresses. "Okay, this is uncanny," I said, continuing to stare. "This package with the runestone was mailed from the same address on Telegraph Hill where Edward Samuels lived back in the 1800s. How could that be?"

"Let's find out," Liz said, postponing lovemaking in favor of reverse-searching the address, finding a phone number, but no Edward Samuels next to it.

I called the number, and an elderly woman answered. When I asked if this was the Samuels residence, she replied that it once was. I then asked if she had recently mailed a package with a runestone in it to someone in Dallas, and she said, seeming quite pleased, that she had.

I told her I had received it.

"Brice?" she asked, in a tone that an old relative might use if she hadn't heard from me in years and couldn't believe it was me. Her voice speaking my name sent a shiver up my spine.

"Yes," I said tentatively. "Do I know you?"

"It's hard to tell." She laughed lightly.

"Well…how did you find me?"

"I just follow my dreams, and they generally tell me what to do," she said in a bell-like voice.

"But my address is—"

"In the dreams, dear," she interrupted in a tone that indicated I was a little thickheaded. "If you're ever in San Francisco, you must come and see me."

"I will. What does sending the rune mean?"

"You know about runes, Brice," she said, slightly chastising. "They're oracles. You've always listened to oracles. I must go now." And she hung up.

"What did she say?" Liz asked when I flopped back on the couch stunned into silence.

"Do you know her?"

"She thinks I do. She's kind of daffy, mailing runes to people from her dreams."

"Did you ask her about *your* dreams—the battle?"

"No."

"Call her back."

I dialed the number and let it ring and ring; the woman didn't answer.

CHAPTER TWENTY-FOUR

We were worn out from driving back and forth several times a day from our two city homes to the ranch construction site, then driving over to see the horses. So the minute the house was habitable I decided we should move to the ranch, having kept my part of the bargain and given Liz every piece of me.

Admitting I had done so, she agreed to the move and put her home up for sale, despite the longer drive to get to work. We were both idealizing our future on the Ponderosa.

The moment the last metal screw went into the ranch building and the last hinge went on the pasture gates, we gave notice to everyone— good-bye to Liz's old oil-town mansion, my condo, and Paula's exclusive barn. We all headed for the ranch.

We knew we had to have two items: a horse trailer to get the horses to the vet and an all-terrain vehicle to haul trash and logs, pull the riding mower out of muddy ditches, and a million other dilemmas one could get into on a ranch.

Today, we were getting to use the horse trailer for the first time as we hauled our horses out to spend their first night in our new home. Once within the ranch gates and safely inside the horse paddock, I stopped the truck and wrapped my arms around Liz, giving her a long, sensual kiss designed to dampen everything but our spirits, then, suddenly ecstatic with my life and Liz, I jumped out and entered the side door of the horse trailer to untie the horses. Liz opened the trailer's wide back door, and that's when I realized we were much better kissers than cowgirls.

Unloading horses was trickier than it looked. The horses had to back up slowly and feel their way to the edge, then step down carefully. They were excited, and before I realized it, Rune was trying to turn around in the narrow trailer, despite Hlatur's body blocking her way. I shortened her lead rope to stop her, moved fully into the trailer in front of her, and gave her the signal to back up.

Once we had the horses out of the trailer, we removed their halters and they both took off as if they'd just seen Iceland again. They ran and kicked and whinnied and farted, then picked up speed and did it again. Their joy was indescribable. Hlatur lowered his head at a dead run and swept through a clump of Johnson grass, grabbing long blades of it as he ran and carrying it around the pasture like a flamenco dancer with a rose in his teeth.

"Oh, I wish I had this on film," Liz said. "I've never seen them so happy."

That moment I'd expected to see when I first laid eyes on Icelandic horses in Yakima—beautiful, proud, energized, dynamic animals flying through the fields—I was finally seeing on my own ranch. This was how Icelandic horses should look. This was where they should be. We watched them until they wore themselves out rolling on the ground, nipping at each other playfully, and finally, peacefully, grazing.

"They love it here. *I* love it here!" I gave Liz a big hug. "I'm so excited I could eat grass."

❖

I drove Liz down to the main gate on the south end of the property, a gate we didn't use because it was so massive. Turning to face it from the road, I asked her what she thought. She stood still for a moment, trying to figure out what I was asking, and then she saw it. The big CCR welded onto the gate.

"The Chandler & Chase Ranch," I said.

"How did you get this done?" She had tears in her eyes.

"It was the first thing I ordered the day I bought the land, and I know good ole boys who know good ole boys."

"You amaze me. First I couldn't even get you to kiss me, then just like that you make this our place."

"Once I make a decision, I go with it. Sign of a strong, decisive executive—unemployed but decisive," I said, rather proud of myself.

Liz put her arm around me, and we stared at the big metal letters welded to the pipe rail as the setting sun hit it and cast a purple-pink glow across the giant iron letters that for us spelled happiness.

"You took a big chance, Ms. Chandler. Suppose I had decided not to move out here with you, and you already had those big gate letters up there—"

"I always have a backup plan. It would just be Celibate Chandler's Ranch. Thank God I didn't have to fall back on that," I said, leaning in to kiss her, then pulling back just as quickly.

In my peripheral vision I saw officers in flack vests tromping across our land, talking into their shoulder radios and waving assault rifles in the air. It looked like an attack by aliens. The SWAT officer approached and introduced himself.

"We've busted twelve meth labs out here in the last three days. Group of 'em just went over the back side of your land last night in four-wheelers. We've got 'em on the run, but you need to be on the lookout." The deputy handed me his card. "Mostly now they're looking for computers, electronics, things they can hock to get the cash they need. Do you have a gun?"

"Yes," I replied.

"Good," he said, and with that the officers were gone, leaving us to contemplate meth dealers after dark.

"Did you *bring* a gun?" Liz asked.

"Yes, but when you're nervous a pistol is hard to aim. I think we should buy a lighter-weight gun. We need another one anyway."

"I'd like to bring the horses into the barn tonight," Liz said. "The meth-dealer alert makes me jumpy."

"We need country dogs out here. You know, eating scraps and scaring the hell out of people."

"I don't want our dogs to eat scraps and be scary."

"Not scary to you, just scary to other people," I said happily. "Dogs, guns, trucks. Overnight, I've turned into a redneck, but I'm beginning to see the logic in the lifestyle."

We brought the horses in and put them in the cushy stalls, kissed them good night, then stood in the doorway leading to our house, very pleased with ourselves. We could wander out into the barn in our nightshirts without going outdoors, check on the horses through the door that separated them from the breezeway, or hang our heads out our bedroom window and see them down the long porch, hanging their heads out of their stalls. I set the alarm and assured Liz that if meth dealers appeared, we were covered.

❖

I playfully hauled Liz into the bedroom, kissing her at every step. As I began unbuttoning her shirt, she got the giggles, which made me laugh. Lovemaking was temporarily aborted.

"What is wrong with us?" I finally asked.

"We're in shock from what we've done. I married a corporate executive who's turned into Annie Oakley."

"I'll be an executive again," I said, "but my background comes in very handy out here." I tried to kiss her and she pulled away again, still giggling.

"Are you going to hold board meetings with the cows? I *mooooove* that we adjourn." And she giggled more. "Who knew *stock* options meant Hereford or Guernsey," she shrieked.

"That'll be just about enough out of you." This time I kissed her decisively, and her muffled laughter turned into soft endearments.

"I love you but I'm exhausted," she said, slipping out of the remainder of her clothes and crawling into bed.

"I completely understand," I murmured as she turned her back to me and rested her body in the curve of mine. I massaged her shoulder and down her arm and into the bend of her waist and over her sensual hips and down her legs, retracing my steps and sliding my hand up the crevice between her legs and onto the delicate, incredibly soft areas that nestled there.

She moaned and pushed her buttocks into my hand, and I slid my fingers into her and put my mouth on the back of her neck. Liz rocked into me, murmuring that I had tricked her.

"A savvy television personality should be long past the tricked stage. I think you were coming on to me," I whispered, then gave an involuntary sigh over how she came long before I was ready to let her go.

She turned over to face me and kissed me with a mouth as wet as the vistas I had most recently visited. "You're going to get it," she threatened softly.

"I was hoping."

❖

The next morning the sun came up over the back forty acres with nothing to obstruct it, not a building or car or person to get in the way. It filled the sky and fields and ponds with its glorious radiant light, and I felt as if I had found the only true church, as if God had visited me and had given me the most blessed gift I would ever receive. We stood with our arms around each other, Liz and I, in the rapturous light of the rising sun.

Then we fed the horses and led them out into their second and larger pasture. They flew around the five acres and whinnied and kicked. They too felt the magic of this place.

Later that morning, we mucked out the stalls where the horses had spent the night and turned on the barn radio to hear country music. A newscaster broke in to say a tornado had been spotted thirty miles south of us.

I went outside and whistled up the horses, still unsure about when to put horses into a barn for protection. I figured if we had lightning or hail, they were better off inside, but I fretted; if the barn took a direct hit from a tornado they would be trapped inside and killed. However, I reasoned, if left in the pasture and the tornado blew metal debris into them at a hundred miles an hour, they would be injured.

I had to make a decision and hope for the best, so I coaxed the horses inside by putting sweet feed in their stall bins. Then I closed the south barn door and put the big double latches on it, remembering the posted warning on the barn doors that strong winds could lift the double barn doors right off their hinges and toss them up on our roof, requiring a crane to retrieve them. The image of gigantic barn doors sticking out of the top of my roof stuck with me.

"It's headed right up the freeway. Local radar reports say it's coming within a mile of us, if it stays on track."

"Shit," I said quietly.

Within a few more minutes the sky had grown dark, with a large wall cloud on the western horizon. It looked like a great black landmass moving in on us, its form made more ominous by the wide open spaces, where forces of nature take on gargantuan proportions. The winds were kicking up, pieces of hay and debris swirling around the porches; it was at once exhilarating and frightening.

Unlike the storm we'd experienced at Ann Colton's farm, when Liz and I had our first horse adventure, we couldn't just jump in the car and drive away from this one. It suddenly dawned on me that we had roots now. We lived here on this wild piece of land. These were our animals, and if we ran, they would be left behind to face it alone.

We were getting our first experience at riding it out and my first experience at being committed to what I'd created. I understood why our ancestors had stuck it out fighting famine and fires and unfriendly neighbors to save what was theirs. And I also understood why it might have scared them senseless, as it nearly did me.

"It's right here!" Liz said loudly.

"We need to take cover!"

"Wow, look at this!" Liz whooped.

Off the porch, sheets of dark rain swirled in a hypnotic and powerful water dance. I didn't know if we were under the storm or off to one side.

"Let's get into an interior closet!" I yelled.

"It's okay," she said, marveling at the buckets of rain pummeling the ground.

Suddenly the rain shifted like someone redirecting a water hose and it came at us at a ninety-degree angle, the porch roof now meaningless as weather protection, the world as wet as if the earth had tilted on its axis and rain pelted us sideways.

"This is amazing!" Liz was joyous.

"Where the hell is the tornado? We could be killed!"

"It's off to the north a little. These are the winds on the edge of it."

Within twenty minutes the entire event was over. The world was dark and wet and a lot less windy. I checked on the horses. Their bedding was wet from the sideways rain and they were soaked, but no other damage. I let them out of their stalls, then walked down to the pastures looking for any problems.

"The paddock fence posts," Liz shouted.

Little white squares lay all over the ground, a veritable confetti of vinyl fence caps ripped off their posts to join in the swirling water dance, ultimately landing dozens of yards away from their original locations. I started to pick them up on foot, then realized the entire back forty was dotted with small white squares.

We finished picking up the fence-post caps and drove our new four-wheel Kubota ATV up to assess the damage out by the main road. The CCR gate, so beautifully hinged to swing its three hundred pounds smoothly even in a stiff wind, was intact.

Liz pushed the gate open with little effort, took a look around, then came back in, the gate trailing behind her. Suddenly, the heavy gate picked up speed, traveling faster than she was walking, snagged her heel, and flipped her up in the air like a steer. She came down hard and fast on her arm.

"Omigod, can you get up?" I ran over and secured the gate before checking on her.

"My elbow," she moaned.

I carefully helped her to her feet and got her back into the Kubota. We drove over the lumpy ground as she cried over every painful bounce, and I worried over how badly she might be hurt.

At the house I wrapped her arm in ice packs and a towel, located keys, and helped her into the truck. She rode toward town cradling her hurt arm.

Emergency room X-rays showed a chipped bone near her elbow and torn muscles in her arm. By three a.m. she hadn't slept; she couldn't turn over or even let a quilt brush her arm, and she was in agony. Lying there in the predawn darkness, we were both exhausted and depressed.

"Did we do the wrong thing moving out here?" she asked. "In twenty-four hours we've had meth dealers, a tornado, and a trip to the hospital."

"I don't know, but we're here now. What's the worst that can happen? We hate it, and we end up selling it, and we make a profit, because it's one of the last gorgeous pieces of land in the county." I was despondent at the mere thought.

I knew that this accident had ramifications beyond our horse accidents. Everything on the ranch weighed thirty to a hundred pounds: bags of horse feed, bales of hay, cases of bottled water, furniture to be stored, furniture to be moved, boxes to be packed and unpacked as we transferred our lives from our city homes to our ranch, and now instead of four arms to lift and haul and carry, we had three. I suddenly understand the literal meaning of ranch hands.

CHAPTER TWENTY-FIVE

L iz was angry, difficult, and impossible to help.
"Will you let me get that?" I barked.

"I can get it myself." She yanked the muck bucket away from me and proceeded to muck out the stall, using her hip to leverage the loaded pitchfork of manure up into the air, then tilting it into the bucket.

"You'll have the muscles of a lumberjack in your right arm," I snorted.

"Fine with me."

Her tone angered me. "Could you step out of the way so I can lift the shavings into the stall, then lift the feed bags into the barrels so I can *then* go in and unload the groceries?"

"Look, I know you're doing all the lifting, if that's your point. I can't help it!" she yelled, and threw the plastic-tined pitchfork across the aisle like a javelin, just missing my head.

"Did you throw that at me?" My voice rose an octave.

"No!" The insanity of the moment made her laugh despite herself. "If I'd thrown it at you, I would have *hit you*, which is what I'd like to do!"

I got in her face. "You want to hit me?" My executive nature failed me in domestic situations. I wanted to be angry, but instead I felt tears welling up in my eyes.

"Oh, that's good. Now after being totally obnoxious, you're going to cry, and I'll have to give *you* sympathy." Liz's voice softened.

Tears were already running down my cheeks. "I'm sorry. I'm just so tired, and everything on the damned planet weighs fifty pounds. My back is out, my right knee hurts, and an old tennis injury in my foot is flaring up."

Liz was giggling now. "You're pretty pitiful."

"And I'm feeling pretty pitiful," I said, reveling in the attention. "I mucked the alleyway between the pastures to keep manure off your beloved Kubota wheels, and off our boots, and when I lifted a pitchfork full of manure up in the air to throw it over the north fence, the wind shifted and blew horse shit back in my face. It bounced off my cheek and into my shirt and fell down into my shoes and, frankly, I've had it!"

"So I'm hugging someone who's full of shit? Come on," she said. "I'm going to make you a cappuccino."

"With one arm?"

"You'd be surprised what I can do with one arm." And she kissed me sweetly.

"I love you."

❖

A week had gone by, and we both awakened in our usual pain, having slept little over the past few nights. My knee and back and shoulders felt like knives had been slid into them in the middle of the night. The pain from Liz's arm was so intense that she awoke each morning with tears streaming down her cheeks. We could barely stagger out of bed to get dressed. Going out into the barn to muck out the stalls, feed our new rescue dogs, Lily and Lila, take the horses down to their pasture, and lift a never-ending load should have been an effort, but an odd sensation had begun to take place within me.

As I staggered into my sweatpants, jacket, and barn boots, then opened the door to the bracing air and furry animals, all of whom wanted a pat or a hug, the pain in my aching body eased up. The sunshine cut across the sky in the most radiant colors—colors I had never seen from my city home.

We lifted thirty-pound muck buckets and dumped them into the manure spreader, determined not to act like city people paying to have our manure hauled off, then paying to have fertilizer hauled in. So every day, regardless of weather conditions, we turned our manure into fertilizer, hopefully a metaphor for our new lives.

Afterward, I sat down on a bench outside the barn, with our

ninety-pound dogs who had big furry coats and gigantic paws and never stopped imploring me to hold them. They leapt up on either side of me and put their heads on my knee and jostled my coffee until it went down my sweatshirt, and I laughed.

I marveled at the beauty of the land, and I wasn't sorry I had done this. The damp, sweet morning dew, the kaleidoscopic sunrise, and the animals joyously nickering and barking made me smile more than I had in a handful of years. I was discovering that after the initial shock of knowing the vast amount of physical work that awaited me, I was happy to wake up.

Rune wandered over to the fence and I stood up to greet her. When she dropped her head, putting her face in my hands, I looked into her eyes, the morning sunlight making me squint, and suddenly her eyes were blue—lagoonlike, iridescent pools that mesmerized me. *How can they be blue?* My mind registered that thought as I stared into them and she stood perfectly still. Goose bumps covered my body as, in her eyes, I saw— *A woman—that's insane!* I thought. *My horse as woman?*

We stared at each other lovingly, and then she raised her head, putting her lips on my forehead. I closed my eyes and saw what she saw—the sunlight cresting the eastern hills bursting through my closed eyelids with shards of color; the celestial light of golden fields and deep blue sky and green patches of grass and splashes of orange from the wintering shrubs, rays of light like lasers forming stained-glass windows from heaven's church. And at that moment, I felt as if I'd been kissed by a goddess.

When I opened my eyes, Rune's eyes were brown again and I was jarred out of this spiritual experience by my cell phone ringing. It was Jack.

"What do you, me, Hugh, and Maxine have in common? We were all doing such a great job that we had to be fired! Can you explain that?" he said. "I hate the sound of 'fired.'"

"Well, they did you a favor. You're a smart guy and you need to be with a company that will appreciate you."

"I love you. It's like calling Mom. Can I use you as a reference on a possible job in Chicago?"

"I assume you want me to lie."

"Tell them that I'm the most wonderful man you've ever known. Hey, you'll be happy to know that they're selling the company. Ran it into the wall and now they have to sell it for parts."

"Not all breakups are bad," I replied, feeling no malice toward my former company or any of its people, but only peace for having moved on.

"What are you up to?" he asked, changing his tone.

"Right now, I'm cleaning out the barn and every day I'm looking for work. Maybe I'll hire out as a cowgirl."

"Oooh, tight chaps. Send me pictures," he said, and we said our good-byes.

Jack's call put my stomach in knots, reminding me that executives were having to leave town to find jobs. How was I ever going to find an entertainment job near my ranch, for God's sake? I had always had a big job. I was, in fact, defined by my job. Without it I was adrift and tense and worried.

One problem, of course, was money, and the fact that ours was being depleted. I didn't know how to reinvent myself with speed and certainty. Liz was still working, of course, but ours wasn't a one-income lifestyle. However, if I looked more closely, the bigger problem was power—and that mine had been usurped. Certainly, power as I'd come to know it—an anointing by men who knighted me with money. Deep down, I knew that true power wasn't bankable—but I was hard-pressed to believe that truth in my gut.

Liz put her arm around me, startling me with her stealthlike presence. "You don't want a traditional job. You want something with animals and the ranch and the earth. Leave the bullshit back in the corporate pastures," she said, nuzzling my neck like a horse.

"My horse's eyes turned blue this morning," I said, and looked at Liz for a reaction. "I swear. And I thought I saw…a woman in there."

"In your horse's eyes?"

"Yes." I shook my head. "Don't say anything. It'll only make me feel crazier."

Liz gave it a beat. "She does have nice legs."

❖

Another week went by. I glanced over at the stack of mail as the bills piled up. Liz had taken over handling them, as their mere existence threw me into depression. Beside the bills sat another package just like the first one, postmarked San Francisco. I opened the package and found another runestone, a repeat of the first stone—almost as if the old lady who'd sent it wasn't sure it was getting through.

"Teiwaz." I held up the runestone with mock sanctity. "What's she doing?"

"Maybe saying you were a warrior then and you're a warrior now. Twice a warrior, in case you're missing the point."

"I doubt she's thinking it through at that level," I said, exasperated at the old woman who was so daffy she was sending me runestones without either of us knowing why.

I located her number on my desk and rang her. No answer. And yet I believed—I knew—she was there. Was she not answering because she was crazy, or because I was bothering her, or because…she wanted to see me in person? I don't know why I believed the last thought was true, but I did. *She wants to see me in person.* I decided I was losing my mind just by association.

Chapter Twenty-six

D o you need help?" Liz handed me pliers and an electric screwdriver. Her arm was doing better now, but I still didn't want to take the chance she could reinjure it.

"No, I'll figure it out." I trudged off toward the far pasture to fix the horse waterers in the field. I was certain, once I unscrewed the center lid separating the two watering holes, I'd see the apparatus and figure out how to fix it.

Once in the pasture, I realized I needed a socket wrench to get the lid off, so I trudged back to the feed room for more tools. It was thirty-four degrees out, and not unpleasant. I marveled at how I used to think fifty degrees required a coat. Now a sweatshirt in thirty-degree weather was fine.

Field waterers for horses were fairly limited in design, and we'd chosen a style that looked like large encased plastic tubs with two balls on top. The balls covered the water and kept mosquitoes out, thus thwarting the spread of West Nile virus, a deadly killer of horses. When the horses wanted to drink, they pushed the balls down with their noses and drank the water beneath. But now the entire apparatus was leaking, threatening to freeze and burst the valve once the temperatures got down to fifteen degrees for any period of time.

I returned to the waterer and, after angling the wrench, I got the nuts unscrewed, released the lid, and lifted it off. Underneath, the apparatus looked exactly like the tank of a toilet: the large black float had two joints with interlocking screws. I chose the larger joint, which looked like it had more control over the tilt of the float, and gently unscrewed it.

The result was catastrophic. Water shot out of the top of the waterer like a geyser and never let up. I retightened the screw, but nothing happened to change the water show. Water was gathering around my feet at the base of the waterer, and with a hard freeze predicted in twenty-four hours, this wasn't good. I pulled the flotation device up and out of the water, trying to temporarily stem the flow. Nothing slowed it. As the pasture flooded, I ran toward the house.

"Call the plumber! I turned the wrong valve."

"Turn it back!" Liz shouted to me.

"Don't you think I tried that? Call the plumber!"

I ran back to the feed room and found a long metal rod, intending to cut off the water flow below ground at the waterer's shutoff valve. I also grabbed a huge wrench to wrest the PVC pipe cover off, then looked down the narrow three-foot hole in the ground that housed the shutoff valve below the frost line. Instead of the valve that I expected to see, I stared into a three-foot-deep tube of mud and water. Sticking the iron rod down into the hole, I felt around for the shutoff valve, while every second the pool of flood water around me was growing, the clay ground unable to suck up any of it.

"Shit!" I shouted to the heavens as I realized I was going to have to put my arm down the hole, feel for the valve, and turn it off by hand. I pushed the sleeves of my sweatshirt up and started to put my arm into the water, then realized my shirt would be soggy with mud. I gave it up and jerked off my sweatshirt, realizing I hadn't put on a bra this morning, then threw the shirt on the ground. Naked from the waist up, in thirty-four-degree weather, I hoped the neighbors didn't own binoculars.

Rune had her nose down a few yards from me, watching with real interest as my naked breasts lay pressed against the mud, my cheek smashed into the dirt. I jammed my arm into the mud and water, right up to my armpit. "Crap!" I muttered for good measure. After a few seconds I located the valve and strained to shut it off, but it was so deep, my fingers could only brush it, not grasp it. I pulled my arm out and grabbed the iron turn key. This time I knew where to aim it. I locked it onto the valve, carefully turned it, and watched the water shut down. I stood up, naked to the waist and covered in mud.

"Good news, the plumber was right around the corner. He's here!" Liz waved her arms in the air to make sure I could see her, as she stood a hundred yards away shouting at me, the plumber standing at her side.

I yanked my muddy shirt back on as he and Liz jogged toward me.

"I thought you couldn't get the water shut off," he said, obviously startled by the sight of me.

"Just did."

He gave me the once-over. "You see this valve?" he asked, pointing to the one I'd loosened inside the horse tank and taking the tone of a vo-tech instructor. "The key thing is…don't ever mess with it."

"I'll make a note of that," I said as the plumber left, promising to return later if need be.

I was washing up at the barn sink, letting the warm water take the chill off my arm. "I had to put my arm down that three-foot mud hole up to my armpit." I scrunched up my face at the mere thought of what I'd endured.

"I can't believe you did that. Water moccasins spend the winter underground, and there could have been a snake in there."

"Are you kidding me?" My voice rose.

"You didn't know that?" Liz grinned.

"No, I didn't know that, or I would have approached it a little differently!"

"How would you have approached it?"

"I would have put *your* arm down there," I said, and she grinned at me again.

"Aren't you glad I insisted that we have shutoff valves at each waterer? Otherwise you'd be turning that water off three hundred yards away, then running back to see what was going on."

"Yes, you were very smart to do that."

"You fought me on it," she said in a tone that questioned my giving in so easily, but I had gotten more comfortable giving in of late.

Perhaps out here nature set the example: summer giving in to winter, cold ground giving in to the first shoots of spring grass, and mares giving in to a cycle that ensured the life of the herd. I had no doubt that I would fight many more battles, but for now I was at peace.

❖

I stepped out of the shower, dried off, and immediately pulled Liz into bed with me and curled up around her. My intention was to make love to her, but the bracing wind and cold temperatures had made me more tired than I realized, and I passed out as she was talking.

In the predawn, a dream fragment floated through my head and I heard my own voice, the voice of the redheaded warrior speaking to his young aide as he stood currying his horse.

"Don't focus on loss, focus on what you're going to obtain. You can't be a warrior if you focus on loss."

"Did you think you were lost when you lay at the bottom of that ravine, sire?" he asks me.

"Momentarily, but as with all warriors, just when you believe you are finished, the world turns, because the gods save their warriors."

I awoke to the light piercing through a purple and orange sky and saw two big white-tailed deer leaping across the back forty. The horses had their heads hanging over their stall windows, and Rune nickered at me as I opened the back door. The dogs bounded toward me as if I'd been gone for a year, and the two stray kittens we'd adopted after they appeared at our doorstep scaled the fence to see me.

Everything was surreal and beautiful: the wildlife, the weather, the quiet. I had chanted, prayed, looked for work, and tried to remain positive. For months I had tried not to think too far down the road, and now the road had risen to meet me. *Who am I now? What am I here to do? More than ever, I need to know that.*

Liz came outside and put her arms around me, unwilling to let me fret alone, dissolving my fears in love and lust.

"I'm sorry," I said. "I should have a solution."

"We *are* the solution. Forget the world. Make love to me," she whispered and pulled me back into the house and into bed. "Remember that it's who you are, Brice Chandler, that I love and have always loved."

Liz's hot mouth enveloped mine, her legs, radiating heat, wrapped around my thighs, and her breasts pressed so tightly to my chest could not muffle the beating of her heart. "You belong to me," she said, and her tongue created a writhing rhythm in me, moving in time to her fingers drumming inside me until my hips could no longer refrain from the wild, erotic dance, and I thrust my whole being into her—coming to be one with her, all the while feeling this had happened to us before.

❖

The phone rang about the time I was starting to breathe regularly, and I answered it without checking the caller I.D. It was Madge.

"Haven't heard from you two in a while. You doing all right?"

Saying that we were, I tried to focus my brain, which was swimming through the euphoria of endorphins brought on by sensational sex.

"I'd say from the sound of things, you're doing better than could be expected. I told you the day you met Liz Chase that she was perfect for you."

"You did not!" I fired at her and she laughed loudly.

"I knew it inside. I was just making sure that you came to it on your own…that you knew it and didn't rely on my telling you. Important to come to things like that on your own. Call me sometime when you're not in bed," Madge said and hung up.

"How long have you known her?" Liz asked, giggling, having heard Madge's loud voice through the phone.

"Forever."

"Sounds like it."

CHAPTER TWENTY-SEVEN

The bills were through the roof. Not just the ordinary cost of living, but construction costs and now the cost of horses.

"Healthy as a horse" was obviously a phrase coined by people who never even saw a horse, much less owned one, horses being expert at finding something to run into, step on, bite into, or trip over. Their intelligence and curiosity made them as dangerous as a five-year-old kid on a sugar high. And even if they managed not to wrestle one another into a bloody state, or eat themselves sick on fresh grass, they always needed shots, worming, teeth floating, or hoof trimming.

Dr. Brown and his assistant, Sarah, unloaded the buckets, syringes, teeth braces, and other paraphernalia that January always brought. They were a relaxed pair, Brown and Sarah. They leaned up against the hitching post and petted the horses, then admired the land.

Finally, we got down to the shots—EWE, tetanus, rabies, West Nile—then the injection to relax the horses so they could have their teeth floated. As Sarah tightened the halter buckle, the metal teeth brace slammed into Rune's teeth. Even with sedation, Rune's eyes went wide. Sarah apologized and loosened the buckle, and I cringed.

When the work was complete, Rune was left in her stall to recover from all the bodily insult. I stayed with her, held her sagging head up, and talked to her while the sedative wore off.

When Brown and Sarah moved on to Hlatur for his sheath cleaning, Liz was in deep conversation with them, examining even the most private parts of Hlatur for signs of any waxy blockage.

"Lose your diamond up there?" I teased her as the vet finished, packed his gear, and Sarah lugged all his equipment out to the truck.

"Bet you like the sunsets out here," Dr. Brown said as he backed his big truck out of the drive.

"I like everything out here. I hate to go into the city."

"Me too," he said and tipped his hat, taking his leave and a sizeable chunk of our money for only an hour's work.

❖

That night I was working at my computer, when suddenly my mouth was in terrible pain. My front teeth hurt so badly that I couldn't touch them. My lips felt feverish and I began tasting metal, like I'd eaten green beans from a bad tin can. I got up and walked around to see if the pain would go away, then wandered out into the barn where Rune was standing in her stall, her hay still lying on the ground at her feet. She hadn't eaten since the vet left. Taking her temperature, I discovered it was 102.5.

I got the bute paste, dialed up two grams, and gave it to her, then stroked her head; she looked sad. "You can't chew, can you? Your mouth is sore." She looked me full in the face. "When that big metal thing clanked against your upper and lower teeth that hurt like hell, didn't it? Okay, I got the message. The bute will take away that pain, and by tomorrow you'll be able to eat again, I promise."

Fifteen minutes later, the pain in my own teeth ended, just as abruptly as it had started. I went back out in the barn and found Rune lying down with her feet tucked up under her and mentally told her not to get up. I entered her stall, sat down on the shavings beside her, stroked her chest and neck, and put my arm around her. It was magical. My mare on the floor with me, her legs tucked up under her like a large dog, letting me hug her.

When I went back in the house, Liz was playing computer games and I told her about my experience with Rune and her teeth. "This is so weird. I'm listening to the horse, Liz, and she was telling me her teeth were hurting. Now I'm listening and I think she's telling me to go to San Francisco."

Liz stopped playing and turned toward me. Studying me for a moment she said, "Is she putting it on her charge card?"

❖

Our plane flight to San Francisco had been uneventful, and we'd obtained a rental car without waiting. *Auspicious*, I thought. We drove up and around the winding roads overlooking the brightly shining bay and were glad we would be here in San Francisco for a day.

Liz checked the directions and told me to take a hard right, then head straight up the hill, and the house we were looking for would be on the right-hand side. She was right.

I parked on an uphill slope, cranked my steering wheel to the far right, and set the parking brake. "People live like mountain goats here," I remarked.

Liz was staring up at the three-story rococo flat bearing the correct address.

"Brice, it's vacant."

"What!" I sagged back into the leather seats and peered across her up into the tri-level flat. "Maybe it just looks vacant, come on." I refused to believe we'd spent time and money to come to a vacant house.

We clambered up the steep front steps and I rang the bell, but already I could see through the giant bay front windows the house had no furniture; it *was* vacant. I rang again and got no answer. We were turning to leave as the door opened.

"Come in." A tall woman smiled at us.

I was overjoyed someone was there, although she looked nothing like I had envisioned the voice on the phone. In fact, she was rather stunning with a long white fur coat and a white fur hood; the only sign of color was the trim around the bottom of the coat, which looked like sapphires.

"Are you—"

"No," she said. "The older lady you're most likely seeking isn't here any longer."

And I immediately knew that she'd died.

"I'm here wrapping up the shipment of her belongings to her son, who's going to auction them off, I think."

"I can't believe it." I was distraught over not getting my questions answered and also sad over the demise of the sweet woman I knew only by her voice.

"You must be a longtime friend."

"No, I really didn't know her at all. I'd spoken to her on the phone. She sent me a gift on occasion and invited me to come and visit. I wanted to talk to her about why we're..." I struggled with the words.

"Here."

I thought she was completing my sentence, but realized she was offering us a seat on the couch.

"Well, not *here* here but—in a more cosmic sense—why we're back. I'm sure that sounds completely insane to you." I tried to laugh, feeling self-conscious now.

"She would have loved that conversation. She probably would have said, 'Can you prove you ever left?'"

Where have I heard that? I thought. *Who else played games with me about leaving?* It all sounded so familiar.

"So no one's back, they've never really left?" I probed. "They're just sort of around?"

"Perfecting their archetype or transitioning to a new one," she said. "Warrior, queen, working on love and fear while wearing different costumes."

"When it comes to the warrior archetype, there wasn't much love, as far as I can see."

"Fear gets love out of balance, doesn't it?" she said, checking bookshelves and looking into cabinets. "I was thinking about leasing this place myself, what do you think?"

"It's a lovely place," Liz said, as I tried to sort out what was going on.

"So we're each just an archetype?" I quizzed her.

"And the perfection of your archetype perfects the whole."

"One atom at a time until we all become what—a happy drop of rain?" I asked sourly.

"You know about the planets. The sun dwarfs them all—all the ones we talk about—but the sun is dwarfed by Arcturus, and that star is dwarfed by Betelgeuse. The earth is not even a pixel on your computer next to the star Betelgeuse. So, you see, there are limitless experiences and possibilities. Oh, she left something for you," the tall woman said and handed me another small package, like the first two I'd received in the mail. She watched me unwrap it. "Ahh, just as I suspected—a rune!"

"Did she send runes to a lot of people?"

"I don't think so." She seemed surprised by my question.

"It's blank."

"Some people don't believe the blank rune exists, but there it is. The unknowable, the beginning and the end. Karmic shifts. Karma shifts, you know, as you continue to evolve. The rune is called Odin."

"That was the name of my Viking hound, my Norwegian elkhound…" As the words came out of my mouth, an elkhound padded into the room and stood beside her obediently. It was Odin. *I'm sure it's Odin!*

I gasped and knelt to the floor, tears in my eyes. "Odin!" I called out. He walked over and licked my cheek, then quickly turned and went back to her, standing at her side, leaning up against her, obviously claiming her.

"Is that my dog? My dog is dead."

"Is he?"

I watched him look adoringly at her. "He looks just like Odin."

"Then he is." She smiled. "Energy is neither created nor destroyed, only transformed. You know that old saw. Physics, actually."

Liz took my hand, squeezed it reassuringly, then asked, "How did the older lady find us?"

"The dog led us to you."

"When, how?" I whispered.

"You both remember the restaurant, dear, in the storm?"

I stared into her piercing blue eyes, astonished at what she was saying. She was the waitress that night asking about my dog. "You were there as—"

"I found you several times: the docent in the museum, the woman who gave you the postcard by the river where you washed your feet, the shopkeeper with the antique horse, remember?"

And with each mention of a person her features shifted just slightly, reminiscent of the form I had seen. "Let your journey begin!" She snapped her fingers, mimicking the gesture the elderly shopkeeper had executed. "I must go. Oh, and don't forget, dear, to look for the signs."

"Who is the man on the horse with the queen?" I blurted out.

She stopped abruptly and faced me, obviously shocked at my impudence in bringing up the subject.

"Why are you asking questions to which you already know the answer, Brice?" she said, and I recognized the voice I'd heard over the phone.

"You're the woman I spoke to on the phone! What's going on here?"

"And that's the question I came in on." She turned to go.

"Wait! Please, I'm sorry. Is he…was I that man? Please tell me." I heard myself begging.

"You are that man. I'm here if you continue to have questions," she replied lightheartedly. "And you already know about the triplicities."

"What are the triplicities?" I hurried to ask before she could leave.

"Google it, dear," she said impatiently, and walked up the stairs. The dog followed her, never looking back.

"How will I know when you're speaking to me?" I called after her.

"Listen to the horse," she said, and a wind began to pick up and swirl around her feet and enveloped her body; her white robe blew around her thighs like a soft white blanket, and a rush of wind caught her long platinum hair and whipped it around her head like the mane of an exquisite horse whose ethereal eyes were as blue as sapphires.

"Omigod, Liz!" I said, nearly faint.

Liz grabbed me by the arm, the hair on our bodies standing straight up from the electricity in the air as the woman-now-horse, with Odin at her heels, departed into the ethers.

"What time is it?" I murmured.

"1:11 p.m."

As we made our way back down the steps to the car, my mind remained in a heightened state of awareness while my knees shook uncontrollably.

"How did she know your name and how did she—" Liz began.

"Forget my name, how did she become a horse? I didn't imagine that!"

"We always say horses have spirit. We don't say any other animal has spirit."

As we unlocked the car door, there, clearly visible on the dashboard, lay a book. "Did you buy this?" Liz asked as she got inside. "It's a book on runestones."

When I assured her I hadn't, she began thumbing through its pages to find the blank rune. "Oh, my God, check this out!" She held the book up, open to the last illustration on the back page. It pictured a tall woman in a white fur coat and fur hood, with jewels around the hem of the coat and a talisman bag around her waist. It was captioned, "Mistress of the Runes, Iceland 1642."

"Maybe that woman is a performer; and she plays the part of a—" I stammered.

"Maybe she is who she is," Liz said, and we both looked back up at the house on Telegraph Hill, its lights out, doors locked, and completely empty.

We pulled away from the curb slowly and rode in silence.

"She was the Mistress of the Runes who painted the picture that had me as the warrior and you as the queen in the Viking battle that was never recorded and she never saw, of two people who weren't born until hundreds of years later. How did she know what that battle looked like, what we looked like?"

"Because she was there. You told me you saw her heal your horse after it was injured saving you. She's timeless—we're all timeless," Liz said, staring out of the car window as we drove back to the airport.

"It's just so hard to wrap my mind around it."

"'Around' is apparently the key word," Liz said softly.

CHAPTER TWENTY-EIGHT

Weeks later our trip was an unsettling but distant memory. Because my mind had to reject what it couldn't process, I didn't marvel again over the events in San Francisco, and Liz only brought it up as a puzzle to be solved.

She Googled "triplicities," reading to me from various links. A triplicity was a series of repetitive numbers, and the number 111 signified seekers—those who wanted to know more about human existence. Different people around the world reported seeing different sets of numbers; some saw threes, some saw only twos. One article said those who saw triplicities of one were the enlightened.

"This is so strange." Liz continued to read the article. "While we've been quietly wondering what all the one-one-ones mean, thousands of people are having the same experience we are."

I shrugged it off, laughing. "If I'm so enlightened, why am I unemployed and crawling around on haystacks?"

"Maybe part of being enlightened is simply realizing that you are."

❖

I hauled the last of twenty bales of hay in the Kubota to the porch outside the horse barn. We were headed for a high of sixty-eight degrees, when only two days earlier, the high had been twenty-one. After unloading the hay bales, I dusted off my jacket, hosed the mud off my boots, and went inside for a bowl of oatmeal. It was such a glorious day, and the oatmeal was comforting—womb-y. I began thinking that oatmeal must be akin to a warm bran mash that horses are often fed, and I wondered if our horses had ever had that kind of treat. If not, oatmeal was merely oats, water, and sugar, none of which should hurt a horse.

I wandered out to the horse-holding area by the hitching post with a shiny white Mikasa bowl filled with oatmeal and offered it to my mare. Suddenly the color white wasn't frightening, a china bowl wasn't nerve-wracking; my mare seemed quite at home putting her entire mouth into the pile of oats and slurping it up with her tongue like a dog. I couldn't help but smile.

Liz decided Hlatur was being left out, so she brought him a bowl. He put his nose in the oatmeal and snorted loudly, throwing little globs of oats onto her shirt and leaving a large piece of oats stuck to his upper lip. He was in high distress and curled his large upper lip back like a chimp, rubbing his nose back and forth on the grass to get every sticky morsel off.

"You would think I'd rubbed his nose in Elmer's glue!" Liz laughed.

Rune leaned over and finished off the oats from his bowl, then I retrieved a paper towel from the barn and gently cleaned Rune's face. She looked happy and nuzzled my chest, but when I tried to wipe Hlatur's mouth, he acted as if I'd come at him with a pitchfork.

"Forget it, horse!" I said, laughing, and left him to his grass rubbing. I was learning that I couldn't conquer everything…sometimes it was okay to let it be.

❖

At dawn Sunday morning, I crept out of bed so Liz could rest. Dimming the light in the closet so it wouldn't hit her eyes, I dressed inside it, putting on sweats, boots, and a double layer of turtleneck and ski sweater, then slipped out of the bedroom and carefully closed the door before deactivating the burglar alarm. I put sweet feed in the horses' food bins so they could eat while I fed the dogs and cats, who'd begun sleeping in the heated breezeway during the cold winter.

Then I went back out to the horses and led them down to their pasture, carried four flakes of hay out to them, checked their field waterers, and dusted off my clothes on the way back to the barn. After turning on the radio I picked up a muck rake and began mucking out the stalls. The world, I had decided, was full of shit; but this was shit I could do something about, and I slung it into buckets with an efficiency brought on by morning after morning of the same activity.

When the rising sun crested the horizon and hit my face, I felt a sudden rush of joy for this heaven we'd created and a greater rush of fear over how short life is and how little time we have to find meaning in it. I'd wasted so many years toeing the corporate line, treating the corporation like a family member, worrying about meaningless work, and before I knew it, I was standing alone in the stall staring into the sunlight, silently crying.

I tried to form a prayer, but a prayer seemed ridiculous. If God was God, then (S)He knew full well what was going on and didn't need me to recite it. I finally murmured, "God...help. What is it about?" My eyes remained transfixed on the glorious scenery visible through the top of the barn stall—the beautiful rolling land, white fences, and electric orange ball of fire setting it all aglow.

I see the scene as if a camera has pulled back to reveal a wider view; it is the painting. I sit astride a different horse, a massive black war horse, with legs like tree stumps, and I am leading a string of horses out of the fire and flames, taking them up into the hills with me. My horse is afraid of nothing; I am at peace.

Nothing had changed but the angle of the sun, but I knew my ancestors were sending me a message of hope. Something was on its way.

Feeling better, I dried my tears. By the time Liz came out in her flannel nightshirt, smiling sweetly, I showed no signs of my small breakdown. I certainly didn't want her to think I was losing faith.

"Thanks so much for doing everything this morning." She hugged me. "This is the third day in a row you've done it. It's not fair."

"It's fair. You get up and go to work. I don't. But I like working in the barn, actually. I like kissing the animals before the sun comes up...all their sounds and smells. I like it."

"Did you dream?" Liz always asked about my dreams.

"Crazy dreams last night. Some voice in my head said be sure and get a copy of the morning paper, there's something in there for you. Now how odd is that?"

❖

An hour later, Liz plopped a copy of the paper in front of me, and in it was a classified ad about a job: operating officer for a national auction company, reporting to the CEO. I applied on line.

That accomplished, I asked Liz to follow me down to the waterers, which were once again leaking and causing our water bills to skyrocket. Smarter this time, we brought along a small hand pump to jettison the excess water above the frost line that covered the shut-off valve, a longer pipe key, and so many tools we looked like a plumbing flotilla. Over the past week we'd completely disassembled the entire mechanism four times to find the faulty part.

"Okay," Liz said half an hour later, sliding the hood back over the valve and tightening the gear teeth on the arm. "Fire her up and let's see."

Putting the three-foot valve key down into the PVC ground pipe, I located the valve by feel and gave it a forty-five-degree turn. A hundred pounds of water pressure flew into the pipe and up into the horse waterer. The gasket held, the valve didn't leak, the overflow holes in the tank showed no signs of water escaping.

I stood up from the cement ledge of the waterer, ignoring the wet mud caking my sweatpants and squishing ankle high over my boot laces, and gave Liz a big muddy high five. "It's a beautiful thing!" I shouted.

"We did it!" She shot me a huge smile that cracked the mud glued to her cheek. "You look like you need a major hosing down." I laughed.

We gathered up the raft of tools, themselves caked in mud, and trudged slowly up the alleyway toward the barn, the cool air and soft sunshine feeling like nature's soft pat on the back for a job well done. We were so pleased with ourselves that the mud we would normally despise sticking to us seemed a ritual christening.

We washed off in the barn, cleaned the tools and put them away, then went back into the house. An e-mail was waiting. The CEO wanted to meet me.

❖

Two days later, in a double-breasted Armani suit, I walked into the office of the tall, angular, sandy-haired CEO. I hadn't dressed like this in so long I'd forgotten the power of an expensive wardrobe. The young CEO rose quickly from his desk and faced me, revealing his freckled face and sweet smile—I was speechless.

Stretching across the centuries, leaping from my dreams and off the canvas, was my young aide. I heard him thanking me for saving him in battle, then my own words echoing back across the ages: *"One day you may return the favor, saving me."*

Conversation between us was easy, as if we'd merely picked up where we left off in some long-ago meeting. Three hours went by without our even noticing. Suddenly, he paused for a moment and then appeared to make a decision. "With your background, you're a lot of horsepower." The young CEO grinned. "So many corporate battles—you're way ahead of me. You can teach me a lot."

And with that, he offered me the job, as if he'd been waiting for me to arrive. I took it—grateful to be saved.

He turned me over to a young man who gave me a tour of the office, walking me past another man who was sorting photos taken at a mansion they were about to sell at auction: beautiful antiques, furniture—and there it was, the oil painting of the red-haired warrior on horseback—the me I had come to know.

I was dumbstruck, finally managing to ask where the painting was physically located. The young man said a lot of the items from this mansion had been sold before they got the property, so these photos didn't reflect what was truly left.

"Do you know who bought the painting?" I gasped.

"No. Well, maybe. I think they said a very wealthy guy bought it at our last auction."

I thought of the woman at the house in San Francisco saying the items had been sent to an auction company and asked him if I could get a color copy of the photo and any other information about the painting, knowing how odd that request sounded.

"Sure." He shrugged and went out to scan the photo for me.

While he was gone I fingered a tattered piece of paper and read, The battle—one of many raids by early Viking clans—depicts the siege of a large castle compound by the red-bearded warrior who killed the king and claimed the infidel queen, becoming the first barbarian ruler.

His men rode on without him and were ambushed and slain in the following battle leagues away, putting an end to the clan.

Feeling slightly dazed, I went home to the ranch and told Liz, "I got the job."

"Congratulations, darling, I knew you would!" She kissed me. "Aren't you happy?"

"Yes. The CEO was the aide in my dream," I said breathlessly.

"You're kidding me."

"They auctioned the painting. They had a photograph of it!" I pulled it out of my pocket. "Look at the arrow on his shield pointing toward the heavens, just like my dream and just like the Teiwaz runestone."

Liz looked stunned. We were both stunned. We couldn't share this type of thing with anyone because no one would believe it, but it did feel as if linear history was circling around and catching its own tail.

"You were very handsome," she said.

I pulled a piece of paper out of my pocket. "Read this. My men died because they went on without a leader. I stayed behind to rule the city, and they went forward and died."

Liz read the entire paragraph, then folded it up and put it on the dresser and looked at the picture again. "So you think that was your fault? If indeed this is you?"

"I think it explains some things. Maybe I'm back because I owe them a debt."

"Or maybe you're back to help them evolve. After all, they didn't listen to you last time and got themselves killed. You, on the other hand, stayed behind to rebuild the city and take care of its people," she said, and I listened in silence, thinking about a decision of that magnitude.

Liz screwed up her face at the blond-headed queen in the photo, the facial features too small to be recognizable as anyone's, much less Liz's. "Who was doing my hair?"

I placed the photo on the dresser and pulled Liz into bed.

"I'm going to make love to you until dawn," I promised, then wrapped my arm around her and felt strong again, pulling her under me, then balancing my weight on the palms of my hands, and lowering myself gently to her lips before letting my entire weight rest on her body.

She had managed to position one hand between my thighs, and I found myself inside her mouth as she was inside me, creating a bonding heat that welded us to one another, like cast iron forged across the centuries. Our bodies pounded against one another, wet and wanton, every opening of mine fitting into or over hers, and we came together, like the wind and the rain, swirling in each other like the elements of time.

"My God, it gets better every time," she whispered as my mouth left hers to glide down her belly and rest between her legs, and I entered her with a suddenness that made her moan. The earth began to move around us and the images were of us, but we were suddenly the red-bearded warrior and the golden-haired queen, and I knew his love for her transcended all time.

❖

Happily dizzy after our prolonged lovemaking, I kissed Liz's breast and got up to go to the dresser to look at the photo one more time before going to sleep. "It's gone…it's faded!" I said in desperation, and Liz bounded out of bed to see for herself. "This runestone was sitting on top of the picture, and it wasn't there when we went to bed."

"Are you sure you didn't bring the runestone in here?"

"No, I didn't! Besides, it's a different stone altogether."

I took the rune with me into the living room and located the book of runes. The book calls it the Horse Rune—Movement/New Life/ Progress. Did the woman in San Francisco send it?"

"This never came in the mail. It just appeared."

"But how?" I asked and we stood looking at one another not knowing what to say.

"This runic symbol is shaped like the letter 'M.' This is the rune the warrior ripped from his neck and gave to his queen. It must have had deep meaning for him."

"We're in the middle of something very powerful," Liz said quietly but with certainty, and we were both silent.

I clutched the rune, taking it back to my bedside, not knowing why but believing one day it would lead me to understand who I was and why I was back at this time in history, in this form, with this woman. Then I fell asleep without angst for the first time in over a year. I had a job and a purpose, and I dreamed the Rune Mistress was speaking to me.

You have three runes. Your past is bound in the Warrior Rune, reminding you that the biggest battle takes place within. The Blank Rune is your present state of beginnings and endings, and the circle of both. The Horse Rune is before you, teaching you that as we develop who we truly are, all else follows and all else is revealed.

I don't know what woke me, but I rolled over and looked at the clock. The backlit LCD clearly illuminated the large red numbers reading 1:11 a.m. *One eleven again!*

Liz was sitting straight up in bed.

"What?" I asked softly, surprised to find her awake.

"You're the owner, the female master of your horse, right?" she asked, still and listening to something unseen.

I nodded in the affirmative, thinking she must have had a dream.

"Then you're the mistress of Rune—your horse."

I sat quietly absorbing that thought.

"Could it be that you are the Mistress of the Runes? Maybe, you're she and she's you."

"No, she was there. You saw her."

"She was there, but what if she's your Higher Self, your Knowing?"

"No. I don't want her merely to be a piece of myself. I need for her to be real. She *is* real. I saw her. She said she'd be there as long as I have questions and that she'd help me find out who we are and why we're back."

I sank back into the pillows and Liz curled up in the crook of my arm, resting her head on my chest, and I could feel my heartbeat against her cheek.

"She will," Liz said, looking up at me, and in the light from the bedside lamp, her gorgeous eyes, almost surreal, were bright and deep...and exquisitely blue.

Outside the horses nickered softly in the moonlight.

About the Authors

Andrews & Austin live on their horse ranch in the Central Plains. Their strong lesbian characters, great storytelling, and distinctive style derive from years of writing for television and film. Andrews & Austin operate several large business ventures and still find time for one of their biggest passions—writing lesbian fiction that entertains and enlightens.

For more information visit www.andrewsaustin.com.

Books Available From Bold Strokes Books

Wall of Silence, 2nd ed. by Gabrielle Goldsby. Life takes a dangerous turn when jaded police detective Foster Everett meets Riley Medeiros, a woman who isn't afraid to discover the truth no matter the cost. (978-1-933110-90-5)

Mistress of the Runes by Andrews & Austin. Passion ignites between two women with ties to ancient secrets, contemporary mysteries, and a shared quest for the meaning of life. (978-1-933110-89-9)

Sheridan's Fate by Gun Brooke. A dynamic, erotic romance between physiotherapist Lark Mitchell and businesswoman Sheridan Ward set in the scorching hot days and humid, steamy nights of San Antonio. (978-1-933110-88-2)

Vulture's Kiss by Justine Saracen. Archeologist Valerie Foret, heir to a terrifying task, returns in a powerful desert adventure set in Egypt and Jerusalem. (978-1-933110-87-5)

Rising Storm by JLee Meyer. The sequel to *First Instinct* takes our heroines on a dangerous journey instead of the honeymoon they'd planned. (978-1-933110-86-8)

Not Single Enough by Grace Lennox. A funny, sexy modern romance about two lonely women who bond over the unexpected and fall in love along the way. (978-1-933110-85-1)

Such a Pretty Face by Gabrielle Goldsby. A sexy, sometimes humorous, sometimes biting contemporary romance that gently exposes the damage to heart and soul when we fail to look beneath the surface for what truly matters. (978-1-933110-84-4)

Second Season by Ali Vali. A romance set in New Orleans amidst betrayal, Hurricane Katrina, and the new beginnings hardship and heartbreak sometimes make possible. (978-1-933110-83-7)

Hearts Aflame by Ronica Black. A poignant, erotic romance between a hard-driving businesswoman and a solitary vet. Packed with adventure and set in the harsh beauty of the Arizona countryside. (978-1-933110-82-0)

Red Light by JD Glass. Tori forges her path as an EMT in the New York City 911 system while discovering what matters most to herself and the woman she loves. (978-1-933110-81-3)

Honor Under Siege by Radclyffe. Secret Service agent Cameron Roberts struggles to protect her lover while searching for a traitor who just may be another woman with a claim on her heart. (978-1-933110-80-6)

Dark Valentine by Jennifer Fulton. Danger and desire fuel a high-stakes cat-and-mouse game when an attorney and an endangered witness team up to thwart a killer. (978-1-933110-79-0)

Sequestered Hearts by Erin Dutton. A popular artist suddenly goes into seclusion, a reluctant reporter wants to know why, and a heart locked away yearns to be set free. (978-1-933110-78-3)

Erotic Interludes 5: Road Games, ed. by Radclyffe and Stacia Seaman. Adventure, "sport," and sex on the road—hot stories of travel adventures and games of seduction. (978-1-933110-77-6)

The Spanish Pearl by Catherine Friend. On a trip to Spain, Kate Vincent is accidentally transported back in time—an epic saga spiced with humor, lust, and danger. (978-1-933110-76-9)

Lady Knight by L-J Baker. Loyalty and honor clash with love and ambition in a medieval world of magic when female knight Riannon meets Lady Eleanor. (978-1-933110-75-2)

Dark Dreamer by Jennifer Fulton. Best-selling horror author Rowe Devlin falls under the spell of psychic Phoebe Temple. A Dark Vista romance. (978-1-933110-74-5)

Come and Get Me by Julie Cannon. Elliott Foster isn't used to pursuing women, but alluring attorney Lauren Collier makes her change her mind. (978-1-933110-73-8)

Blind Curves by Diane and Jacob Anderson-Minshall. Private eye Yoshi Yakamota comes to the aid of her ex-lover Velvet Erickson in the first Blind Eye mystery. (978-1-933110-72-1)

Dynasty of Rogues by Jane Fletcher. It's hate at first sight for Ranger Riki Sadiq and her new patrol corporal, Tanya Coppelli—except for their undeniable attraction. (978-1-933110-71-4)

Running With the Wind by Nell Stark. Sailing instructor Corrie Marsten has signed off on love until she meets Quinn Davies—one woman she can't ignore. (978-1-933110-70-7)

More Than Paradise by Jennifer Fulton. Two women battle danger, risk all, and find in each other an unexpected ally and an unforgettable love. (978-1-933110-69-1)

Flight Risk by Kim Baldwin. For Blayne Keller, being in the wrong place at the wrong time just might turn out to be the best thing that ever happened to her. (978-1-933110-68-4)

Rebel's Quest: Supreme Constellations Book Two by Gun Brooke. On a world torn by war, two women discover a love that defies all boundaries. (978-1-933110-67-7)

Punk and Zen by JD Glass. Angst, sex, love, rock. Trace, Candace, Francesca…Samantha. Losing control—and finding the truth within. BSB Victory Editions. (1-933110-66-X)

The Devil Unleashed by Ali Vali. As the heat of violence rises, so does the passion. A Casey Clan crime saga. (1-933110-61-9)

When Dreams Tremble by Radclyffe. Two women whose lives turned out far differently than they'd once imagined discover that sometimes the shape of the future can only be found in the past. (1-933110-64-3)

Stellium in Scorpio by Andrews & Austin. The passionate reunion of two powerful women on the glitzy Las Vegas Strip, where everything is an illusion and love is a gamble. (1-933110-65-1)

Burning Dreams by Susan Smith. The chronicle of the challenges faced by a young drag king and an older woman who share a love "outside the bounds." (1-933110-62-7)

Fresh Tracks by Georgia Beers. Seven women, seven days. A lot can happen when old friends, lovers, and a new girl in town get together in the mountains. (1-933110-63-5)

Too Close to Touch by Georgia Beers. Kylie O'Brien believes in true love and is willing to wait for it. It doesn't matter one damn bit that Gretchen, her new and off-limits boss, has a voice as rich and smooth as melted chocolate. It absolutely doesn't… (1-933110-47-3)

The Empress and the Acolyte by Jane Fletcher. Jemeryl and Tevi fight to protect the very fabric of their world…time. Lyremouth Chronicles Book Three. (1-933110-60-0)

First Instinct by JLee Meyer. When high-stakes security fraud leads to murder, one woman flees for her life while another risks her heart to protect her. (1-933110-59-7)

Erotic Interludes 4: Extreme Passions, ed. by Radclyffe and Stacia Seaman. Thirty of today's hottest erotica writers set the pages aflame with love, lust, and steamy liaisons. (1-933110-58-9)

Unexpected Ties by Gina L. Dartt. With death before dessert, Kate Shannon and Nikki Harris are swept up in another tale of danger and romance. (1-933110-56-2)

Broken Wings by L-J Baker. When Rye Woods, a fairy, meets the beautiful dryad Flora Withe, her libido, as squashed and hidden as her wings, reawakens along with her heart. (1-933110-55-4)

Combust the Sun by Andrews & Austin. A Richfield and Rivers mystery set in L.A. Murder among the stars. (1-933110-52-X)

Tristaine Rises by Cate Culpepper. Brenna, Jesstin, and the Amazons of Tristaine face their greatest challenge for survival. (1-933110-50-3)

Passion's Bright Fury by Radclyffe. When a trauma surgeon and a filmmaker become reluctant allies on the battleground between life and death, passion strikes without warning. (1-933110-54-6)

Sleep of Reason by Rose Beecham. Nothing is as it seems when Detective Jude Devine finds herself caught up in a small-town soap opera. And her rocky relationship with forensic pathologist Dr. Mercy Westmoreland just got a lot harder. (1-933110-53-8)

Grave Silence by Rose Beecham. Detective Jude Devine's investigation of a series of ritual murders is complicated by her torrid affair with the golden girl of Southwestern forensic pathology, Dr. Mercy Westmoreland. (1-933110-25-2)

The Traitor and the Chalice by Jane Fletcher. Tevi and Jemeryl risk all in the race to uncover a traitor. The Lyremouth Chronicles Book Two. (1-933110-43-0)

Carly's Sound by Ali Vali. Poppy Valente and Julia Johnson form a bond of friendship that lays the foundation for something more, until Poppy's past comes back to haunt her—literally. A poignant romance about love and renewal. (1-933110-45-7)

100th Generation by Justine Saracen. Ancient curses, modern-day villains, and a most intriguing woman who keeps appearing when least expected lead archeologist Valerie Foret on the adventure of her life. (1-933110-48-1)

Whitewater Rendezvous by Kim Baldwin. Two women on a wilderness kayak adventure—Chaz Herrick, a laid-back outdoorswoman, and Megan Maxwell, a workaholic news executive—discover that true love may be nothing at all like they imagined. (1-933110-38-4)

Erotic Interludes 3: Lessons in Love, ed. by Radclyffe and Stacia Seaman. Sign on for a class in love…the best lesbian erotica writers take us to "school." (1-9331100-39-2)

Punk Like Me by JD Glass. Twenty-one-year-old Nina writes lyrics and plays guitar in the rock band Adam's Rib, and she doesn't always play by the rules. And oh yeah—she has a way with the girls. (1-933110-40-6)

Forever Found by JLee Meyer. Can time, tragedy, and shattered trust destroy a love that seemed destined? When chance reunites two childhood friends separated by tragedy, the past resurfaces to determine the shape of their future. (1-933110-37-6)

Sword of the Guardian by Merry Shannon. Princess Shasta's bold new bodyguard has a secret that could change both of their lives. *He* is actually a *she*. A passionate romance filled with courtly intrigue, chivalry, and devotion. (1-933110-36-8)

Sweet Creek by Lee Lynch. A celebration of the enduring nature of love, friendship, and community in the quirky, heart-warming lesbian community of Waterfall Falls. (1-933110-29-5)

Wild Abandon by Ronica Black. From their first tumultuous meeting, Dr. Chandler Brogan and Officer Sarah Monroe are drawn together by their common obsessions—sex, speed, and danger. (1-933110-35-X)

Of Drag Kings and the Wheel of Fate by Susan Smith. A blind date in a drag club leads to an unlikely romance. (1-933110-51-1)

Turn Back Time by Radclyffe. Pearce Rifkin and Wynter Thompson have nothing in common but a shared passion for surgery. They clash at every opportunity, especially when matters of the heart are suddenly at stake. (1-933110-34-1)

Promising Hearts by Radclyffe. Dr. Vance Phelps lost everything in the War Between the States and arrives in New Hope, Montana, with no hope of happiness and no desire for anything except forgetting—until she meets Mae, a frontier madam. (1-933110-44-9)

Innocent Hearts by Radclyffe. In a wild and unforgiving land, two women learn about love, passion, and the wonders of the heart. (1-933110-21-X)

Justice Served by Radclyffe. Lieutenant Rebecca Frye and her lover, Dr. Catherine Rawlings, embark on a deadly game of hide-and-seek with an underworld kingpin who traffics in human souls. (1-933110-15-5)

Justice in the Shadows by Radclyffe. In a shadow world of secrets and lies, Detective Sergeant Rebecca Frye and her lover, Dr. Catherine Rawlings, join forces in the elusive search for justice. (1-933110-03-1)

A Matter of Trust by Radclyffe. JT Sloan is a cybersleuth who doesn't like attachments. Michael Lassiter is leaving her husband, and she needs Sloan's expertise to safeguard her company. It should just be business—but it turns into much more. (1-933110-33-3)

Storms of Change by Radclyffe. In the continuing saga of the Provincetown Tales, duty and love are at odds as Reese and Tory face their greatest challenge. (1-933110-57-0)

Distant Shores, Silent Thunder by Radclyffe. Dr. Tory King—along with the women who love her—is forced to examine the boundaries of love, friendship, and the ties that transcend time. (1-933110-08-2)

Beyond the Breakwater by Radclyffe. One Provincetown summer, three women learn the true meaning of love, friendship, and family. (1-933110-06-6)

Safe Harbor by Radclyffe. A mysterious newcomer, a reclusive doctor, and a troubled gay teenager learn about love, friendship, and trust during one tumultuous summer in Provincetown. (1-933110-13-9)

shadowland by Radclyffe. In a world on the far edge of desire, two women are drawn together by power, passion, and dark pleasures. An erotic romance. (1-933110-11-2)

Love's Masquerade by Radclyffe. Plunged into the indistinguishable realms of fiction, fantasy, and hidden desires, Auden Frost is forced to question all she believes about the nature of love. (1-933110-14-7)

Honor Reclaimed by Radclyffe. In the aftermath of 9/11, Secret Service Agent Cameron Roberts and Blair Powell close ranks with a trusted few to find the would-be assassins who nearly claimed Blair's life. (1-933110-18-X)

Honor Guards by Radclyffe. In a wild flight for their lives, the president's daughter and those who are sworn to protect her wage a desperate struggle for survival. (1-933110-01-5)

Love & Honor by Radclyffe. The president's daughter and her lover are faced with difficult choices as they battle a tangled web of Washington intrigue for…love and honor. (1-933110-10-4)

Honor Bound by Radclyffe. Secret Service Agent Cameron Roberts and Blair Powell face political intrigue, a clandestine threat to Blair's safety, and the seemingly irreconcilable personal differences that force them ever farther apart. (1-933110-20-1)

Above All, Honor by Radclyffe. Secret Service Agent Cameron Roberts fights her desire for the one woman she can't have—Blair Powell, the daughter of the president of the United States. (1-933110-04-X)